"What's

"Nothing. I thought we were going to dance," Kendall said. "I mean, I can feel your body against mine, but I don't think we're dancing."

"Sorry, you just get my body all excited. I can't control it, Kendall. You're a beautiful woman and you're really working that outfit."

"Are you always such a smooth talker? I bet you say that to all the girls."

"Oh, you got jokes. I'll just have to show you what I mean." Cole knew this was a mistake but he couldn't deny himself one more second. He kissed her on the lips softly. He was determined to go slow, to savor her like a glass of fine imported wine. He tasted her lips with his tongue and gently bit her bottom lip. He felt her surrender as her hands encircled his neck, bringing his face closer to hers.

Cole was too engrossed in the kiss to realize that the music had ended until he heard the applause from their table. Kendall would definitely think he was out to embarrass her now. Gradually, he ended the kiss.

"Sorry, I got carried away. I was just trying to relax you."

ANYTHING BUT LOVE

CELYA BOWERS

Genesis Press, Inc.

INDIGO

An imprint of Genesis Press, Inc.
Publishing Company

Genesis Press, Inc.
P.O. Box 101
Columbus, MS 39703

ISBN: 13 DIGIT : 978-158571-287-8
ISBN: 10 DIGIT : 1-58571-287-6
Manufactured in the United States of America

First Edition 2009

Visit us at www.genesis-press.com
or call at 1-888-Indigo-1

DEDICATION

This book is dedicated to my mother, Celia Mae Bowers Shaw Kenney, and a very dear person I recently lost, Falice (Fay) Lee.

ACKNOWLEDGMENTS

As always I would like to thank my mom for having been a dynamite woman. I know the stars shine brighter in heaven because you're there.

To my family, the best support system in the world: Darwyn Tilley, Jeri Murphy, William Earl Kenney, Sheila Kenney, Kim Kenney, Celya Tilley, Yolanda Tilley, Rod Kenney, and Shannon Murphy.

To my great niece, Kennedy, you are my heart.

To all my BFF's: Cherry Elder, Erica Black, Eulanda Bailey, Sharon Hickman-Mahones, Roslin Williams, Dawn Moore, Kenneth Portley, Lester Brown, DeAndra Garrett, Melody Alvarado, Judy Brown, John Brown, Donna Lefear, Beverly Cofer, Lewis Stewart, and Lisa-Lin Burke.

To Eddie Lee, it was an honor meeting you and I'm so glad I did.

To my readers and new fans: thank you for letting me into your heart.

To my old college friends: Alice Pollock, and Nalen Busto, thanks for looking me up!

To my critique group, the Sizzling Sisterhood: Diane O'Brien-Kelly, Angela Cavener, and Vanetta Chapman.

To Celya's Corner: Paula Washington, Pam Washington, Mattie Washington, Christine Washington,

Clara Washington, Brenda Washington, Lisa Peters, Ingrid Johnson, Lesley Paine, Gail Surles, Winston Williams, Northa Hollins, Jessica Kenney, Kathy Solsberry, Shaunette Smith, Darlene Ramzy, Kerry Elder, Stacey Plummer, Sherry Ramsey, Tammy Hill, Shirley Washington and Kim Williams.

If I forgot anyone, please forgive and charge it to my head.

Thank you for keeping me in your prayers.

Peace

Celya
Celya.bowers@sbcglobal.net
www.celyabowers.net

CHAPTER 1

For some women, it was frilly underwear. But for her it was stilettos. Dr. Kendall Matthews sat in her corner office at Briarwood Hospital, relishing a few quiet moments before having to pull emergency room duty for the afternoon. She propped her stiletto-clad feet on the desk, crossed them at the ankles, and relaxed. Most of her colleagues thought she was crazy for wearing those shoes to work, but it was part of her style.

She loved showing off her legs. Perhaps it was vanity, but she didn't really care. She loved looking and feeling like a woman.

She picked up her stereo remote and clicked on her favorite classical music CD. Debussy's "Claire De Lune" filled the room, instantly calming her frazzled nerves. After such a hectic morning, her eyes drifted closed.

She heard her office door open. Since no one knocked, she knew it was her physician assistant, Max Cork. Everyone else at the prestigious hospital valued their job too much to enter her office without knocking first. "Kendall, we've got a problem in the emergency room and need your diplomatic skills."

She opened her eyes and sat up straight. "I'm not due in the ER until one. It's not even eleven. Get someone else."

Max closed the door and strode to the desk, apparently not paying attention to the tone in her voice. "Look, Kendall, do you know Coltrane Highpoint, the best-selling author?"

She did, she knew the African-American author and had had a secret crush on him all those years ago, when she was too young to know better. "Yes, I went to school with his greatness, back when he couldn't construct a simple sentence properly."

"I thought you were only approaching the big 4-0?"

"Okay, he wasn't in my class. He was a little older. He knew my brother Charlie, and he was always at our house. He should be about forty-five. Charlie told me he moved back last year and was working on his next best-seller."

Max shook his head at her. "Whatever. Get to the ER."

Kendall smiled at him. Max was the only person in the hospital she let talk to her like that, and she allowed it for one simple reason: He was her best friend. That was saying quite a bit since Max had blond hair, blue eyes, and was a man. At a time in her life when she was very pro-black and pro-woman, Max had stormed his way into her life just as he had her office that morning.

Knowing that Max wasn't leaving until she did, Kendall stood and walked to the door. "Okay, okay. I'm going."

Max let out a breath. "Thank God. Dr. Phillips is about to pop an artery 'cause this guy is ranting about the poor level of service he's getting."

"Just great," Kendall whispered. "His cocky attitude hasn't diminished in twenty-five years." She turned toward her friend. "Come on, Max, let's go open a can of whup ass."

"Mr. Highpoint, if you would just calm down, we can wrap your ankle," the nurse pleaded, hands planted on her hips.

Coltrane Highpoint looked at the mature woman and immediately moved his foot out of her reach. "Not if you're going to move it and make it hurt more than you did when you took the X-ray. As a matter of fact, I want that doctor back in here. Your bedside manner is deplorable."

She stood with her hands on her plump hips, ready for battle. "Mr. Highpoint, if you would just sit still, this would already be over and you could be on your way home. I told you we had to get pictures from several different angles to make sure there wasn't a break, and you refused pain medication."

"You didn't tell me you were going to try to take my foot off in the process!" Cole crossed his arms over his chest in defiance. "Unless someone dressed in a white jacket and with a nametag that says 'doctor' comes in here, you're not touching my foot."

"Will I do, Coltrane?" A tall, slender African-American woman with the most beautiful dark chocolate skin he'd ever seen walked into the tiny examination room. Not paying him any attention, she headed to the X-rays on the vertical lighted table. "I don't see a break."

"And you are?" He noticed her purple dress was much shorter than her white lab jacket. He also noticed the dress was molded to her slight form, but he wasn't going to complain about that.

She finally tore her gaze away from the X-rays and walked toward him. "I'm Dr. Kendall Matthews. I'm on call this afternoon. Now I do recall you saying something about someone being in a white lab jacket with a nametag. I believe I meet your criteria." She nodded at the nurse. "You can leave now. I'll take care of Mr. Highpoint."

Coltrane watched the other woman scurry out of the room. He turned his attention back to the attractive woman before him. "Do I know you?"

"Vaguely. I'm Charlie Stone's youngest sister." She touched his ankle gingerly.

Coltrane watched her carefully as she probed his ankle. Amazingly, it didn't hurt. She had a delicate touch. "You're little Kiki? My goodness, it's been what, twenty-five years since I last saw you?"

"Yeah, probably."

He took a closer look as she rummaged through the cabinets, obviously not at home with the contents. For some reason, he couldn't seem to keep his eyes off her legs. They seemed to go on forever. He cleared his throat. "I talk to Charlie pretty often and he keeps me up on the happenings around Arlington. He mentioned you married a while ago and were now divorced."

She didn't face him as she answered, "Yes, about four years ago. I was tired of being 'the young Stone girl,' so I kept my married name." She located the wrap for his ankle and shook it at him. "Shouldn't hurt."

He knew she didn't mean that. It was probably going to hurt like hell, and he probably deserved it and more for the scene he'd caused earlier. "Look, I know you're probably here so I won't sue for the horrible service I got, but don't worry."

Kendall stopped cold. "Coltrane, I'm here because you were in here screaming at everyone like you were in labor. It's just a sprained ankle. You've gotten the highest level of care in this hospital and it was your choice to deny painkillers. We treat all our patients the same. No one is better than the next. No matter how many best-selling novels you've written, you're no better than the construction worker, accountant, mayor or whoever walks through those doors. Briarwood has a reputation for excellence, and you will not detract from that."

Apparently he'd struck a nerve. He hadn't meant to upset her. In fact, the more she talked the more he admired those full lips. His gaze went to her long legs and stopped at the stilettos. He'd never seen a doctor dress so sexy.

"Would you like me to model for you?"

Busted. "No, I was just admiring how much you've changed."

Kendall shook her head at him. "How about let's wrap your ankle so you can get on with your writing and someone else can use the table."

"I didn't mean to offend you, Kendall. You have to remember the last time I saw you, you must have been fifteen or so."

"Yes. Lie back please."

Had he missed something? Why was she being so short with him? Granted, he wasn't the most ideal patient, even if it was his friend's youngest sister.

He reclined on the table, determined to suck it up and not yell when the pain became too much. But oddly enough, his mind wasn't on the pain as he watched her delicately wrap his ankle.

He inhaled her scent. It was a clean scent that only reminded him of how long it had been since he'd been on a date. Having just celebrated his forty-fifth birthday, and with his life somewhat settled down, he probably just needed a little companionship.

"There. All done." She smiled at her handiwork. "I'll get Max to bring you some crutches. It'll probably take a few weeks to heal. Try to stay off it as much as possible. I'm sure your mom will be happy to have you at her house for a few weeks, or I can give you the name of a service that can also provide for you while you're recuperating."

"Thank you, but I just signed the closing papers on my house yesterday. I have everything under control," he said. "I'd like to catch up on your life when I'm a little more mobile."

She smiled. "Thanks, but no."

"No?"

Kendall started picking up the materials she'd discarded and pitched them in the trash can. "No, Cole. I know a man as good-looking as you isn't used to a woman not falling at your feet. You just want to know if those hazel eyes can work on me. They didn't work then, and they don't work now." She left the room.

Cole looked at the swinging doors, wondering what the heck had just happened. He was usually more in control with women. Granted, he'd had his share of willing females. He had just never had one throw him back.

Kendall leaned against the wall near the emergency room. What happened to her brain? After all this time, Coltrane Highpoint still jumpstarted her heart. She'd had a crush on him when she was a teenager and he was too old to consider her anything but his best friend's baby sister. She'd hoped the last twenty or so years would have dulled the ache she had for him, but she was wrong. So wrong.

She couldn't go back in that room and face those hazel eyes again. Couple those eyes with a dazzling smile, athletic build, and nice legs, and she was just like every other woman on the planet. She was done for.

After a few deep breaths, she walked to the nearest phone and paged Max over the intercom system. A few minutes later, Max called her back.

"Max, Coltrane Highpoint is going to need some crutches, and then he can be dismissed. You might need to write him a script for pain meds." Being a PA, Max had the authority to do just that.

"Hey, I thought you like seeing your patients to the door? Especially with him being a brother and all," Max teased.

"Not this time. You can have the honors. If I ever see that man again, it will be too soon."

Max walked into the recovery area of the emergency room expecting to see a very pompous celebrity waiting to be pacified in every way possible. What he actually saw was a man deeply confused, obviously Kendall's latest victim in the man-woman war.

The large African-American man was sitting on the examination table, his bandaged ankle on the table, while the other dangled off the end. He was shaking his head, probably trying to figure out what he'd done wrong and coming up empty.

Max realized Kendall's earlier call was out of character. She'd never asked someone else to take on any of her responsibility. She made it a policy to see every patient out the door personally. This man had rattled a woman famous for never being rattled.

This was a match made in heaven if Max ever saw one. However, neither Kendall nor Coltrane Highpoint knew it yet.

"Mr. Highpoint, my name is Max. I'm Dr. Matthews's physician assistant." He nodded to the crutches in his hand. "She said you might be needing these. I also have your dismissal papers and your prescriptions for your pain medication."

Coltrane nodded at Max. "I guess that means she's not coming back in here, right?" He made a move to stand on his healthy leg.

Max stopped his patient before he made the costly mistake of thinking he could manage on his own. "A wheelchair is on its way. Is there anyone that can come get you?"

"Yeah, too many people," he answered cryptically. "How about you call me a cab or something and I can get out of your hair, too."

Man, Kendall had done a number on this guy, Max thought. The famous author's ego was shattered. "Dr. Matthews isn't actually used to nurturing men right now. She deals mostly with pregnant women. But there's no rush about you leaving."

Coltrane looked at Max. "Don't you know who I am?"

Max nodded. "Right now you're a patient of this hospital, and that's all I'm concerned with. You have a sprained ankle and you're going to need some help getting into the car."

Coltrane laughed. "That put me and my celebrity status in place. Please call me Cole. I'm sure Kendall's recollections of me in my youth weren't good, but that was then."

"Okay, Cole." Max glanced at his watch. Kendall would kill him for what he was about to do. But what was life without a little death threat every now and then? "Look, Cole, it's almost my lunch time. Why don't I give you a lift home? I have an SUV, so there'd be plenty of room in it for you to stretch out."

"Why?"

Typical, Max thought. People with Cole's kind of status weren't used to someone doing something for nothing. "Look, man, I don't want anything from you. It sounds like you don't really have anyone to call, and I was just trying to help you out. I know what it's like to be in a place where you don't really want to be."

Cole nodded. "Sorry. I'm just used to dealing with a certain type of person. I have to remember I'm back home and not everyone is trying to get something from me. In New York, you don't know how rare that is. I would very much appreciate a ride home. I'm actually not that far from here. My house is in Biscayne Meadows."

Max couldn't help grinning. Looked as if destiny was already at work; Kendall's house was in that same upscale subdivision. "Yeah, I know the place. A friend of mine lives there." He didn't mention that the friend was Kendall. "It's very secluded." Not to mention the very high price tag of those custom homes and the armed security guards.

"Yeah, that was the main reason I bought it. I love privacy and don't like everyone in my business."

Max snickered. "Sounds like my friend."

CHAPTER 2

"Max, surely you're kidding! You know they do have taxi services around here." Max had just informed Kendall he was taking Cole home. "Cole has a ton of money. He can easily afford car service, or even a limo if His Majesty so desires. He can always call his mama. I just happen to know that his mother drives a Cadillac Escalade. Plenty of room in it for him and his leg."

"Kendall, I'll be back before you know it. I just felt sorry for the guy. Who wants to go home alone?"

Kendall knew her friend was right. No one wanted to leave the hospital alone. "All right, Max. Why don't you take some time off? We have a busy day tomorrow."

Max chuckled. "You want me to get all the dirt, don't you? Be his friend so he'll tell me all his secrets."

"No, I don't," she lied, though she would love to know what Cole had been up to all this time. Although her brother had mentioned him from time to time over the years, he'd never given Kendall any details on Cole. "Just make sure he doesn't hurt himself on the way. I don't want him crying lawsuit or something."

"Yeah, right. I'll come by your house later with a full report. Later."

Kendall shook her head as she hung up the phone. When Max got a burr in his butt there was no deterring him. Hopefully her dear friend of six years wouldn't embarrass her or Cole by trying to play matchmaker.

A few hours later, Kendall pulled up in her driveway, hit the garage remote, and sighed as the door slid up, revealing her mother's Lexus already parked there. "Oh no. What's she doing here?" The one thing she didn't need was her mother's weekly visit and plea for more grandchildren. She parked her Jaguar next to the Lexus, slid out of her car, and walked inside her house.

Her mother was sitting on the couch reading one of Kendall's medical journals. "Hi, Mom. Am I going to have to take my spare key from you, again?"

Zenora Stone-Evans looked her daughter up and down, then placed the heavy journal on the marble coffee table. "It says here that it's perfectly all right health-wise for a woman over forty to give birth to a healthy baby."

Kendall nodded. They'd had this same conversation every week for the last few years. It was her mother's attempt at subtlety. "I know that, Mom. I am a reproductive endocrinologist. I deal with high-risk pregnancies all the time. A woman can be in her fifties and still give birth to a healthy baby." She kissed her mom on her smooth brown cheek. "Now what brings you to my house today?"

"I thought I would come by and see Jordan, since he's the closest thing I have to a grandchild from you. I also talked to Martha Highpoint and she told me that you treated her son today. You know, that Cole is a handsome rascal. Too bad about his marriage."

Kendall looked sideways at her mother. "What marriage? When was Cole married?"

Her mother smiled. "Well, it sounds like someone is a little curious. I'm glad to know that you at least still notice when your path crosses with that of a handsome man."

Her mother had the irritating habit of always baiting her. "Mom, what about his marriage? He didn't mention that."

"Well, if you weren't so quick to turn him down he might have told you."

Kendall sighed. Trust Cole to run to his momma at first chance. "I turned him down because I'm not looking for a mate, Mother." She stood and whistled for Jordan, her black and white Pembroke corgi. She smiled when she heard the familiar sound of his paws tapping against the hardwood as he made his approach.

Jordan bounded into the room, headed directly for Kendall, and attempted to climb her legs.

Kendall picked up her canine companion and hugged him. "Mommy is glad to see you, too."

Zenora laughed. "You need to try doing that with a human being. Martha said Cole hasn't been on a date in almost two years."

So much about Cole didn't make sense to Kendall. "Okay, Mom, I'll bite. How long has Cole been divorced?"

Her mother patted the seat beside her. "Sit down."

Kendall complied.

"I know you think I'm meddling in your life, and you're right. I just don't want to see you become one of those women leaving all her money to her dog because she didn't have any children. I know you love kids because you're always doing things for your nieces and nephews. You take them to the zoo, movies, and you baby sit when needed. You have too much love in your heart not to give another man a try. Just because James Matthews wasn't worth the time of day and cheated on you at every turn, it doesn't mean that there's not another man out there waiting to love you."

"I know, Mom, but I'm not looking for love. James was thinking with his most used body part, rather than his brain. When I found out he'd gotten that girl pregnant, I thought I'd never live that down at the time, but it passed. That was almost five years ago."

Zenora hugged her daughter. "I know, baby. But now it's time for you to find some happiness. You bring all those babies into the world. It's your turn to have one."

Kendall rested her head on her mother's shoulder. She'd always thought she was happy. Wasn't she? She made a good living, had a comfortable home, but was she really happy? Maybe she could get her dating feet wet. She didn't have to drown in a pool of love, just wade in a little to see how the water felt. But the last thing she wanted was to get involved with someone her family already knew. "Thanks, Mom. I will find a man. Just not right now."

"Well, at least you're thinking about it. Why don't you like Cole?"

Kendall sat up and stared at her mother. "He's too good-looking."

"And that's bad because . . . ?" her mother asked.

"It just is."

"Spoken like my daughter with all those degrees. You better start listening to your heart. Now, what are you making for dinner?"

Okay, something was definitely not right. Her mother didn't approve of Kendall's dietary lifestyle. "Mom, I'm making stir-fry. If you're staying I can put chicken in it."

"Are you eating chicken?"

"Maybe. Now tell me what's really going on."

Her mother sighed. "Nothing. I just wanted to spend some time with my only daughter. Is that so wrong?"

Kendall knew there were many things wrong with that statement, but like any good daughter she didn't mention them.

"No, Mom, there's nothing wrong with that. We can enjoy a good meal and gossip."

"And we can talk about how you're going to get me some grandkids."

Some things never change.

A few hours later, Kendall was at the end of her mental rope. She and her mother had finished dinner

and were now sitting in her oversized kitchen sipping fla-
vored coffee. Her mother still had not divulged the
gossip. Instead, she was making Kendall stew in curiosity
soup. "Mom, you were telling me about Cole. What happened in his marriage?"

Zenora stood and placed her cup in the sink. "Well,
Martha said he married Gabriella Hunt right after he
moved to New York. The marriage was rocky from the
start. They've been divorced about ten years."

Kendall nodded. "What happened?"

"The usual. They had nothing in common. Gabriella
was pretty and she gave him a son. But after that it was
just downhill. She never came to Arlington and didn't
want to be married to someone more famous than her."

Kendall nodded, filling in all the blanks her mother
didn't. Gabriella Hunt was one of the most popular
African-American actresses in New York and Hollywood.
It seemed you couldn't watch a movie without seeing her
light-brown face on the screen. It must have been hum-
bling watching Cole come into his own popularity as a
premier fiction writer. Two creative types together was
definitely a recipe for disaster.

"Well," her mother continued the story, "when Cole's
first book was optioned for the big screen about fifteen
years ago, the bottom dropped out of the marriage. She
couldn't take it. It was fine when she was supporting his
struggle to the top, but once he got to the top, it was a
different story. They separated, then divorced, and his

son refused to see him. After that Cole kind of shut that part of his life down. Martha said up until a few years ago he was all but living with some newswoman, but something awful happened and he came back to Arlington."

"Why would his son refuse to see him?"

"Why do you think? His ex-wife was trying to get back at him, feeding that boy lies about his daddy. They just started mending fences last year."

Even though Kendall hated herself for it, she felt sorry for Cole and the hurt he'd experienced. God help her, it was just like she was sixteen again and she was reliving her crush on Coltrane Highpoint.

With the last of his energy Coltrane hobbled into his living room and collapsed on the couch. Thank God his mother wasn't there fussing over him and embarrassing the holy crap out of him.

"It's about time you got here, baby."

Cole sighed. His mother was there. Even in a city as big as Arlington, news traveled fast. He glanced at Max. But Max just shrugged as if he'd expected it.

Martha Highpoint entered the living room with a tray stacked with sandwiches and lemonade. She reminded Cole of a pleasingly plump Lena Horne. Her light-brown skin was flawless and didn't look anywhere near her almost seven decades on this earth. "Some reporter called me a few hours ago and told me you were rushed to the hospital. Were you unconscious? Is that why you couldn't call your mother? I've been worried sick."

"Mom, slow down. I'm okay. It's just a sprained ankle, nothing serious. By the way, this is Max. He works at the hospital."

Martha set the tray on the coffee table and shook Max's hand. "It's nice to meet you, Max. I'm glad Cole had someone to bring him home. I know he's a famous writer and all, but he hates to lean on people."

"Mom," Cole pleaded. "Max doesn't want to hear that." Cole himself certainly didn't. That was the main reason he didn't want to call his mother, brothers or sister. His family often treated him like fine china: something that could only be admired, and never handled.

Max laughed. "It's okay. I'm used to Kendall's mom and stepdad. My family is in Washington State and I do miss them, but Kendall's family fills that void for me."

That answer seemed to pacify Cole's mother. "Yes, Zenora is one of my dearest friends. I just talked to her a few hours ago."

Max had the strangest look on his tanned face. If Cole didn't know better and was more acquainted with Max, he'd swear Max was up to something.

Max cleared his throat, grabbed the crutches and placed them against the wall. "Yeah, I talked with Zenora this morning as well. She said she was going to have dinner with Kendall."

Martha nodded. "What took you guys so long to get here? That was hours ago."

"We stopped for a bite to eat." Cole didn't mention the couple of beers he'd also consumed.

"I guess you saw Kendall at the hospital. She turned out to be quite a beauty."

Cole nodded absently. "Yes, she's pretty, Mom." And for some reason she didn't want to have dinner with him. "She said she was divorced."

Martha nodded. "Yes, that was so long ago. She's not seeing anyone at the moment."

"Mom, could you stop? Max works for Kendall."

Max waved the remark away. "It's okay, man. I'm used to everyone always speculating about her 'cause she's totally dedicated to her job. Men have no reason for existing in her mind."

Martha laughed. "Sounds like a challenge if I ever heard one, baby." She picked up the tray. "Since you apparently drank your lunch, I'll return this to the kitchen." She headed out of the living room. "You probably shouldn't mix alcohol with your medication, but what do I know?"

Cole shook his head and glanced at Max, glad his mother was out of the room. "Mothers. What can you do?"

Max glanced at his watch and took a seat. "It's cool, Cole. Like I said, I'm around Kendall's family a lot. It's nice to be loved."

He couldn't argue with that statement as much as he'd like to. "Yeah, but sometimes I get smothered." He sighed. "I'm sorry, Max. I'm sure it's just the pain talking."

"It's okay, Cole."

"When I'm up and mobile I want to repay you for your kindness."

Max shook his head. "That's not necessary."

"Yes, it is." But Cole wasn't asking him to be nice. Well, partly he was, but partly he was being slightly devious. The only way he'd get to know the puzzle that was Kendall was through Max.

"You got a deal. You should take some medicine for the pain before it gets unbearable." Max handed him the vial of pills.

Before Cole could agree, his mother walked in with a bottle of water. He smiled. Even after all this time, his mother apparently could still read his mind.

He took the water from his mother and opened it. "Thanks, Mom." He took the medicine with a long drink of water and let out a sigh. Soon the pain would ease and he could hobble to the guest room and collapse.

Max rose, as if he too could read Cole's mind. "If you need anything, Cole, give me a call."

Cole nodded. "Thanks, Max. I just may take you up on that."

Max waved and left the room. Cole watched his mother escort Max to the front door and shook his head in wonder. Max had never once asked for anything and was well on his way to becoming someone that Cole could call friend.

A friend was one thing he needed the most.

That evening, Kendall watched her mother drive down the street. Finally she could breathe again. She knew her mother meant well, but sometimes that woman jumped on her last nerve.

Like tonight. Her mother's sole purpose in life was to point out every available single man in the Dallas-Fort Worth-Arlington area to Kendall. Zenora hadn't let the issue of Cole just die, as a normal mother would have. She hadn't stopped badgering Kendall until she promised to be nicer to him the next time she saw him. Which, if God were a woman, would be never.

She needed something to settle her nerves. Once around the park should do it. Walking upstairs, she whistled for Jordan as she walked into her bedroom to change. She slipped on some nylon running shorts and a short T-shirt. Pulling her hair back in a ponytail, she was ready to skate away some frustration.

Jordan ran into her bedroom and hopped on her king-sized bed. She ruffled his brown fur.

"Ready for a run? Your granny has put me on edge, and this is the only way I have to release my frustration right now."

Jordan barked and shot out of the room.

Kendall laughed. "I guess that means he's ready." She felt better already.

Jordan was waiting for her by the front door. Kendall grabbed her in-line skates and Jordan's retractable leash and they went out the front door. As was her custom, she put her skates on outside, so as not to hurt her hardwood floors.

Soon the night air and the quiet calmed her nerves better than any alcoholic beverage. She used the skater's path that outlined Biscayne Meadows. She'd lived in the pricey subdivision for the last three years and loved it. There were only twelve houses in the gated community and, as she skated by it, she noticed the last house had finally sold.

Curiosity got the best of her and she skated closer. A black Range Rover was parked in the driveway. Kendall was nosy, a trait she'd inherited from her mother. She wanted to know who her new neighbor was. She hoped it wasn't another professional athlete. The last one who'd moved in didn't last too long after he learned about the party clause in the homeowner's agreement. Parties could only be held at the clubhouse and had to end by midnight.

She figured the house had to be about four bedrooms, three baths, like the rest of the community. It had to be a family, she reasoned. Who else would need all that room?

CELYA BOWERS

"Hey baby, need a lift?"

She froze at the words, then laughed as she recognized the voice. "Max, what are you doing here?"

He walked up to her. His vehicle was nowhere in sight. He gave her a mock salute. "Reporting as ordered, ma'am."

"Ha ha. Not funny. Where's your SUV?"

"It's a secret. You told me to report on Cole."

"I did not."

"Whatever. Anyway, he has a nice place. Plenty of room to have lots of parties," Max said.

"Good thing he doesn't live here."

"Yeah."

Kendall didn't like Max's tone. "What are you up to, Max?"

"Not a thing. I just came by to tell you that there was no mystery family hiding at the house. I met his mom. She's a hoot."

"I know. I think that's why she and Mom are such good friends. They're both overbearing mothers."

"Yeah, there's that little detail."

Kendall started skating around Max. "Do you know Cole told his momma I turned down his invitation to dinner? And she told my mother, of course. What a wimp."

"Actually, that was me," Max admitted.

"You blabbed to her!"

Max shrugged. "You know I'm putty in her hands."

Kendall laughed. Here she was ready to hang Cole from the nearest tree, and it was Max's fault. "I'm going to have to remember how weak you are around mothers."

"It won't do any good. Now why did you turn Cole down? He seems like a nice guy. And he fits your first requirement. He's a brother. He also fits your second. He has a good job. And third, he doesn't live with his mother."

"I don't want to talk about it," Kendall said.

Max put his hands on her waist to stop her movement. "I think you're afraid of him. You're afraid there's a freak inside you and Cole might unleash it."

Kendall was stunned. Her mouth hung open in astonishment.

"You know I'm right. It's been a long time since you had a date. We won't even talk about the last time you got some. I say give the guy a break. Who knows, you might even like him."

CHAPTER 3

Three weeks later, Kendall walked into her house exhausted and not quite ready to deal with a hyperactive corgi with pent-up energy. Jordan barked and jumped until she had to pick him up and give him a hug. She laughed as he then struggled to get down and started barking at her again.

"Just like a man," she teased. "You get what you want and you're done. I guess this means you're ready to go for your run?"

Jordan continued barking at her.

"This is what I get for spoiling you," she said. "Do you know for the last two weeks I've been run off my feet at the hospital?" Kendall stopped as she realized she was whining to a dog. "Sorry, I'll go change clothes." She took the stairs two at a time.

She quickly changed into her shorts and a T-shirt, grabbed her skates and joined Jordan at the front door. "See, that didn't take long."

Dog and mistress headed outside into the hot Texas evening. Although it was almost eight o'clock, there was still a little daylight left. But Kendall knew it would be dark before she finished. She went back in the house and got the fluorescent retractable leash. "Now we're ready."

They took off at a leisurely stroll. Jordan trotted quietly beside her, not making a sound. She loved skating at this time of day when everything was quiet. Most of the children were inside and the path was hers alone. Kendall could actually think while she skated.

She knew she needed a breather from her schedule. Since her divorce four years ago, she'd worked hard to pack every minute of her spare time with something to do. It would be next to impossible to cut back now. She'd had a meeting with the accountant for her pet charity, InfaCare, a charity hospital for underprivileged children, and the meeting hadn't been good. She needed to find some funding or the hospital was going to be in the red for the first time since opening its doors five years ago.

Kendall prided herself on the fact that she never had to ask for funds. The equipment, as well as the doctors' and nurses' time, was donated. The only overhead she had was administration and medicine, two things she couldn't control.

Jordan growled, alerting Kendall that a stranger was approaching. The stranger was tall and walking at a brisk pace directly toward her. He was dressed in a dark running suit and she could feel her heart pumping hard and fast and trying to pop out of body as she recognized the stranger.

"Hello, Kendall." Cole stopped directly in front of her.

Kendall stopped as well. "Hello, Cole. What are you doing here? Are you stalking me now? I told you I wasn't interested in dating you."

A fine sheet of perspiration dotted his forehead. "How can you hold up your head? With that ego it must be huge. What are you doing in this subdivision?"

"I asked you first," Kendall said. "You're not supposed to be able to wander the grounds. They have a public park a few blocks away."

"Why in God's name would I go to a public park when I live here?"

Kendall gasped. "You live here?"

"Do you really think that poorly of me, Kendall? Okay, I might not have been the best teenager in town, but I don't think I warrant this attitude from you."

Kendall felt like a fool. "It's not that, Cole. I just didn't know."

"Max didn't tell you when he brought me home?" Cole started laughing. "That Max is a character. He was just over to my house the other day. You know he'll do just about anything not to go home."

Kendall knew Max always stayed late at the hospital most nights, claiming he needed to catch up on paperwork. Although she didn't question him, Kendall knew something wasn't right in his marriage and was just waiting for Max to tell her. She knew all about male pride and didn't want to hurt Max's feelings.

"Hey, are you at least listening to me?"

"Of course. You were talking about Max."

"No, I wasn't. I was asking you when you were going to drop the whole 'man hater' routine. You're not the only woman to have had a cheating husband."

"I see Max has been talking," Kendall whispered.

"Have you ever just talked to Max as a friend?"

She was outraged at the question. "Yes, he's my best friend. How dare you imply I don't know my friend?"

"Because you don't. You don't know one thing about him, but he knows everything about you. He loves you."

Kendall's mouth dropped open in shock and she reacted before she thought about it. She stepped toward him, expecting him to react like most men and step back, but Cole stood his ground. They stood body to body, but Kendall wasn't about to back down. "Look, I know Max is going through something, but he'll tell me when he's darn good and ready. So why don't you go finish your book or something?"

Cole smiled at her, a definite challenge sparkling in his hazel eyes. His hands settled on her waist, halting her getaway. "How about the 'or something'?"

Kendall didn't like the way her body was reacting to Cole's nearness or his touch. It wasn't like she hadn't been near a man in her life. She'd had her share of intimacy and she was usually in control of her body. This time, however, her body had a mind of its own. She watched his face inch toward her and she was helpless to do anything but wait for his lips to touch hers.

Cole hadn't meant to kiss her, but what man could deny himself a taste of those lips? He lowered his head and let his lips graze hers as his arms drew her closer.

She wasn't fighting him, so he deepened the kiss. Her hands crept up to encircle his neck and she moaned. Cole took full advantage of her relaxed mouth, tentatively teasing her lips further apart and letting his tongue speak for him. The kiss was electric and swept him into a tidal wave he wasn't quite ready for. He should release her, say something sharp and go back to his house, but something in his body wanted to pull this woman closer and lower her to the ground with his body on top of hers. He didn't expect to get his wish.

As they both fought for control of the kiss, Kendall lost her footing and they ended up on the ground with him sprawled on top of her. It wasn't an unpleasant situation, but he didn't want her to know how turned on he was. He quickly rolled off her as Jordan barked at him. "Sorry," he mumbled. "Got a little carried away."

"Apparently." Kendall scrambled to her feet and stared at him. Then she squatted down beside him and began pulling up his pants leg.

While this might have meant a green light for most men, Cole knew she was checking his ankle for injury. Her gentle caresses were playing havoc with his hormones. He was quickly on his way to having a full-blown erection, and there would be no way he could hide it. He pulled his leg away. "It's fine, Doctor."

"I just wanted to make sure you didn't re-injure your ankle. Actually, it looks pretty good."

"Yes, I was officially released today. Harry Connors said I should walk to get my strength back."

Kendall nodded and gracefully rose to stand. Unfortunately, since he was still on the ground, he caught a glimpse of a white sports bra under her short T-shirt. Why was something so functional turning him inside out?

She reached out a hand to help him up. But Cole shook his head. "I'm too heavy for you."

She laughed. "You weren't thinking that a few minutes ago. Give me your hand." She held out her slender hand.

Cole sighed and hoped for the best. The worst thing that could possibly happen would be that they both ended up on the ground again.

He took her hand and stood. Kendall Stone Matthews was a lot stronger than she looked. They stood face to face, feeling the awkwardness of the moment.

"Did you say you live here?"

She asked it so innocently that Cole was a little confused. "Yes, I did." The light finally went on in his thick skull. "You're the friend."

"What?"

He wanted to laugh at Max's now-blatant attempts to push him toward Kendall. Max hadn't bothered to tell either of them. "Max told me he had a friend who lived here. He just didn't mention your name."

The expression on her face was priceless. It made her look softer, more vulnerable, and much more approachable. Until she opened her mouth.

"I'm going to kill him. I'm going to give him a vasectomy the hard way." As she skated away from him, mumbling to herself, her little dog jogged behind her.

By all rights, Cole should warn Max of the trouble he was in, but he wasn't going to. Max had played both him and Kendall and they'd fallen innocently into his trap.

Cole walked toward his home and sighed. He was behind on his novel and that was where his attention should be, not on the woman who'd just skated away in a huff. The only thing Cole couldn't decide was why. Was it that she hadn't enjoyed the kiss as much as he did or that she was pissed at Max for not telling her where Cole lived?

As he unlocked his front door he decided that only time would tell. And Kendall's time was coming due in just a few days. She just didn't know it yet.

Kendall walked into the hospital the next morning with one objective in mind and damn the consequences. She was definitely going to rip Max a new one for his latest stunt.

It was a little past nine when she spotted Max in his usual position, perched on the edge of the desk of Jami Allen, her medical receptionist, annoying her while she attempted to work. Jami was a chocolate-skinned sister with shoulder-length hair, which she always wore pulled back in a ponytail. She was giggling at something Max was saying.

"Max Cork, I'm going to kill you!" Kendall announced as she approached Jami's desk, which adjoined the nurses' station.

Max slid off the desk and faced her. A wide smile split his tanned face. "And why are you mad at me?"

Kendall looked from Max to Jami. They both wore the silly high school grins of people in deep like, but they were both married to other people. Surely she was misreading the situation. Cole's kiss from the night before still had her on edge, and it was showing.

"Kee, why are you mad at me?"

He knew she disapproved of him calling her by his pet name in front of the hospital personnel lest it undermine her authority with the staff. He was doing it to bait her, but she wasn't losing her cool today. "My office."

Max saluted her in military fashion. "Yes, sir." He winked at Jami and headed down the hall.

Jami giggled at Max's retreating figure. "He's so funny."

Kendall cleared her throat, her usual signal for her staff to get back to work. "Do you have my agenda for today, Jami?"

The laughter abruptly stopped. "Yes ma'am. Max pushed the Donovan sonogram back to two o'clock."

"Why is Max moving my appointments around without consulting me?"

Jami looked flustered. "Max said he'd take care of it."

Kendall knew Max probably had a valid reason for changing the appointment times around, but he was on her bad list at the moment and should be taught a lesson. "Please remember that all changes should be authorized by me."

"Yes, ma'am."

At least someone treated her with respect, she thought. "Where's Keerya?"

Jami looked like a guilty child. She pretended great interest in the file on her desk. "I believe she's running a little late this morning," Jami offered in a low voice.

And no doubt from partying all night, Kendall fumed silently. At twenty-eight, Keerya Sanchez was on her way to being a great OB nurse, but her night-time activities were playing havoc with her daytime job. Twice Kendall had had to reprimand Keerya for being late, and there wasn't going to be a third. "Tell Keerya to see me when she gets in."

"Yes, ma'am."

Kendall walked straight for her office without another word. It was starting out to be a devil of a day.

She entered her office and found Max sitting in her chair behind her desk. Did the man not know how big a mess he'd created with his so-called matchmaking attempts? She closed her door with a thud, dropped her briefcase on the leather chair in the corner of her office. "Max, how many times do I have to remind you that I can find my own dates?"

Max ignored her question. "I was merely trying to speed up the timetable. Admit it, Kee, you know you want Cole. I think you've met your match. He doesn't back down from you like most men. He challenges you. It's going to be interesting to see who falls first."

Kendall's brain was on overload. Max wasn't even denying his underhanded plan! "Max, listen to me," Kendall started slowly. "I am not dating Cole. Not today, not tomorrow, not ever. If I see his face again it might be harmful to your health."

Max rose from the chair and shrugged his shoulders. "Whatever. You're still going out with Staci this weekend for girls' night?"

With all the drama with Cole the last few weeks, Kendall had completely forgotten about her monthly dinner date with one of her closest friends, Staci Diaz. "Thanks, Max, it had completely slipped my mind. Staci would kill me if I cancelled on her."

Max nodded and walked to her. "You know, I do all this for your own good. Kendall, you need some love in your life."

Kendall shook her head. "I tried love and it didn't work. I'm settling for a little friendship, which I have with you."

Max looked at her with serious blue eyes. "You know I love you, but you need someone to do the things I can't."

Kendall knew what Max meant. Yes, it would be nice to cuddle and watch a movie with someone, but she didn't have that option. "Max, it would be nice, but I'm not looking for that. How about I just settle for Mr. Will Do? You know, someone that will do when I need a date and not much else."

"I think you're selling yourself short."

"Maybe. But for now that has to be enough."

Max kissed her on the cheek.

Kendall smiled at her friend of six years and laughed. "This is when you say, 'If I wasn't married, you'd be my woman.'"

When Max didn't answer, Kendall knew it was time for her to drop all pretense. "Okay, Max, I'll tell you what."

"I'm listening."

"I'll be nicer to Cole if you tell me what's going on in your life. By life, I mean marriage."

"Why do I feel like I've just been escorted to the corner of the room and there's no way out but yours?"

Kendall batted her eyelashes, something she'd never do in front of anyone other than Max. "Because you'd be right."

"How about you come to Nurses' Night Out, next Friday? If you do, then we have a deal."

Kendall knew this was another example of getting what she paid for, but decided to play along. She extended her hand to Max. "Deal."

Max smiled. "Pleasure doing business with you." He headed for the door.

"Wait just a minute. Spill it."

He stopped at the door and took a dramatic breath. "All right." He turned around and walked back to her. "Remember, you wanted to know, so I'm telling you. And only you."

Kendall nodded.

"For the last few years, Caitlin and I have been having problems. She didn't like the idea of me returning to school after Carson was born. She says I spend too much time at the hospital. And I'm just tired of arguing with her. I know I tell you you deserve some happiness, but I think I deserve some, too. Do you know I've haven't been intimate with Caitlin in almost three years? Carson is four."

Until recently, Kendall had always thought her friend was happy. "I'm sorry, Max."

"It's not your fault. Caitlin and I have been married ten years, and I guess when it took her so long to get pregnant, the tension started to build between us. I've been trying to talk her into counseling, but to her that's admitting failure."

Kendall sat down in her chair. She felt like a fool for berating him for playing matchmaker. "Why is getting help for something you believe in failure?"

Max knelt in front of her and caressed her hand. "Why don't you try online dating?"

Kendall knew exactly why she didn't try online dating. That was admitting failure, that she couldn't find a man on her own. "Touché. What about you? How are you dealing with this? You can't stay like this forever."

Max shrugged. "Right now, I'm more concerned about Carson. Caitlin keeps throwing him in my face. She knows how much I love my son. She says she might move to get a fresh start."

"Oh, that's just awful. Women can be heartless sometimes."

"Spoken like the queen," Max drawled.

"I'm not heartless!"

"No, you're just focused on everything but a man."

Several hours later, Max's words still rang loudly in Kendall's ears as she prepared for the Donovans' monthly visit. Peri Donovan was one of her favorite patients. Although Peri's pregnancy had been full of complications, Peri's outlook had been outstanding. Most of the nurses looked forward to Peri's visit, mostly because of her husband, Brendan.

His Irish accent and intense blue eyes, plus the fact he didn't notice all the nurses swooning over him, just made him sexier. But Brendan only saw his African-American wife.

Kendall was washing her hands in the private bathroom adjoining her office when she heard a gentle tap on the door. She knew it was Keerya coming in for her reprimand. This time Kendall had a surprise for her.

"Just a minute," Kendall called.

"Dr. Matthews, it's Keerya."

"I know. I'll be right out."

Kendall dried her hands and walked into her office. Keerya sat on the couch, her purse in her hand, obviously knowing the reason for this meeting.

Kendall walked to her desk and sat down. "Keerya, we've had this discussion before. I understand what it's like to be young, but you have a responsibility to this hospital. I pride myself on having the best of the best on my staff so I can give my patients the best care possible. You're a dynamite nurse and I know you'll get better with time, but this coming in late and reeking of alcohol is not going to cut it."

Keerya's dark brown eyes filled with tears. "I understand, Dr. Matthews. I do love working here, even with . . ." She let the sentence drop.

"Me being a bitch."

Keerya's mouth hung open in shock. "I didn't say that."

"You didn't have to. I know everyone in this hospital is afraid of me. I don't want people to fear me." Lie. "I want people to understand that my main concern is the integrity of the hospital. I don't want to have to worry about my nurses smelling like a brewery while attending patients."

Keerya rose from her seat. "I know I messed up. It's my fault. I know you've already given me more chances than I deserve."

"So why do you keep doing it? Do you want to be fired?"

"No."

Kendall sat in the chair opposite Keerya and looked the young woman in her face. "Then tell me what's going on with you."

Keerya reached for a Kleenex and blew her nose. "Well, Dr. Matthews, my parents have been married about thirty years. A couple of months ago my mother told me that she doesn't love my dad and doesn't love me and told us both to get out of her house. It threw my dad for a loop and didn't do me much good, either. My dad moved in with my aunt until he can find a place, and I just moved into a new condo a few days ago. I had to go help my dad this morning. It took longer than usual."

Kendall nodded, realizing everyone around her seemed to be in some sort of crisis. "Keerya, have you talked to your mom?"

"No. My dad is a diabetic and has a heart condition. This has about devastated him. I'm really mad at her for destroying him like this."

Kendall understood. "You can take the day off, Keerya. Spend time with your dad."

Keerya shook her head. "No, I need to stay busy. At first I was trying to drink my troubles away, but that wasn't the answer. I know the Donovans will cheer me up, especially that dishy husband of hers."

Kendall nodded. "Okay, Keerya, now that I know the situation, I understand your behavior, but you could have just come to me. I'm not an ogre."

Keerya nodded. "Sorry, Dr. Matthews, I thought I had it under control."

"It's okay, Keerya. Remember, you can always come and talk to me."

"Yes, ma'am." Keerya rose and left the room.

Kendall breathed a sigh of relief. That could have ended horribly if she had followed her first inclination. But something nagging at her told her to listen to the nurse, and she was glad she did. With all that was going on around her, she felt like she was in the eye of the hurricane and the wind was only going to blow harder.

CHAPTER 4

Kendall squared her shoulders and walked into the examination room. This visit was probably going to zap all of her practical brain cells. The Donovans always did that.

Watching the couple interact with each other always made her want to run out, buy a romance novel, and dream of perfect husbands.

Brendan Donovan was seated near the examination table, talking on his cell phone. His wife was missing from the room. He stood the minute Kendall came into his line of vision.

"Hello, Dr. Matthews. Peri is changing into her dressing gown," he said in that sexy Irish accent.

Kendall nodded and went to the table where Max sat discussing something in hushed whispers with Keerya. "That's fine, Brendan. No hurry."

Both Max and Keerya gasped, but Max was the one who voiced their concerted opinion. "What happen to 'things must run according to schedule'?"

Kendall grabbed Peri's chart and studied it. "I still believe that, but there are exceptions to every rule." She smiled at Max's startled expression. "Stop looking at me like that."

"Hey, I just want to know what happened to the real Dr. Matthews." He walked closer to her so that only her ears could hear. "Personally, I like it."

"When Peri and Brendan are here, it's like I lose all my edge. I become an emotional female. They make me feel so, I don't know how to describe it, but because of them I know love is possible. That kind of love you always read about but never witness. Brendan helps her onto the table, not because he has to, but because he wants to. He accompanies her to every test, sonogram, and office visit." She watched as Brendan did exactly as predicted. "It's sickening."

Max laughed. "You're jealous of a pregnant woman!"

Kendall laughed. That was all she could do. She sounded jealous. Was she also bitter? "Point taken."

"Hey, how about dinner after this?"

Kendall shook her head. "I have to take Jordan to the groomer's."

"Is he staying overnight?"

"Yes, my mom is picking him up in the morning."

"So you have a free evening?"

Kendall shook her head. "No, I have to brainstorm tonight. InfaCare is almost in the red. I think I need a miracle."

"You just might get it." Max rose from his chair. "Ready?"

Kendall nodded. "Yes." She walked to the examination table where Peri and her husband sat holding hands. It was going to take all Kendall's wits to get through this visit.

"Hello, Peri," Kendall said, reaching for the gel. "How have you been feeling? Any problems since last month?"

Peri Donovan smiled at her. Her caramel skin was smooth and had the glow of a woman in love. "I've had a few cramps in my back, but Brendan would just give me one of his wonderful massages."

Kendall sat on the chair next to bed as she called Keerya over. "That's normal, Peri. Actually that's a good sign. You're entering your seventh month. Cramps are normal. I do want you to stay in bed as much as possible."

Peri snorted. "With a seven-year-old?"

"Yes, with a seven-year-old. How is Chelsea?" Kendall asked of Brendan's daughter from a previous marriage.

Brendan rubbed his wife's tummy. "She's at school until three. Peri's mom is picking her up."

Kendall raised a brow. "Your mother is visiting?"

"Yes, my parents have been here about a week. Mom won't let me do much. And I thought Brendan was bad. I don't even get to cook anymore. Brendan's been cooking Irish dishes for us. I've probably gained ten pounds." Peri smiled at her husband.

Kendall nodded, pretending not to notice the love evident in the room. It had settled over her like a thundercloud. "If you've gained any weight, it would be beneficial for the baby."

Peri sighed. It wasn't the sigh of a tired, pregnant woman, but rather a happy one. "That's what he keeps saying. But you know men don't count calories."

"You're still beautiful to me." Brendan kissed his wife's forehead. "You're the most beautiful woman in the world."

Kendall sighed. She wanted that. A man to lie to her, but in a good way. There was no doubt in her mind that Brendan loved his wife and he made it his mission in life to make sure Peri knew that.

Three hours after the Donovans left her office, Kendall was still reeling from their visit. She needed to come back down to Earth. Only one thing would help her clear her mind of all that mushy romance, and that was a workout in the employee gym in the basement.

Used to keeping strange and long hours, Kendall kept a change of clothes as well as exercise clothes at work. After checking with the night nurse, Kendall went downstairs.

When she was dressed in her exercise clothes, she immediately felt better and more energized. Until, that is, she stepped out onto the exercise floor.

Coltrane Highpoint was running on the treadmill, wearing nylon shorts and a tank top, showcasing his huge biceps and long, muscular legs. He had the attention of the four nurses that were also working out.

"Hey, Kendall," Max said. He was also on a treadmill, but jumped off and walked to her. He was covered with sweat, but wrapped her in a bear hug anyway.

"Max!"

He stepped from her, smiling. "What?"

Kendall nodded toward the nurses.

"Oh, they're busy checking out Cole. We've been here an hour and they've just watched him work out. If someone doesn't step up to the plate soon, she might lose out."

Kendall laughed. "You're about as subtle as an elephant in the corner of the room."

He put his arm around her and guided her to the treadmill. "Now you're going to walk on the treadmill and behave like a good little girl, right?"

"All right."

In a loud voice, Max called to Cole, "Hey, look who's come to join us? We can have a threesome."

The nurses laughed. Cole laughed. Max chuckled. Kendall was mortified.

Cole slowed his pace on his treadmill to a speed walk. "Sure, Kendall, you can be in the middle." He nodded to the vacant treadmill.

Max nudged her. "Come on, don't be a party pooper."

Kendall stumbled but was determined not to let her embarrassment show, especially in front of the nurses. She regained her balance and hopped on the treadmill ready to out-exercise both men. "How about a challenge?"

Max groaned. "Oh, no. You're too competitive for me."

"I accept your challenge," Cole said. "What do I get if I beat you?"

Kendall stammered, not knowing how to respond or if she should. But the woman in her would not be defeated. "Loser, which would be you, will visit the patients for an entire day." That should fix him.

He continued power walking and agreed to her challenge. "Done, but if I happen to win, I need eight hours of your time. One on one, if you get my meaning."

She did, and lost her footing and fell on her butt. "I think you should keep your libido out of this." She struggled to stand, knowing those nurses would have the story all over the hospital by morning. This man was going down.

He pushed the button to increase his speed. "I was referring to your stellar decorating taste. I saw what you did to Charlie's house and thought you could decorate a room for me. But I think I like your idea better. Ready?"

Furious at herself for falling into his trap, Kendall nodded. She needed to keep her concentration on her goal, to beat Cole at all costs. She pushed the controls for a run. "Yes."

Max stood between the two runners like a mom between two battling children. "Now guys, you type A personalities are too competitive. Remember that there are innocent people around here."

"Shut up!" Kendall and Cole said at once.

Thirty minutes later Kendall didn't know if she could keep up the pace. For a man with a recent injury, Cole appeared to have the stamina of a seventeen-year-old. Any other time she wouldn't have minded, but today she wanted this man to cry uncle first.

That was a nice theory, but somehow it didn't seem like it was going to happen. Every time she thought he was ready to give up, he got a spurt of energy.

"If you want to quit," he panted, "I won't hold it against you. You just come over to my house ready to work."

"You're older, you should really watch out for your heart," Kendall shot back. "I wouldn't want you to have a heart attack on hospital property."

"My heart, along with the rest of my body, is in perfect working order. I can show you later if you want. On a person-to-person level, of course."

Okay, that did it. One little not-so-harmless remark and she was thinking about his body in not such a medical way. *Stay focused, Kendall,* she chastised herself. *He's just trying to get to you.* "No, thanks, I've had enough small things for one day," she said, smiling as the barb hit its mark.

It was just enough to knock him off balance on his very muscular butt. He stood gracefully and walked to Kendall and held out his hand. "Well, Doctor, looks like you got me."

Kendall tried her best not to smile as she took his hand. "Yes, I have."

"The bigger question is, what are you going to do with me once you have me where you want me?" He grabbed his towel from the treadmill handlebar and walked toward the dressing room.

She should have felt victorious, but she didn't. What was she feeling? She stopped the treadmill and stared at Max as he stared back at her, shaking his head in disgust.

"Don't you look at me like that." Kendall wiped her face. "It was a fair race."

"Yeah, right. You know you can't joke about a brother's manhood. I'm white and I know that. You were fighting dirty."

"Not."

"Yes, you were. I knew that was going to happen, but I can't cry over spilled egos. I'm going to go shower. As a measure of goodwill why don't you join Cole and me for dinner?"

"Avoiding your home life isn't making it better."

"Said the woman with a dog."

Said the woman with a dog.

Max's words haunted Kendall through her shower and as she dressed to go home. Was her life on the path to true boredom, with dog included? Even Jordan, the dog in question, had a main squeeze in the subdivision.

Maybe she did need a date. Cole wasn't the worst person in the world. He'd do in a pinch, which was where she was at that moment in her life.

She sat on the bench and mentally ticked off Cole's qualities. Rich, handsome, and he was a brother. Okay, so they didn't have a lot more in common. He was a Mr. Will Do, not Mr. Right.

A Mr. Right would cause too many problems in her well-ordered life. A Mr. Right would probably turn his nose up at a forty-year-old doctor who loved to in-line skate at night with her dog. A Mr. Right would expect her to change her life for him and that was the one thing she wouldn't, couldn't, or shouldn't do.

A Mr. Will Do wouldn't make any demands on her lifestyle and if he did, too bad. He wasn't going to be a permanent fixture in her life anyway, so it didn't matter what he thought. Cole would work out nicely. And if she could get a little revenge for him treating her like a leper at the tender age of sixteen, so much the better.

She decided to let Max play matchmaker.

Gathering her bag, she marched into the men's locker room knowing that Max was still in there meditating. He'd taken up the relaxing exercise two years ago, and now she realized why he did it. Max needed calmness in his life and he surely couldn't get that at home. Kendall felt awful for not knowing her friend better.

She stopped in her tracks as she beheld the sight in front of her. It was the most beautiful example of the male body she'd ever seen in her life. The man before her didn't have a stitch of clothes on, and he didn't need any. At least not in her opinion.

Unfortunately, the person that body belonged to was Coltrane Highpoint. He was parading around the room chatting with Max about some upcoming party at his house.

Kendall held her breath as he walked to the shower stall and entered. Why couldn't he have a beer gut or some flab somewhere on that perfect body?

"I'm shocked at you," Max whispered in her ear, suddenly appearing out of nowhere. "You were ogling a naked man. I'm telling your mother."

Kendall opened her mouth to counter Max's comment, but what could she say? She did the next best thing and scurried out of the dressing room to the safety of the women's.

Max wasn't to be deterred. He followed her. "Kendall, there's nothing wrong with looking at a naked man as long as he knows you're doing it. Your mouth was hanging open like you've never seen a naked man, which I know is not true. You were married." He motioned for her to sit on the wooden bench.

Kendall finally found her voice. "James didn't look like that. And he definitely wasn't hung like that."

Max snorted as he sat beside her. "Kendall, I don't believe you were checking Cole out like that. I thought that was standard issue among the brothers."

She knew Max only said those outrageous things to make her laugh, and for once she was entirely grateful. "No, just another myth. I have to say Cole surprised me."

"I guess that means you'd be willing to take him out on a test run?"

"Maybe."

Cole stepped out of the shower and wrapped a towel around his body. He glanced around the room. No Max. "Just great," he muttered as he reached for his clothes. He and Max were supposed to have dinner, but apparently his new friend had forgotten. As he struggled into his boxer briefs, he heard voices.

He moved closer to the sound and realized it was Kendall and Max talking. She'd probably have his head, and other body parts, if she knew he was eavesdropping. He'd really have to find out what man did a number on her. From the conversation with his mother he'd found out that Kendall's former husband cheated on her, but it was a long time ago. Surely she should have been over it by now. Why was she still hanging on to hurt? Was she using it as a shield against him?

Yes, he thought. She was definitely using it against him. But he had faced tougher opponents than a woman shielding her heart from the world. He'd just have to wear down her defenses one at a time. And that was where Max would come in. If anyone knew how to help him get Kendall, it was his new best friend.

He continued listening to the conversation and wanted to laugh out loud as Kendall and Max were discussing the very thing he wanted. A date with her.

Things had just gotten a lot easier.

Later that evening, Cole watched as Max downed his third beer in less than an hour. He hated taking the sensible role, since a well-lit Max would be an easier mark than a sober one, but he had to do the right thing. "Max, maybe you should slow down."

Max signaled the waiter for another beer. "I'm perfectly aware of what I'm doing, Cole."

"Of course you are, Max. I just don't want Kendall blaming me when you have a hangover tomorrow. I would like to get on her good side and you showing up to work smelling like a brewery isn't going to help."

Max grinned as if he knew a secret, which he most likely did. "I know what would get you on her good side."

"What?"

Max shook his head. "Not so fast, Cole. I need to know why you want her so bad."

Cole didn't know the answer to that. It was something about the way she looked at him as if he were wasted space. He had to prove her wrong. "I wish I knew, Max. I know for some reason she thinks I'm worthless. I just want to prove her wrong."

Max nodded. "So it's a competition thing. You guys are going to kill each other. You're like two kids fighting over a toy."

"Are you going to tell me or not?"

The waiter placed another beer in front of Max. He took a long sip, then set the glass on the table. "Okay, I'll tell you. I'm only telling you because I got a feeling about the two of you. If you want to get on her good side, ask her about InfaCare."

Cole knew of Arlington's only charity children's hospital. It was known nationally for its good work and the fact that underprivileged children were getting quality medical care without their parents having to incur the cost.

"What about it?"

"It's almost in the red."

"What's that got to do with me?"

Max laughed. "Make the red go away." Suddenly, his head plopped on the table.

Cole knew that sound. That was the sound of a man whose life was in the toilet and who was hiding his pain through liquor. Max was out cold and in no condition to go home. "Just what I freaking need," Cole groaned. "Just freaking great."

After getting Max settled in the car, Cole drove to his house and helped Max inside and into the guest room. Max groaned and passed out on the bed.

Cole left the room and headed to the living room to call Max's wife. Cole was surprised no one was home. It was after eight. As the answering machine kicked on, Cole decided just to leave a short message.

"Caitlin, it's Cole. Max had a little too much to drink, so he's at my house." He hung up the phone and went to his computer.

Since Max was not an option anymore, Cole went to his laptop to search the Internet for InfaCare. On his first attempt he hit pay dirt, or at least he thought he had. InfaCare was a hospital, and it was located in Arlington, Texas. But what did that have to do with Kendall?

He clicked on the link to the hospital and got his answer. Definitely wasn't the one he was looking for. According to the website, Kendall was one of the founders of the hospital. Why? She didn't have kids. Maybe she was looking for penance for something in her past, just as he was.

The light finally went on in his thick skull. The few words Max had got out before he passed out finally made sense. InfaCare was in financial trouble. He could see a very devious plan hatching. If it worked, Kendall would be his.

Friday morning Kendall stifled a yawn as the accountant for InfaCare explicitly laid out the trouble she was headed toward.

"Ms. Matthews, although the facility is still financially sound at this time, we should really consider letting investors in."

Kendall shook her head. "No investors. I'll solicit donations or something, but that's it. When people start investing they start trying to tell me how to run this place, and I've done just fine."

The mature gentleman smiled at her. "Yes, you've done an excellent job, but this year the patient load increased by thirty percent."

"That's not my fault. Call the president and tell him to find these parents a job so they can have insurance."

He chuckled. "I know just how you feel. My wife was just caught in the downsizing crunch and I share your sentiment about jobs."

"How are we doing for the rest of this year?" Kendall braced herself for the bad news.

"Actually, you're doing pretty good and have the remainder of the year wired. But if you want to start handling cancer victims, that's going to require a full time person. Well, two actually. Possibly a department."

Kendall hadn't planned on a whole department. Maybe a therapist, a doctor, but not much else. A department would entail too much. She sighed in defeat. "Okay, maybe we could outsource that."

The accountant nodded. "Very sensible."

But then she thought about what that sensible decision would cost a child. "Forget that. I'm doing the cancer center. I'll just have to start doing fundraisers or something. Outsourcing is part of the problem. We have to start taking care of our own problems and not farm them out to someone else."

"Now that sounds like the Dr. Matthews I know. But to do that, we're going to have to get a game plan."

Kendall smiled back at her accountant. "I'm already working on it," she said, brimming with confidence. "I'm actually meeting with one of my board members for dinner later. I'm sure that between the two of us we'll come up with something."

Something indeed, Kendall thought as she walked into her favorite restaurant and jazz club. Brooklyn's was an upscale eatery situated on the edge of Dallas. It hosted only the best jazz musicians on their way to stardom.

After such a grueling day of meetings, consultations, and sonograms, she was ready for a night of relaxation. She wanted no baby talk, and definitely no Cole talk. She knew she'd get both with her best friend, Staci Diaz.

She walked through the entryway not giving one thought to the many men staring at her. This was her night, and no man was going to ruin it.

"Hello, Dr. Matthews, Dr. Diaz is waiting for you." The young man smiled at her as he escorted her to her favorite table.

"Thank you, Dante. Who's playing tonight?"

"Oh, it's a special treat. Javier and the Boys are doing a set. You got here just in time. It's probably going to be packed in another hour."

"I thought Javier was out of the country on tour." Javier Maxwell was a hometown boy and had played at Brooklyn's over the years. He had been rewarded with a huge recording contract the year before and was promoting his new CD.

"He flies out to London tomorrow." They arrived at Staci's table. "I'll make sure he comes and says hello." He pulled the chair out so Kendall could take a seat.

"Thank you, Dante. And tell your dad hello for me."

He handed Kendall a menu. "You know Pops is going to give you a shout the minute I tell him you're here. He still can't thank you enough."

Kendall smiled ruefully. "How is Kenyon?"

"Running us all ragged. Who knew my dad getting remarried would lead to me having a little brother with the energy of five kids? But he's a blessing. That's what my stepmom says."

Kendall nodded. "You know you love it. I've seen you with him."

Dante smiled, his white teeth contrasting with his dark-chocolate skin. "Yeah, you got me, Doc. He's the best birth control I know. When my boys get a load of him, they're running to the drugstore." He bowed and left the table.

"Well, Doctor, what is that we have on and when can I borrow it?"

Kendall unfolded the linen napkin and placed it on her lap. "This is what we in fashion circles call a dress. You remember, I bought it in Paris last year. And no, you cannot borrow it, because it would drag the floor since you're only five-two."

Staci laughed. "Only because you're eight inches taller than me. I could still wear it and have my husband's tongue hanging out of his mouth."

Kendall didn't doubt it for one minute. "You could have on a granny gown and Miguel would probably jump you at the door."

"True. Latin men are the bomb."

"Where is Mr. Romance, anyway?"

"He's watching Carmen. His parents are visiting for two weeks, and his mother is about to drive me nuts. She wants to cook every meal. I needed a break. Miguel wants me to bring him a doggie bag. We've had fajitas or enchiladas every night since she's gotten here. Sometimes you just want something else."

Kendall laughed. "See what happens when you marry out of your race? If Miguel was black you'd be eating soul food."

Staci smirked at her friend, knowing she was joking. "Yes, and I would do it again. No man has ever made me feel the way Miguel does. You'll see what I mean when you meet the man who can melt that wall of ice you have around your heart."

Kendall opened her mouth to issue a retort, but Kenneth Harper, the owner of Brooklyn's, approached the table with two drinks.

"Ladies." He placed one drink in front of each of them.

"Kenny, you didn't have to."

He smiled at her. "I didn't. That gentleman at the end of the bar sent them. He wanted me to tell you hello."

Kendall stared at the drink. It was a caramel apple martini, her favorite. Her eyes reacted before her brain could tell it not to. She stared into the hazel eyes of Coltrane Highpoint. "What's he doing here?"

"If you bothered to read the newsletter I email to you every month, you would know that he was signing books earlier. Did you know he and Javier were friends in high school?"

She had forgotten. "Yes, I remember now that they were until Javier's parents moved to Dallas. I guess they stayed in touch."

Kenny smiled. "Yeah, business has been booming. With him signing and Javi coming to sing tonight, I think I'll have Kenyon's college on lock."

Kendall nodded, easily making the translation that his youngest son's college fund was growing. Though in his forties with a twenty-year-old son, Kenny tried to keep up with the slang.

"So, Kee, what you want me to tell ole boy? You know the gold diggers been hovering around him like birds of prey. You better make your move, girl. He's a catch, although I know that don't matter to you."

Kendall was too stunned to speak. So Staci did her bidding. "Please ask Mr. Highpoint to join us, Kenny."

CHAPTER 5

"I see that I'm going to have to kill you now," Kendall said through gritted teeth. "Why on earth would you invite that moron over here?"

Staci laughed, picking up her menu. "One reason is that you called him a moron. That tells me there must be something fighting its way to the surface. What did the brother do? Make a pass at you? Tell you how incredibly beautiful you are?" She snapped her slim fingers. "I know. He told you that although he has more money than five gold diggers can spend, he would pay any price to have you."

Kendall tried to fight it, but she couldn't help it. She giggled at Staci's words. "You're awful. He kissed me."

Staci glanced in the direction of the bar. "You know you don't have much time. Share."

"Not much to share. Turns out he lives in my subdivision and he was out walking one night, and I was out skating."

"What kind of kiss?"

"The bad kind," Kendall admitted. Not that Cole wasn't a good kisser. He was. He could probably make cement have an orgasm with that tongue.

"Was he that bad?"

Kendall shook her head, ready to explain, but Cole was fast approaching their table. "I'll explain later. Hush."

"Hello, ladies. Thank you for inviting me to your table. I hope you enjoy the drinks." Cole sat down at the vacant chair closer to Kendall.

Staci, being Staci, said, "Oh, thank you, Mr. Highpoint."

He gushed. "Please call me Cole."

Staci extended her hand to him. "Staci Diaz, and please call me Staci. I'm a pediatrician."

Cole shook her hand, but glanced at Kendall. "Another doctor. Nice to meet you, Staci."

"How did your book signing go? I got here just as you were finishing up," Staci explained. "I can't believe you know Kendall."

Cole smiled at Kendall. "Yes, her brother and I go way back. I was best man at his wedding. He's also my attorney."

Kendall knew she should probably say something, but her tongue refused to move. They were talking as if she didn't exist!

Staci nodded. "It's good to have friends like that. Kendall and I are like that. We met at a medical convention years ago, in Florida, I think. We have kept tabs on each other over the years. She's one of the best friends I have. "

Cole nodded. "Are you married?"

"Yes. We have a four-year-old daughter. Her name is Carmen."

"Kids are a joy at that age. I remember my son asking about a zillion questions about everything," Cole stated.

Staci snickered. "Yes, Carmen does. And lately it's been, 'Where do babies come from?' "

"Why on earth is she asking that?" Kendall finally joined in the conversation. "Carmen is a smart and intelligent child. She probably could tell me."

Staci smile faded. "Oh, I meant to tell you the minute you sat down, but the dress took all my attention."

This wasn't boding well for Kendall. "What is it? You know you don't have to beat around the bush with me."

"I'm pregnant."

"What? Are you nuts?"

Staci gasped. "I know. Here I am over forty and pregnant with my second child. Miguel cried when I told him. You know he's hoping for a son."

"What about your practice? I mean, you just got things like you wanted and now you're pregnant."

Staci threw the napkin on the table. "You know, I think my mother was happier for me than you are. Are you that pissed about me having another baby?"

Kendall felt emotions coming to the surface, and there was no stopping them this time. "You're right, Staci. I apologize for my behavior. That was inexcusable." The first tear trickled down her face. She couldn't let them see her bawl because her friend was one hundred percent correct. She hastily rose, mumbled an excuse, and took off for the ladies' room.

Staci looked at Cole's shocked face and felt his confusion. Usually when she and Kendall traded barbs like that, they ended up laughing, not Kendall running to the bathroom like a siren from an old movie.

"Must be her time of the month," Staci said.

Cole shrugged and pretended to be interested in the menu. "Maybe you should go after her. She seemed pretty upset."

"Maybe you should tell me about the kiss."

He closed the menu and placed it on the table. "A gentleman doesn't kiss and tell."

This should be fun, Staci thought. "A gentleman also doesn't stalk a woman. I know for a fact that the book signing was over hours ago. While I was waiting for Kendall, Kenny told me you had been hanging out at the bar, nursing some mineral water for about two hours."

"I see."

"Cole, if you're trying to get on her good side, forget it. You're a man, and it's not going to happen. Think of Kendall as your most challenging project. Most women you can romance, but Kendall isn't like that. You're going to have to break her wall down one brick at a time."

"Yeah, I'm getting that picture."

Cole was definitely getting the picture when Kendall returned to the table ten minutes later. She was composed and ready to face her dinner companions. In other words, another brick had been placed in the wall.

"Excuse my outburst." She took her seat and sighed.

Staci winked at him as if to say, "I told you so." "Do you have room in your schedule to handle my pregnancy?"

"Of course," Kendall said without hesitation. "When are you due, anyway?"

"Mid-February, around Valentine's." Staci smiled proudly.

"Perfect." Kendall reached into her bag and extracted a PDA and began tapping on the small display screen. "February is a slow month, baby-wise, so it will be a perfect time to deliver."

Cole felt as if he had just walked in on a bad joke. He just didn't understand these two women and their special relationship and realized he probably never would.

Knowing he was licked, he sat back and watched the women as they discussed the pregnancy. It was as if the earlier episode had never happened. He noticed Kendall's wistful expression. Could the good doctor harbor dreams of motherhood?

The waiter appeared, ready to take their orders. Both he and Staci ordered steaks. Kendall, to his surprise, ordered a vegetable plate.

"Kendall is a lacto-ovo-vegetarian," Staci explained. "She only eats things that are grown from the earth, eggs and milk."

Cole nodded. He would never understand why someone chose to eat only vegetables. He was definitely a meat eater.

Kendall turned to him. "Go ahead and ask me."

Cole was at a loss. "What?"

"Why I'm a vegetarian," Kendall said. Without waiting for his nod to continue, she did. "I dated this guy in college and he was a vegetarian. I didn't like it then, but over the years and after the meat scandals, I started cutting meat out of my diet."

Cole shrugged, not knowing exactly what to say. "Well, I guess that means more meat for me."

It had been over a week since her dinner with Staci, and Kendall still couldn't get it out of her mind. Cole didn't kiss her that night, didn't touch her in any way, but it had seemed to heighten her awareness of him. And Max singing Cole's praises for the last few days wasn't helping matters any.

She sat on the edge of her king-sized bed with Jordan by her side. She held a silk blouse in her hands, and there was a black short skirt lying on the bed. In the spirit of trying to connect with the nurses, Kendall was going to attend Nurses' Night Out, a monthly occurrence. The nurses usually picked a restaurant/club for the night out. Usually, Friday night was reserved for laundry, but this was the start of something different and quite scary.

Kendall arrived at the club determined to have a good time if it killed her. She was now wearing in a silk blouse and short skirt with black stilettos. The blouse's bottom half was sheer and displayed her flat stomach. The short skirt revealed her long, slender legs, and her three-inch stilettos finished off the ensemble. Her shoulder length hair hung over her shoulders. She was ready for a night of bonding.

Cole had the feeling he'd been set up. Max arrived as promised for a Friday night of partying. As soon as they cleared the security gate of the subdivision Max dropped the bomb.

"By the way, I think Kendall is going to be at the club," Max said quietly.

"Why is she going to be there?" Cole couldn't keep his voice level. It had risen at least two octaves. "I thought it was beneath her to associate with the nurses?"

Max laughed as he navigated the road. "She's trying to change. I think if she can let go of some of the hurt she's walking around with in her heart, she'll be able to connect with them."

"So why is she trying to connect with them all of a sudden?"

"Actually, it's because of something you did."

Cole looked at Max sideways. "What could I have done?"

"Remember when you came up and we had lunch?"

Cole remembered it well. It was the first peaceful visit he'd had at the hospital. Kendall wasn't in her office or on the floor. "Yes."

"She overheard you talking to Jami."

Cole didn't really understand. "I didn't say anything off-color. Jami is a very nice young woman going through some major changes in her life. I was giving her the name of a good lawyer. Kendall's brother, as a matter of fact."

"I know, Cole. I've been telling Jami she needs to divorce her husband, but she thinks her son won't have a male influence. I think she could do just as well without her husband. She needs someone who will love her."

Cole nodded. Max sounded like a man in love, or at least deep like. "Max, do you have feelings for Jami?" He expected his friend to deny it.

"Does it show that bad?"

Cole sighed. "Man, you do realize that you're not in a position to have feelings for anyone but your wife?"

"Yes, Cole. I haven't acted on anything. She has no idea of how I feel, and I plan to keep it that way. Besides, I don't want to lose her friendship over something that could turn out to be nothing."

Cole wished he had that kind of control. "That's why you've been drinking so much."

"No, my wife is my reason for my drinking. But I'd rather not talk about her, if you don't mind."

"Got it."

Max laughed. "What I would like to talk about is how you're going to approach Kendall when we get to the club."

Cole had figured he was being set up, and his new best friend had just confirmed it. He was headed for trouble, he knew, but he was going to take Kendall down with him.

"He's just a man," Kendall chanted to herself as she walked to the table in Arlington's hottest place to be seen. "He's just a man."

In her first effort to bond with the nurses and other members of her staff, Kendall was in the one place she'd always thought she'd never return to. Larry's Ribs and Blues was the place where she'd caught her ex cheating on her the first time. She hadn't been inside the place since.

But that was the old Kendall. The new Kendall was trying to make a change in her life. The new Kendall was going to face her demons from now on, and that included one Coltrane Highpoint. She approached the table, plastered a smile on her face, and greeted her co-workers. Of course everyone but Jami and Max looked at her as if she were definitely in the wrong place. Cole was staring at her until she returned his gaze. She instantly realized he was looking at her attire.

Okay, staring or gawking would be a better word. Exactly the effect she'd hoped for after Jami informed her that Max was bringing his new best friend. She decided to make the best of a semi-awkward situation by greeting everyone. "Hi, guys, thanks for inviting me."

Cole tried his best to hide his nervousness behind his glass of Scotch. Kendall looked hot! He'd never in all his days seen a woman so beautiful. He couldn't keep his eyes from straying to her cleavage until Max cleared his throat.

"You're gonna blow it," Max whispered. "Quit looking at her chest. She hates when men do that."

Cole knew Kendall would be a challenge even if she hadn't dressed in a revealing blouse. He took a swig of Chivas Regal scotch, feeling the drink warm his soul. "Please sit down, Kendall. I promise I won't bite." He nodded to the vacant chair next to him.

Kendall sighed, took the seat, and hung her purse on the back of the wooden chair. Cole didn't need to be a rocket scientist to feel the tension at the table. He felt it from Kendall, too, and there was only one thing to do to relieve it. He leaned closer to her and whispered, "Let's dance."

Kendall shook her head. "No, thank you."

"Do you disapprove of me that much? It's just a freaking dance, not a proposal of marriage."

She turned to him with a look of anger that made Max gasp. "I don't dance," she said just above a whisper. "My ex-husband said I'm stiffer than cardboard."

He'd stuck his foot in his mouth, of course, but he'd fix it. He reached for Kendall's hand and stood. She'd never make a scene, so he felt pretty secure that she'd follow him to the dance floor.

She did. Suddenly, he realized that now Kendall was at least an inch taller than his six feet, one inch. How tall were those stilettos?

As the band settled into a slow number, Cole pulled Kendall closer to his body. She did move rather stiffly, but he would soon fix that. His hands settled around her waist. She was a perfect fit.

"See, this isn't so bad, is it?"

Kendall shook her head, glancing around the room, obviously waiting for the dance police to arrest her.

"Kendall, this is supposed to be fun. If you don't relax, I'll be the only enjoying the sensations of one body rubbing against another," Cole teased, hoping to put her in a better mood. "Why don't you take a deep breath and relax? This is a slow number, and no one is watching you."

"Liar. The whole table is watching me. I told you I couldn't dance and you still dragged me onto the dance floor. Are you trying to humiliate me in front of my staff?"

He heard her voice tremble. "Kendall, no one is trying to embarrass you. I'm trying to get you to melt that block of ice around you so someone can get in." He looked into sultry brown eyes that were now moist. Surely she couldn't be on the verge of tears? "What's this really about?"

"Nothing. I thought we were going to dance," Kendall said. "I mean, I can feel your body against mine, but I don't think we're dancing."

"Sorry, you just get my body all excited. I can't control it, Kendall. You're a beautiful woman and you're really working that outfit."

"Are you always such a smooth talker? I bet you say that to all the girls."

"Oh, you got jokes. I'll just have to show you what I mean." Cole knew this was a mistake, but he couldn't deny himself one more second. He kissed her on the lips softly. He was determined to go slow, to savor her like a glass of fine imported wine. He tasted her lips with his tongue and gently bit her bottom lip. He felt her surrender as her hands encircled his neck, bringing his face closer to hers.

Cole was too engrossed in the kiss to realize that the music had ended until he heard the applause from their table. Kendall would definitely think he was out to embarrass her now. Gradually, he ended the kiss. "Sorry, I got carried away. I was just trying to relax you."

Kendall looked up at Cole. She should be furious, but the kiss had felt too good. "I know. But you know what they say about paybacks." She grabbed his hand and led him off the dance floor, enjoying the look of shock on not only Cole's face, but everyone else's at the table as they took their seats.

Jami laughed. "Kendall, when you let your hair down, you don't mess around."

"I'm just making up for lost time." Kendall signaled for the waiter. She'd let her hair down, all right. She had been seen sucking face with the man least likely to return her feelings. Her heart would be the victim again. But she could prevent Cole from stomping on it. She just had to beat him at his own game.

The waiter approached her. "Yes, ma'am."

"Scotch on the rocks. Make it a double."

The waiter nodded and left the table. Max voiced his concern from across the table. "Kendall, are you sure? Remember what happened the last time?"

"That was an isolated incident." She didn't want to dredge up the past. She already felt exposed with Cole's hot kisses heating up her body.

Max nodded, not believing her. He grabbed Jami's hand and led her to the dance floor. There was something tender in the way Max held Jami close to his body as they swayed to the music. Kendall wished she could be that free.

"How are things at InfaCare?" Cole whispered in her ear.

That brought her back to the present with a jolt. "What are you talking about?"

"I'm talking about your hospital. How are things? I was thinking of making a donation."

Kendall's head started buzzing. How did he know it was her hospital? "We can always use a donation. What were you thinking of?"

The waiter returned with her drink. Before she could reach for her wallet, Cole paid for it. "I'll get it."

"T-thank you, Cole." Kendall grabbed the drink and took a long sip. Initially, she'd thought the liquor would put out the fire in her body, but it only added fuel to the inferno.

"Hey, you better slow down. That's some strong stuff."

Kendall took another long drink. "I hate to tell you this, but I'm capable of making my own drinking decisions." She downed the remainder of the liquor in one swallow to prove her point.

Which was not the smartest thing she could have done. The burning liquid left a trail of fire from her throat to her stomach. She closed her eyes against the pain.

"I bet you're regretting that little cowboy-at-the-bar moment," he drawled. He shook his glass, making his ice clink like a bell. "Scotch is like kissing you. It should be done slowly, so one can savor the flavor."

Kendall's eyes popped open and she looked at Cole. "What did you say?"

"I was asking you about your hospital."

He was lying, she knew it, but decided against calling him on it. "What about my hospital?"

He set his glass on the table and faced her with a smile so mischievous that he reminded her of one of her nephews when they were naughty. This was not going to go well.

"I would like to make a donation to the hospital, and there's only one condition."

Kendall needed another drink. Anytime anyone wanted to do something for her or to her, there were always conditions. "What is it? You want your name on the hospital?"

"No, I'm not that vain. I was thinking I could present the check to the hospital next month at the Arlington Annual Charity Gala and you can be my date."

"I can be your what?"

"You heard me."

"You can just make a donation anonymously," Kendall countered. She had no intention of going to the city's one charity event with this man. It would look too much like a date.

"I want to present the hospital with a check. I know you are close to going into the red, and I do believe in your cause." He signaled the waiter. "I don't think even you would refuse a large donation."

"How large?"

He smiled a smile so masculine that it could only mean more trouble. "Magnum."

She had a feeling he wasn't just talking about his charitable donation. "Dollar amount?"

The waiter interrupted their conversation. Cole ordered another round of drinks. "You want another Scotch? Or have you had enough of the rugged manly drink?"

"Another scotch."

The waiter nodded and left the table. Kendall watched as the members of the table headed to the dance floor. The band had picked up the tempo of the music and had started playing old school music.

Cole cleared his throat. "Would you like to dance?"

Kendall shook her head. If she danced with him, he'd probably try to kiss her again, and she didn't have her wits back yet. "No, thank you." She coughed. "You were saying something about donating to the hospital?"

He winked at her. "Yes. I will donate one million dollars on the condition that you attend the charity gala with me as my date."

"Why do I have to go as your date?" Kendall picked up her glass, then put it back down when she realized it was empty.

"Maybe I enjoy your company."

The waiter returned with their drinks and placed them on the table. After the young man was gone, Kendall took a quick sip of courage, then asked, "Why?"

Cole took a long drink of his Scotch and set the glass on the table. He picked up Kendall's hand. "Whether you believe me or not, I think you're a very attractive woman. I would love to be in your company. Kendall, I don't know why you hate me so."

"I don't hate you."

"You don't like me," Cole pointed out.

If he only knew the truth. "I like you fine," Kendall said quietly.

"Oh, yeah, I can tell you really mean that. Your ex really did a number on you, didn't he?"

"What are you talking about?"

Cole took another sip. "It's clear that you see me as the enemy, but you treat Max like a dear friend. You treat him differently. But me, I can feel the tension between us."

She felt it too. It was tension, but not the kind Cole thought. It was the kind Kendall couldn't ignore much longer. "Cole, it's not what you think." It was a billion times worse.

"Why don't you tell me?"

Kendall shook her head. "You just had your tongue down my throat. Now you want me to tell you all my secrets."

Cole studied her for a short moment. "Actually, I want to kiss you again and again. Until you can't breathe or think. But for now I will settle for a date to the charity dinner."

Kendall pondered her situation. That donation which she knew was nothing for Cole would go a long way toward setting the hospital up for at least the next year. Maybe she could open the cancer wing sooner than she anticipated. She had only one answer. "Looks like you just bought yourself a date for one million dollars."

CHAPTER 6

Exactly four weeks later, Kendall stood in front of her floor-length antique brass mirror laughing uncontrollably. It was almost as if she were sixteen again and her prom wish had come true: Coltrane Highpoint was her date for the evening.

Okay, back to reality. Cole was escorting her to the charity gala for one reason, and one reason only: It was part of the deal he'd struck with her nearly a month before. So technically it wasn't even a date.

But tell that to her teenaged heart.

Kendall took one last look at her attire and nodded approvingly. The pink bias-cut sequined gown accented her curves, and the v-neck hinted at her full cleavage. However, she wasn't particularly fond of the front slit that ran from mid-thigh. It exposed the length of her legs each time she took a step. Tonight she'd find out exactly what kind of man Cole was. Most men's eyes automatically focused on her breasts, then slowly they made eye contact; others stared at her legs. Was Cole a breast or a thigh man?

She glanced back at Jordan as he lay on her king-sized bed, watching her. "What do you think?"

Jordan barked once.

Kendall looked in the mirror and finger-combed her shoulder-length hair. "I take it you're still mad at me for not taking you out tonight?"

Jordan barked twice.

Kendall nodded. "You think I'm going to way too much trouble for Cole, don't you?" She exhaled. "So do I. But my mother, sister-in-law, and best friend will not let me do otherwise."

Jordan raised his head and his little ears perked up. He cocked his head to one side, telling her he didn't believe one word of her previous statement. He was right, because Kendall didn't believe it herself.

"Okay, you got me," she confessed. "I bought this very expensive dress to knock Cole's socks off. That will show him." Was that her sounding like a bitter woman? "Let it go, Kendall. That was almost twenty-five years ago. This is a new day," she told herself. "You're just gonna blow his pea brain, accept that check, and not let him put those sweet-tasting lips anywhere near yours."

She slipped on her pink stilettos and sat on the bed next to Jordan. As usual when something bothered her, she talked it out with Jordan. He was an excellent listener. Like now, when Jordan was listening to her insane ramblings about the one man she was genuinely attracted to.

"Okay, even I don't believe that. To be honest, Jordan, I could really go for one of Cole's sweet kisses right now."

Cole wasn't sure what he was expecting when he rang Kendall's doorbell. But once the door opened and he took one look at her, he knew that definitely wasn't it. He was expecting the uptight doctor to be dressed in some traditional black tasteful gown for the evening. Never in his wildest and most lustful fantasies would he have imagined this form-fitting pink number.

Instantly remembering Max's warning, Cole averted his gaze from her breasts. It wasn't easy, especially since he was a breast man, but he did it. He maintained eye contact and hoped and prayed the lower part of his body didn't get a mind of its own.

"Are you just going to stand there gawking or are you coming inside?" Kendall stepped aside to let him inside her house.

Hoping to God he didn't voice the retort on the tip of his tongue, Cole nodded and stepped into the foyer. He watched her every graceful move. "You look beautiful, Kendall," he mumbled. "I wasn't expecting such a lovely dress."

She smoothed her hands over the dress, tracing the outline of her gorgeous figure. "My mom picked this out. Can you believe it?"

Cole did, and would have to thank her for her contribution. "It's lovely and complements your complexion."

She picked up a small pink evening bag and smiled at him. "Really? I thought it was a little out there, but I'm glad I let Mom and my sister-in-law talk me into it." She walked toward him. "Ready?"

Cole heard the pad of four paws on hardwood as Jordan trotted in from another room. Cole kneeled down to greet the canine wonder, but Jordan wasn't having it. He trotted past Cole and sat at Kendall's feet and whined. This was definitely a woman's dog, Cole thought.

"No, Jordi, I can't pick you up. I'll ruin this dress. I'll be back soon and we'll go for nice long run," Kendall promised.

Jordan scampered off in the opposite direction. Kendall laughed. "He's mad. He's going to sulk in the garage."

Cole stared at her. She was smiling like a proud parent. "I take it that happens quite a bit."

Kendall started to walk toward the door. "Usually, if I'm going out on a date or something. It's a wonder he didn't try to bite you. That's what happened the last time I had a date."

He wanted to ask how long ago, but that wouldn't be proper . . . or would it? "Well, thank goodness he didn't draw blood tonight or we'd never get to the ball." He opened her front door and waved her outside. "Your carriage awaits, Cinderella."

"Why did you say that?"

He noticed the change in her tone, almost accusatory. "Sorry, I didn't mean anything by it, Kendall."

She took a deep breath, fighting off whatever was rolling around in her head. "It's okay, Cole. I guess I'm just a little on edge about this evening."

Unfortunately, Kendall's disposition only got worse. The minute she and Cole arrived at the Arlington Annual Charity Gala, everyone was treating them as if they were a true couple. She hated it, but Cole loved the attention and quickly fell into character by calling her "honey" at appropriate times in front of the Gala president. They were photographed and placed at a discreet table in the corner of the large ballroom in the Hilton Hotel.

"Away from prying eyes," said the president. "Just in case you lovebirds want to make out." She winked at them.

The Charity Gala was best described as the catch-all affair for every charity in Arlington. Instead of all the local organizations doing fundraisers year-round, there was one large charity event where one could donate to any charity they so desired. This year it was a carnival theme and tonight was the official presentations of the check.

Kendall nibbled on her vegetarian meal as Cole did the same with his filet mignon. She was amazed at the number of people, mostly women, who visited their table. She couldn't decide if it was a territorial thing or not. "Seems like you have quite a following."

He smiled at her. "Jealous? I have been writing for quite a while, you know. I have a dedicated fan base. Some people do love my subject matter and find it entertaining."

Kendall was one of those loyal fans. She'd read every book he'd ever published, but pride would prevent her from divulging that little secret. "I'm sure some people find that kind of book intriguing."

"But you're not one of those people," Cole said.

"I have no idea what you mean." Kendall ate a spoonful of garlic mashed potatoes.

He took a drink of wine and leaned toward her. "I have a photographic memory. I distinctly remember seeing at least four of my books on your bookshelf. So even if you don't read, thanks for at least buying them." He took another bite of steak. "Why don't you quit trying to fight it? Things would move much faster if you'd just admit defeat and fall into my arms."

She leaned forward, making sure he had a good look at her cleavage, and whispered, "Cole, the only way I'd fall into your arms would be if I stumbled and lost my footing."

He knew it was a lie, but said nothing. "Here's to whoever is on the bottom." He picked up his wine glass and toasted her. "You know, it doesn't really matter who falls first, as long as the end result is the one we both want."

"Does everything that comes out of your mouth have to do with sex?" Kendall felt herself growing warm at his mere suggestions. What was she going to do when she could no longer resist his innuendos?

Cole signaled the waiter for another glass of wine. "I think you might want to rephrase that question."

A couple of hours later, it was time for Cole to present his check to Kendall for the hospital. He stood, walked to the podium, and pulled out his prepared speech. Kendall knew nothing about this part, of course.

"Good evening," Cole began. "I'll make this short and sweet." He glanced in Kendall's direction. She was smiling back at him. Whether it was the wine or genuine interest, he didn't know, but as soon as he could he would find out.

"As most of you know, I was raised right here in Arlington, Texas. While New York was very good to me, I couldn't seem to get my hometown out of my head. I returned here last year and can honestly say I'm very proud of the changes that have taken place. One in particular is InfaCare. It's refreshing to know that there's still a place where the less fortunate can take their children and not have to worry about how they're going to pay for quality healthcare. Being from a single-parent household, I can understand the need for it. I would like to present my check for one million dollars to Dr. Kendall Matthews for the InfaCare Hospital."

Kendall was shocked at his speech. Okay, she hadn't remembered he was from a single-parent household until he said so, and it touched her heart. Cole was very good with words, she reminded herself as she rose from her seat. She walked to the podium, accepted the check, and made her speech.

"Thank you, Mr. Highpoint. Our president says he will leave no child behind in education. At InfaCare that's also our motto. No child should be left behind when the system fails them. No parent should have to worry when their child needs medical care and they don't have health insurance because they've been laid off. With your generous donation we will be able to keep our doors open. Thank you for helping us serve our community." She started to walk off but Cole caught her hand.

"We have to pose for more pictures," he told her.

Before she could think straight, flashbulbs were going off in front of her eyes, blinding her. Kendall reached for Cole's hand for a little security as the sea of press photographers began to eat them up.

"See, it's not so hard to lean on someone else, Doc." Cole led her to the safety of his car.

After they were settled in the car, Kendall began to wonder how safe she really was. Being so close to this man was a mistake, but what could she do? She was as helpless as the infants at the hospital.

"I was thinking we could take a little drive since you're all dressed up," Cole suggested. "There's something I want to show you."

"Is this anything like showing me etchings?" Kendall laughed. "Really, Cole, I would have thought you'd have something better than that lame line. After all, you do write for a living."

Cole joined in her laughter and headed to the southern part of Arlington. They were headed to Arlington Lake, she realized. What on earth were they going to do at the lake? "Cole, you know this is private property. You have to have an access code to get in."

"I know that." He stopped at the gate and punched in a long sequence of numbers. "I have it under control." At his words the gates opened and they entered.

The houses surrounding the lake were some of the priciest vacation homes in the county. He stopped at the third two-story structure. "This is what I wanted to show you. I just bought this last week. Actually, Charlie told me about it."

Kendall nodded. Her brother had mentioned the vacation home, but Kendall thought it was too good to be true. Apparently it wasn't. Cole probably got it for a song. "That's great, Cole, but why do you need a vacation home in the same city you live in?"

"I guess it's the artist in me. I think it will be great for me to write in. When I lived in New York, I had two homes, one in Manhattan, and one in the suburbs. Come on, you'll have to tell me what you think."

Kendall took his hand and let him lead her down the path to trouble. He unlocked the front door and ushered her inside. After he turned on the lights, Kendall couldn't believe her eyes. This house looked cozy. The plaid couch looked inviting; the green chaise lounge had a purple wrap tossed across it. "This is beautiful, Cole."

"Thank you, Kendall. I actually think you mean it this time." Cole walked toward her. "Who hurt you so bad that you treat me like I'm lower than dirt?"

Kendall was too tired to fight him. After three glasses of wine, she couldn't keep up the charade. "It was you, Cole."

He stopped dead in his approach. "What?"

Kendall sat down on the couch, wishing she had something strong to drink. Maybe it was time to clear all the dirt from the past. Cole towered over her waiting for an explanation. "Remember when I turned sixteen?"

Cole sat beside her. "Vaguely. I remember I was a senior at Texas University. You had just gotten your driver's license and your mom threw you a party."

Kendall nodded. "Do you remember what happened during the party?"

"Vaguely. Kendall, it was almost twenty-five years ago."

Kendall sighed. "I heard you talking on the phone to some girl. I guess she wanted you to come visit, but you said you couldn't because you were at a stupid kiddie birthday party."

"Say what?"

"I was so crushed because I wanted to ask you to escort me to the junior prom, but I couldn't after I heard that. You still considered me a kid, and that hurt me so bad."

He shook his head. "I'm sorry, Kendall. I was twenty-one at the time, and you were sixteen."

"I didn't see it that way. I thought you were the cutest boy I knew, and you thought I was a kid." Kendall wiped tears from the past from her eyes.

"Kendall, I'm sorry." He picked up her hand and rubbed it. "I was a jerk then, but that's no excuse for doing that to you."

"Everyone thinks I'm so hard on men because of my ex. It was you. I kept that hurt in my heart so no one could ever hurt me like you did. Even when my ex-husband cheated on me, it didn't hurt as bad as that day."

Cole kissed her forehead before taking her in his arms. "Kendall, I'm sorry. I know that means nothing right now, but I'm truly sorry. I had no idea."

Something about being in this man's arms did something to her sense of practicality. Tears held in check for a quarter of a century ran full force. Cole wiped her eyes and kissed her gently on the lips.

Kendall knew she should pull away from those kisses, but they only melted her resolve that much faster. As much as she knew she shouldn't indulge in them, she couldn't resist. After her confession she was weak with desire, and with that she gave in to the one man who had a hold on her heart. Her arms encircled his neck, bringing him closer to her body in total surrender.

Cole pulled her onto his lap.

"Cole, what do you think you're doing?" Kendall finally came out of her passion-dazed trance and realized she was kissing the one man she vowed she wouldn't lay her lips on again.

"I'm trying to make you feel good. Is it working?" He kissed her gently before taking her bottom lip between his lips and sucking.

Kendall couldn't really answer his question and she didn't want to. She wanted Cole with all her heart. She'd worry about the consequences of this reckless act tomorrow. Besides, what could actually happen?

A lot, she realized. His large hands crept up to her breasts and began massaging them gently in the rhythm of their kiss. She gasped at the delicious sensations he was creating.

"Kendall?"

She heard him call her name, but it sounded distant. His hands traveled all over her body and left a trail of hot fire as they headed straight for the exact spot. Kendall knew she was in trouble when she felt his hands hovering around ground zero. He patted her leg and she opened her eyes.

"Up."

She was confused.

"Let's go upstairs. To do that, you're going to have to get up, so we can both go." He smiled at her.

She felt as if Cole had sucked out some of her brain cells when he kissed her. She didn't understand what the gorgeous man was talking about. As she gazed into those hazel eyes, the fog finally cleared. He wanted her to get up. "Oh."

He kissed her. "Oh."

The feeling was like an electric jolt to her system. She stood and waited for him to do the same. "I trust you have something for this little event."

He kissed her again. "Yes, I do."

She gazed into the eyes of the man she'd once thought hung the moon. "I don't think you asked me properly."

He laughed, his hands caressing her behind. "Okay, Kendall. Would you like to continue this conversation upstairs?"

"That will be fine, Cole." Although she tried to put on her most stern face, a giggle escaped. Giving in to the moment, she extended her hand and helped him up. His erection was very noticeable.

Cole followed her gaze. "Yeah, you know that's your fault. And now you must pay." He took her hand and led her up the spiral staircase to his bedroom.

The large room was nothing like what she imagined a multimillionaire writer would have. It was comfortable looking rather than fancy. He had a California king-sized bed with a bright red comforter on it. Everything in the room was large and tasteful. Very Cole.

"Now that I have you in my lair, you're all mine, Doctor." He led her to the bed and motioned for her to sit down.

If she had misgivings about the course of the evening, now would be the time for her to speak up. But for the life of her Kendall couldn't think; she could only feel. And she wanted to feel this man all over her body.

She watched Cole take off his jacket and sit next to her on the bed. "Kendall, I know tonight has been emotionally draining on you and I'm trying not to take advantage of a situation, but if you don't stop smiling at me like that, I'm going to forget all my Southern manners."

Was she actually smiling at him? "Maybe I just like what I see." If she could keep this light, she wouldn't get hurt. But she knew it was already too late for that.

"Would you like to see more?"

She shook her head. Or at least that was what she thought she did. Her brain wasn't cooperating. Cole continued to undress. Soon he was standing in front of her in nothing but a pair of black silk boxers and a smile.

Kendall stood to remove her dress, but Cole stopped her. "Baby, let me do that. It will be like unwrapping a Christmas present."

Excitement coursed through her veins like lightning. She stood before him, waiting for him to undress her. He took his time, unzipping her dress slowly and kissing the area of skin it exposed.

Kendall thought she'd go crazy if he didn't get a move on. She wiggled her hips as he slid the dress off her body, trying to give him a hint. "Sorry, Kendall, I want to savor this moment forever. By the time we're done, we're both going to be crazy."

She was already there. Her legs refused to hold her upright any longer. Kendall stepped out of her dress, then sat down again on the bed. Cole kneeled between her shaky legs and pushed the stilettos off her feet.

"I told you I'd do that." Cole smiled up at her. "Now you must pay the price for disobedience." He pulled her pantyhose down and threw them across the room. He kissed her inner thighs. She reclined on the bed and closed her eyes. Hopefully, she could stay conscious.

She shot up with a start. "Cole, what are you doing?" She knew exactly what he was doing and it felt wonderful. But she had to get some kind of control. She wasn't used to not being in control.

He curled a finger under the waistband of her lacy pink thong and pulled it down her legs. Kendall held her breath as she watched him. He was watching her intently, asking a silent question. Kendall nodded. Cole dipped his head and tasted the apex of her womanhood. And that was when Kendall lost it.

CHAPTER 7

"Cole!" She tried to wiggle away from his ravenous tongue. He tasted her as no man ever had in her life. Cole held her hips in place and continued his mission to drive her out of her mind. She slammed her eyes shut as stars exploded in her mind as she climaxed.

He moved next to her after her body quieted. He held her in his arms and kissed her neck. She felt him move away from her; then he was back unsnapping her bra. She heard it hit the floor. Kendall forgot to breathe when he started caressing her breasts. He dropped kisses between her shoulder blades, then moved to her lips.

She wanted to say something sharp, but the feeling was too intense for her to do much more than moan. He kissed her hard as he entered her body in one strong push. The only thing Kendall was able to do was hang on for the ride.

Cole was trying to hold back. He wanted to enjoy the woman beneath him, but she held him in a grip that defied description. He didn't want to let go, even if he could.

Kendall looked beautiful with her dark-chocolate skin stark against his white satin pillows. Her eyes were closed, and she was smiling! That was something he didn't see her do very often. He was very glad he was the reason.

He felt sensations storming through his body with a vengeance. He increased his tempo as her moans became louder and deeper. She wrapped her legs around him, attempting to get even closer. Then he felt it. Her inner walls were milking him for all he had, and that was when he lost it. They exploded in concert.

Minutes later, Cole, exhausted and spent, separated himself from her and lay beside her. They were both panting. Sweat drenched their bodies and neither could say a word. When he got his bearings, he turned to her, kissed her deeply, wrapped his arms around her, and fell asleep.

A few hours later, a powerful sensation awoke him. Kendall's hands were traveling in her sleep, the one time she couldn't hide her feelings. Her slender hands roamed his body, gliding over his flat stomach and heading straight for the great beyond. She wrapped her hands around him and gently began stroking him.

Cole was rock hard in seconds. He removed her hand before she did some real damage to him, like making him climax. Reaching for a condom, he kissed her awake and pulled her on top of him.

Kendall's eyes snapped open as their lips parted. She noticed their new position and smiled. He'd expected an argument about not asking, but she leaned down and kissed him. "You must have been reading my mind." She took the condom out of his hand and ripped the package opened with her teeth. "I think it's my turn to pleasure you."

Cole watched in amazement as Kendall slid the condom on his very erect manhood. It was torture because she was doing it in slow motion, but it was a turn-on. After she was finished, she stared at him, waiting.

Cole, dazed, pulled her astride his more-than-ready body and impaled her. Kendall gasped and held on for the ride, bestowing kisses all over his face as Cole took over the pleasuring.

Sunday morning, Kendall's eyes slowly drifted open. She attempted to turn over on her back, but found her body was too tired to cooperate. After the third try she gave up, realizing she was also tangled in Cole's satin sheets.

Sleeping with Cole! What was she thinking? She knew exactly what she was thinking, and was glad this time she'd listened to her instincts rather than her head. Cole was an excellent lover, she mused, mentally counting the amount of times he had made her climax during the night and the early-morning hours.

"Hey, I didn't know if you were ever going to wake up this morning," Cole said, walking into the bedroom with a tray of food. The antique tray was loaded with an assortment of food. Pancakes and bacon she avoided like the plague, because she couldn't eat one without the other, but the eggs she could deal with.

The aroma of gourmet coffee filled the room. If her nose was working correctly, it was hazelnut créme. Coffee would help her tired body wake up. Kendall moaned and tried to turn herself over again but failed. She heard the clatter of the silver tray as he set it on the nightstand beside the bed. "Here, I'll help you."

Before she could object and refuse his help, Cole simply picked her up, sheet and all, and turned her over on her back, then helped her to a sitting position. She hated being needy.

"Thank you."

He sat on the bed facing her. "I bet that hurt, having to say thank you."

Kendall felt his stare at her cleavage as the sheet slid down her body. She tugged the sheet up to conceal her nakedness. "Thank you, Cole. I'm not used to being on the other end, that's all."

He was dressed in a T-shirt and shorts and looked very refreshed, if not energized. He shrugged his broad shoulders and reached for the tray. "I know. I probably should be thanking you, anyway. Last night was beyond description." He placed the tray on her lap. "Come on, eat up and we can talk about an instant replay later."

Kendall gasped. Her body wouldn't be ready for an instant replay for many, many weeks. "Cole, there's no way you're getting a replay. It was a slip in judgment." Against her vegetarian lifestyle choice, she reached for the plate of pancakes and bacon.

Cole reached for a plate as well. "The first time, I could see," he chuckled. "But care to explain the other time?"

"I did not have sex with you twice in one night." She'd lost track of how many times she actually climaxed.

"How I could have climaxed that many times and still want . . ." She let the sentence taper off into nothing.

"More," Cole finished. He popped a piece of bacon in his mouth. "I don't know why you're trying to fight it."

She cut up her pancakes, ignoring Cole's comments. Initially she'd had such a good plan to ignore him and show him what he'd missed. Now somehow that plan had gotten shot straight to hell. She took a bite of the pancakes and moaned. They were so light and airy that they melted on her tongue.

"I take it you like my cooking," Cole said.

She opened her mouth to object, but Cole was much too fast for her. He popped a slice of bacon in her mouth. She had no choice but to eat it. She didn't want to hurt his feelings; not after such great sex, anyway.

A few hours later, Cole thought he had indeed lost his mind. Having sex with Kendall had opened up a whole new can of worms he wasn't quite ready to confront. There was his best friend Charlie to consider, who just happened to be Kendall's older brother. There was Kendall to consider: She definitely didn't want a relationship with him, not that he'd ask. And finally there was himself to consider. At that moment in time, he had too many items on his plate to have anything more than an occasional bed partner.

But as he looked at her sleeping form lying next to him, he decided none of those items really mattered anymore. After breakfast, the two people most likely not to engage in sexual intercourse had done so for round two. It was as if they hadn't had sex the night before. Was he crazy?

She shifted against him, her naked form waking up his body in the most insane way possible. Cole groaned as he looked at the clock. It was almost two in the afternoon and they were still in bed. He snuggled closer to Kendall and kissed her neck. He ran his hand under the sheet and caressed her flat stomach. She turned to him, her beautiful eyes closed, and whispered, "I love you."

Cole knew she was just lost in the moment. Surely she couldn't have uttered the three words he wanted to hear so desperately. "Right back at you," is what he should have said, but he let those words die on his tongue as he kissed her neck.

Later that evening in the privacy of her own home, Kendall could reflect on the last twenty-four hours of her life. First she and Cole had had sex. Second, in a moment of sexual euphoria, she had told the one person she loved that she actually loved him! Thank goodness he had been asleep and hadn't heard her.

She'd just pretend that it hadn't happened. Hopefully, it would be a few days before she'd have to face him again. It would definitely take her body that long to recuperate from their little sexual marathon.

But "little" in no way described Coltrane Highpoint. He was definitely all man and built to scale. She was just about to order her dinner when the doorbell rang. "It's probably just Charlie returning Jordan," she told herself as she walked to the front door.

She opened the door expecting to see her older brother and her dog, but Cole stood in her doorway with a dozen roses in his hand. He was dressed in Bermuda shorts, a polo shirt, and sandals. As a rule, she wasn't crazy about a man in sandals, but Cole had nice feet to go with the rest of his nice body. She was in so much trouble.

"C-cole, what brings you by?" She ushered him inside, hugging the door so that their bodies didn't have the chance to brush in the hot Texas evening air.

But Cole had other ideas. "I thought we'd have dinner." He kissed her soundly on the mouth and entered the house.

Kendall's knees buckled at the emotions this man stirred in her exhausted body. Somehow she got strength enough to stand up straight and close the door.

Cole walked to the living room and sat on her couch.

Kendall stared at him. Didn't this man just come to her house unannounced, not even apologizing for interrupting her evening? "Cole, what are you talking about?"

"I'm talking about going to dinner. You know, a meal out, in a restaurant."

Kendall shook her head. "No, Charlie is bringing Jordan home later. So I guess you'll be eating alone."

He stood and walked to her. "You might as well get used to seeing me here, Kendall. We can have something delivered."

Having this man in her house was going to be trouble. But memories from the night before and earlier that morning marred her sense of judgment. "What do you mean exactly?" She tried to stall, but knew it was useless.

He led her by the hand to the sofa. In a move she wasn't quite expecting, he sat down and pulled her onto his lap and kissed her soundly on the mouth. "What I mean, Kendall, is that we're going to have dinner and talk about what's happening between us."

She opened her mouth to protest, but thought better of it when she glanced at those piercing eyes that dared her not to. Why was she fighting him? She might as well go with the flow. "Okay, Cole. You can order dinner."

He smiled in triumph and kissed her. "I'll order it later. Right now I think we have other pressing issues to discuss." He kissed her again.

She wanted to say they had already had this particular discussion enough times in the last twelve hours and didn't need to have another one. That was what she wanted to say, but the sensation of being savored robbed her of thought. The only thing she was really concerned about was that Cole never stopped kissing her.

"Well, I guess this is the reason your front door was unlocked," a very amused male voice said.

Kendall knew that voice. And that voice meant trouble with a capital T.

Cole knew that voice. He moved Kendall out of his lap, his first mistake. She was at least hiding his erection for the moment. But the sight of his best friend catching him with Kendall ended that problem for him.

Cole couldn't read Charlie's expression. He stood looming over them as they struggled to get themselves in order. Jordan ran to Kendall and she picked him up, hugging him fiercely. Cole knew it was time to face the music.

"Charlie, I can explain," Cole said as he rose.

Charlie crossed his arms across his chest. "Oh, I'm sure about that. Kendall, that picky mutt of yours didn't like the food I bought, so I know he's probably starving. You might want to feed him."

Kendall looked from Cole to Charlie, seeing the charade for what it was. Charlie wanted to talk to Cole alone. "Sure, I'll be in the kitchen." She whistled for Jordan and they both scurried out of the line of fire.

Charlie sat down on the couch, clasped his hands together in his lap, and then looked at Cole with a ridiculous smile on his dark brown face. "Sit down, man. It's not that serious." Charlie chuckled. "I'm just surprised. I mean, I didn't know you guys even remembered each other until Mom told me about the donation. Then I knew. Even with all your cheese I know a person just doesn't donate a million dollars without an ulterior motive. But whatever the reason, Kendall's hospital benefits, so it's all good."

Cole relaxed, plopped down on the couch, and laughed. "You had me, Charlie. I thought you were going to kick my ass." Maybe this would be easier than he thought.

"Not yet. Not until I hear the whole story. Kendall's on my bad list, too, since she didn't enlighten anyone, either. So how long have you two been involved?"

"Why would you think we're involved?" Cole hedged. "I mean, we were just kissing."

"I also know my sister. For you to get that far, I know that you're involved, and most likely against her wishes."

He definitely knew his sister. "Yep, on all counts. You could have warned me, you know." Cole didn't mean that. Getting there had been half the fun.

CHAPTER 8

Max knew Monday morning was going to be different, and Kendall's closed office door just proved it. He walked to Jami's desk to inquire about his missing-in-action boss. "Any word from Kendall yet?" He sat on the corner of Jami's desk.

Jami shook her head. "It's only a little after eight, Max, and she doesn't have a consult until eleven."

Max smiled at Jami. If only. If only he wasn't trapped in a loveless marriage, and Jami wasn't tethered to that son-of-a-bitch she was married to, they could be together. If, that is, Jami could get over that whole race thing.

"Max?" Jami laughed as she reached for the ringing telephone. "You'd better wake up or Dr. Matthews is going to have your hide for daydreaming."

Max sighed. One day. One day, he'd stop worrying about things he couldn't control. He watched as Jami became rigid and her answers to the caller became very curt. That meant only one thing. The soon-to-be-ex.

"No, Karl. You cannot move back in, and it's not up for discussion."

Max wished he had some of Jami's willpower.

"Karl, I said no. I know Dylan is your son too, but until you have a drug test proving you're clean, he's off limits." She hung up the phone and took a deep breath. She looked up at Max with eyes glistening with tears. "Do you have any idea how hard that was?" She reached for a Kleenex and wiped her eyes.

Max slid off the desk and hugged Jami, not giving one ounce of care about Kendall's rule of no public displays of affection. "Yes, Jami, I know how hard this is for you. I know what you're feeling. I feel it, too. You deserve to be happy, Jami. So does Dylan." Giving in to his feelings, he kissed her.

He expected her to pull away, but she grabbed him and returned his kiss with the same intensity. When they finally separated they were both out of breath. Jami grinned at him as she wiped lipstick from his face. "Looks like we've been thinking the same thing."

Max nodded. He hadn't dared hope she felt the same. Well, yes, he had, but now what? "Looks like." He leaned forward to kiss her again, but the phone rang. "I bet you a granola bar that's Kendall."

Jami giggled and glanced at the caller ID display. "It's her." She answered the phone with her cheery voice. "Good morning, Dr. Matthews's office."

Max listened as Jami nodded at whatever Kendall was saying. Probably a list of things for Max to have done before she arrived.

"Sure, Dr. Matthews, I'll tell him." Jami ended the call.

Max pulled out his PDA, ready to make the necessary adjustments in the day's schedule. "Okay, what does she want me to do?"

Jami shook her head. "Nothing. She says she's bringing breakfast for the staff and apologized for over-sleeping."

Maxed dropped the PDA on the desk. "What did you just say?"

"Close your mouth," Jami said. "You heard correctly. She's bringing breakfast."

"Oh, you mean her version of breakfast." Max picked up the PDA and began checking to make sure the hand-held computer was still operable. "Bagels, fruit, cottage cheese, soy milk, and juice," Max drawled, imagining the meatless meal.

"No, Max. Dr. Matthews said she was stopping by the Donut Hut."

Max dropped the PDA again. "You're trying to tell me that a strict vegetarian is going to the greasiest food pit in Arlington? Her arteries will clog instantly the minute she walks into the joint."

Jami nodded. "And she sounded unusually chipper this morning. You know how grouchy she is in the morning and how she despises people being late."

Max studied the facts before him. Kendall sounding happy and volunteering to bring breakfast didn't sound so out of the ordinary, but for her to set foot inside the most fattening place in town, something miraculous had to have happened, he mused. He grinned as the light bulb clicked on in his head. Cole was to have escorted Kendall to the charity dinner Saturday night. He'd stood Max up yesterday for a Sunday afternoon of drinking and watching some sporting event at the local pub. Could it be true?

"Max, why are you looking like that?" Jami began typing on her computer keyboard. "Why do you think she's in such a good mood? I've worked for her for over five years and have never known her to sound that chipper on the phone."

Max nodded. "I'm sure she'll enlighten us when she gets here." If his suspicions were correct, she should be singing Cole's praises when she arrived.

Today was the day for changes, Kendall decided as she parked her car in the hospital's underground parking lot. For some strange reason, she felt happy, as if only good things could happen to her that day.

Maybe the man in her bed that morning had a little something to do with it, but still, today was a start. She spotted two transporters taking a smoke break. The young men froze as she waved them over. They hurriedly put out their cigarettes and ran to her.

"Yes, Dr. Matthews, I know we aren't supposed to smoke there, but designated smoking is clear on the other side of the hospital. Our break would be up by the time we got there."

Kendall held her hand up to stop him from babbling. "That's fine. I really just needed some help carrying this to the nurses' station in my department." She opened her passenger door to reveal several boxes and several gallons of orange juice, milk, and apple juice. "I'd be willing to share some with you guys for carrying it for me."

The two men looked to each other for guidance, not quite used to this Dr. Matthews. For ten years she'd ruled with an iron hand. Everyone feared her, even the other doctors.

"Are those donuts in there?" the man asked as Kendall loaded his outstretched arms with the third box. "Smells like those weenie things."

Kendall was quite confused, but then it cleared. "Oh, you mean kolaches? Yes," she said, speaking of the sausage wrapped in pastry and drenched in butter. "I bought quite an assortment, so you can pretty much have your choice."

"I thought there was a 'no food' rule in your department?" the other man commented, hoisting gallons of juice in his strong arms. "I mean . . ."

Kendall knew exactly what he meant, mostly because it was her rule. "Yes, I know. I started the rule, so I think I can break it. What do you guys think?" After she picked up the last gallon jug of reduced-fat milk, she closed the door and activated the car alarm.

"Hey, if you can make the rules, then you can break them." He motioned for Kendall to precede them. "And everybody knows you're the boss around here."

Those words would have once brought her joy, but today they didn't. Those words reminded her that in channeling all of her energy into her job and the charity hospital, she'd lost herself. Outside of Staci, she didn't really have any female friends. She was going to change that starting today.

A few hours later after the chaos of the morning set-tled down, Kendall approached the nurses' station where Jami and Keerya were busy working. She'd worked on her speech for the last hour and could only hope for the best.

Keerya was eating a kolache and typing one-handed on the computer. Jami was filing. Both women had their backs to her, which was just as well. If they saw her coming they'd instantly go into their serious work mode.

Kendall cleared her throat and stepped with purpose to where the women were working. "Good morning. I hope the donuts were good. I should treat you guys more often for all the hard work you do for me. In fact, I would like to start with lunch. You can order anything you want. Don't worry about the cost, and it doesn't have to be vegetarian either. I won't force my food choices on you." She reached into the lab pocket and pulled out her credit card. She pushed the card toward Jami. "Just bring it to me when you've ordered."

"Yes, Dr. Matthews," Jami answered, pocketing the card. "Would you like us to order you something? Dr. Diaz? Her first appointment is today at one."

"I forgot all about Staci with all that's happened this weekend," she murmured. She'd definitely give her friend an earful when Staci came in for her first sonogram. "Jami, you're worth a million dollars. Thank you for reminding me."

Jami glanced at her. "Speaking of money, how did the charity dinner go?"

Kendall averted her eyes, knowing she probably still had the look of a woman in love, or at least deep lust. "It was fine. Cole was a complete gentleman." *And we had a lot of sex,* she mused, knowing she couldn't say that part out loud.

"That's good." Jami resumed her filing.

For Kendall this was do or die, sink or swim, feast or famine. She took another step toward the nurses. "Look, guys, I'm going to say this just once. I know you guys have been with me a long time and you each have been going through crises. I just want you to know that I'm here for you both. I have the reputation of being distant, but that's only because I want Briarwood Hospital to always be known as the prestigious hospital it is today." Kendall laughed. "My goodness, I sound like one of those boring CEO people. What I'm trying to say is that I would like you to consider me a friend as well as your boss. And please call me Kendall." She decided to clear out of the room and give the nurses some time to digest what she'd just said. Hopefully, they would know her words were genuine, but only time would tell.

Jami watched Kendall's hurried steps down the hall. Something was definitely up with the good doctor. Jami shook her head as Keerya grabbed a remaining chocolate donut. "What happened to the diet for the new you?"

Keerya also grabbed a plastic cup for more juice. She filled her cup and stuck her tongue out at Jami. "I decided the old me was just fine. Everyone can't be shaped like you. You have poor Max drooling over you every time he sees you."

Jami couldn't keep the giddiness out of her voice. "Really? Do you think so?"

Keerya gasped. "Jami, are you actually thinking of a relationship between you and Max? I'm not against it. I'm a diehard romantic and believe everyone should get some whenever possible. I know you and Max will work it out. You'll see. He'll finally decide to fight for what he really wants."

Jami wished she knew if what he wanted and what she wanted were one and the same. "Why do you think Dr. Matthews is in such a good mood?"

Keerya laughed. "Only one thing will put a smile on that woman's face. A man."

"But who?"

At high noon, Max burst into Kendall's office, stalked to her desk and planted his hands palm down. "Okay, missy, I think I've respected your privacy for long enough. I need details."

"I have no idea what you're talking about, Max." Kendall pretended to study her calendar, not wanting to look Max in the eyes.

"You know, you lie horribly," Max chuckled. "Come on, Kendall, I know he was your escort for the charity thing, and I know you didn't come home Saturday night.

CELYA BOWERS

It doesn't take a rocket scientist to figure out that you guys are attracted to each other, no matter how much you're trying to fight it. Come on, say it. Say, 'Max, you were right.' "

That did it. She couldn't hold her straight face for one more minute. She laughed. "All right, you win. You were right."

"See, do I know you or what?" He sat in the chair with a satisfied, smug look on his tanned face. "I knew something had to be up for you to allow us to eat on the floor."

"Max, I'm not that bad. I just wanted everyone to make good eating choices," Kendall lied.

"Did you kiss Cole with that mouth?"

Kendall sighed. "Yes, I did. Many, many times, if you want to know the whole truth."

"So did you break in the box of condoms?"

Kendall's memory flashed back to just how many times she and Cole had made love. "You could say that."

Max winked at her. "That Cheshire cat grin you're wearing tells me that you probably used the entire box." Max didn't give her time to answer. "I'm glad you finally let go and had some fun. I haven't seen you look this relaxed in a long time."

Kendall couldn't deny it. Cole had her seeing stars. "I feel relaxed." Actually she felt as limp as a wet noodle. She'd had every intention of sending Cole home when he appeared on her doorstep last night, but one taste of those lush lips and she had been as helpless as the babies she delivered.

Max rose. "You look very contented. Does this mean you're dating? Or you a slam, bam, thank you, sir, woman?"

Kendall didn't know what kind of woman she was at the moment. On one hand, she wanted to see Cole again on a social level, but the more practical hand told her she could never be happy with a writer. No matter how many millions he had.

Cole heard a distant thump somewhere in the recesses of his brain, but he didn't want to open his eyes. If he did, then last night would turn out to have just been a dream. But the laxness in his body told him that it wasn't a dream; it told him that he had participated in a sexual marathon.

Slowly the thumping got louder, and now he heard Kendall's heavy breathing. He fought opening his eyes as long as he could. "Baby, I'm too tired. I can't." He reached out to caress her, but instead felt something hot and furry. His eyes sprang open, and instantly he started to chuckle. "I think you gave me a heart attack."

Jordan looked him and barked.

Cole glanced around the room. Kendall's side was missing one very sexy woman, and he realized why when he set his gaze on the bedside clock. "Oh, my God, that can't be right. It can't be almost one in the afternoon!"

But it was one o'clock. Kendall had left him in her bed and probably expected him to walk her dog or something. Cole had no intention of walking or feeding her dog. He had to maintain the upper hand. Jordan crept over to where he lay and give him a big, fat, wet good morning kiss.

Cole laughed. He was dog-whipped already. "All right, man. You win. You know you're setting the men's movement back by making me feed you."

Jordan barked and scampered off the bed.

Instead of being upset, Cole shrugged off the situation and looked for his clothes. After slipping on his boxer shorts and jeans, he headed downstairs. By the time he reached the kitchen, Jordan was waiting for him beside his feeding bowl. "I know you're probably starving," Cole murmured. "I just have to find your food." Cole planted his hands on his waist and tried to get his bearings. "If I were dog food, where would I be?" He started searching the cabinets to his immediate right. Jordan began barking fiercely.

Cole laughed. "Okay, I guess I'm going the wrong way, huh?" He started to search the cabinet nearest the refrigerator. Bingo! He grabbed the bag and began to pour the contents into Jordan's silver doggie bowl. "I can't believe she feeds you this stuff." He filled the dish and replaced the gourmet food back in the cabinet. "That stuff cost the equivalent of a steak dinner," Cole commented.

But Jordan didn't care, or at least he was ignoring Cole while he ate.

While Jordan munched on brunch, Cole listened to his stomach rumble. "I guess it's time for some human food." He opened the refrigerator and got the disappointment of the day. There wasn't a slice of bacon, a patty of sausage or a sliver of hope of any kind of meat in her newfangled fridge. Vegetarian. He'd forgotten Kendall didn't eat meat. "That's the first thing I'm changing around here, Jordan."

He walked to the coffee pot, deciding on caffeine instead. As he turned on the faucet, his last remark hit him square in the heart. Was he actually making plans of the emotional kind with Kendall? For Kendall? He knew what she used to feel, but what did the woman in her think about him now?

He didn't get much chance to think about it. The phone rang. Should he answer it? The phone rang again. He picked up the cordless phone and glanced at the Caller ID. It was the hospital, but most likely it was Kendall, so he picked it up. It wasn't Kendall, it was Max. Cole groaned inwardly as he greeted his friend. "Hey, Max."

"Don't you 'hey Max' me, dude. I know what you did this weekend," Max teased. "I don't want you to elaborate on details, 'cause that's just too weird. But how do you feel?"

"Exhausted," Cole admitted. "After I walk Jordan, I'm heading home to sleep for about two days."

"Not today, bud. Unfortunately, it's the real reason I called. The board was so taken with your donation to Kendall's hospital that they want to capitalize on it. They want to do a PSA with you and Kendall."

Cole rubbed his head. This couldn't be happening. "You can't be serious. The last thing she wants is publicity about the hospital." He knew she'd blame him for this.

"I know that, but this will generate more money for the hospital. Holly Banton of CNT called today, and that's what really got the ball rolling."

Cole felt his blood chill. He'd thought he'd rid himself of the over-aggressive reporter. "Did you say Holly Banton?"

"Yeah. She kind of suggested a human interest story on the hospital on the 'America's Heroes' segment. Then she suggested a PSA on Kendall and your donation."

"I just bet."

"Cole, I'm sensing there's a problem," Max said. "I did think it was strange she called us, but the chief administrator jumped on board with the idea before I could warn Kendall."

Cole tried not to hyperventilate. "Yes, there's a big problem. I know Holly."

"Why does the tone in your voice tell me that you'd rather not hear that name?"

Cole sighed. "I met Holly years ago, and she's one of the reasons I came back home. She's not just an aggressive no-holds barred ace reporter when she's on the job. She's like that all the time."

"So I'm guessing she set you in her sights."

"Yes, she did. I wasn't interested. She's too bossy and demanding. Everything has to be on her timetable. She wanted me to forsake promised appearances, deadlines, but the deal breaker was two years ago. She used me in a story, and not in a good way. I lost a multimillion dollar book deal because of her lies."

"Well, you were interested," Max concluded.

"After that little stunt, no. My agent filed charges against her and CNT, and they settled out of court. The only good thing that happened was Holly was demoted to proofing copy, but to me it's still not enough. I wish I could make her pay for what she did to me."

Max nodded, understanding Cole's pain. "So what did you do after that?"

"After all the dust settled and CNT publicly apologized, I got a new deal with my publisher and I left New York. I just had to get away. I spent almost six months in Ireland thinking about what was actually important to me. There was really nothing left for me in New York, since Holly had sullied my name. My son didn't want to have anything to do with me, or so my ex-wife said. Finally I came back home. No matter how crappy your life gets, you can always come home."

Kendall stared at Staci as she plopped down in the chair in her office. There were two ways to play this. She could pretend Staci wasn't her dearest friend on the planet and treat her as a stranger, or she could tell her honestly the dangers she faced. She chose the latter. "Staci, we've been friends a long time. I have to be honest with you. Your blood pressure was slightly elevated. I know you have a weakness for Mexican food, but you're going to have to start eating better. You're not a spring chicken, you know."

"Yeah, yeah, yeah. Miguel has been cooking. After his mother left he started on this kick. But I told him we had to stop eating like that, so things will return to normal. What I want to know is, who has put a spring in your step?"

Kendall had known Staci would cut to the chase, but she didn't want to give in so quickly. "I have no idea what you're talking about." Kendall attempted to change the subject. "Now about these test results."

"Oh, forget the tests for now. I want to talk about you and Cole."

How on earth could she have figured that out? "Who said I was with Cole?"

Staci waved a perfectly manicured hand in front of her face. "Oh, please. I know he rocked your world. I could tell when you guys were at the restaurant that you wanted each other. I'm just glad you unlocked the vault and dusted off the cobwebs. How was he?"

Staci always got to the heart of the matter. "I can't believe you asked me that." Kendall opened the file folder, attempting to steer the conversation away from Cole. "Now can we please get back to your consultation?"

"Not until you give me the thrust-by-thrust replay," Staci teased. "I'm pregnant, I need some excitement."

Kendall seldom found herself pinned against a wall, but Staci could be stubborn when it suited her, and today was the day. Besides, she was ready to share the details with someone. "All right, I'll give you some of the details."

CHAPTER 9

Hours later, Kendall just wanted to go home, take a hot bath, and go to bed early. Her body was paying her back for having sex all weekend. Every muscle ached with each and every move she made.

She glanced at her desk clock and sighed. It was barely four o'clock and she was ready to go home. She had planned to work on plans for the charity hospital, but as her mouth stretched wide for yet another yawn, she gave up on the pretense of working and decided to check out for the day.

She gathered her briefcase and her shoulder bag and headed for the nurses' station. Since it was early evening, the only person at the counter was Jami. Kendall neared the counter and heard her gentle sobs.

Kendall walked to Jami's desk. "Jami, what's wrong?"

Jami's brown face looked up. She didn't try to hide her tears. Not that she could have. "Dr. Matthews, I didn't hear you."

Kendall grabbed a vacant chair and sat beside her. Not being a very touchy feely person, Kendall was at a loss as how to approach her. Jami needed comforting. Kendall tentatively placed an arm around Jami's shoulders. "Never you mind that, Jami. Why don't you tell me what's wrong?"

"It's Karl."

"Your husband? I thought you guys were separated." Kendall moved closer to Jami.

"We are. Were. He called me today and told me that he was going to sell the house. He said he couldn't afford child support since he didn't have a job. If he sells the house, Dylan and I will have nowhere to go." The tears started all over again. "He claims he can't keep the payments up on the house."

"Does he realize you'll get half the proceeds, according to Texas law, because you're married?"

"Yes, I told him that. I think that just infuriated him more. He said he would move back into the house since he had no intention of giving me one dime."

"You know, sometimes men make me sick," Kendall said. "What are you going to do?"

"I have no idea. I could rent an apartment, but I don't have a rental history. Karl and I have been married for the last seven years, and before that I lived with my parents, but they've passed away since then, and my sister now lives in New York. The few places I could afford want a huge deposit. I just can't do all that right now. I mean, I make good money, but I have to pay for daycare, car payments, and utilities. I just can't do it."

Kendall knew what it was like to have your back against the wall. "Why don't you move in with me until you get your footing? I live in a gated subdivision, so you'd be safe from Karl."

"Dr. Matthews, I couldn't. Dylan would wreck your house."

"I told you to call me Kendall. I would love to have you guys there. I have the room. I'm not trying to force you, so just let me know if you decide you want to."

Jami looked at her with those teary brown eyes. She grabbed a Kleenex and hastily dried her eyes. "Thank you for the offer, Kendall, but surely Karl will come to his senses."

It wasn't that Kendall thought Jami should have jumped at her offer; she just wanted Jami to know she had an option. "You should never be dependent on a man, Jami. Is your name on the deed to the house?"

"No. He had it when we met and we never bothered to change it."

Kendall reached for a notepad, a gift from the medical sales rep, and scribbled her address and phone number. She handed the small piece of paper to Jami. "I'm not saying that you have to stay at my house, but you do have the option."

Jami took the oversized Post-it and stuffed it in her jacket pocket. "Thank you, Kendall."

"I know it's your decision, Jami. Just know that I'm here if you ever want to talk. I'm ready to listen, and I don't judge."

"I appreciate that, Kendall, but I have to work this out for myself."

"I know. I just wanted you to know that you have a friend. If you need a few days to get your bearings, I understand."

Jami nodded, finding some composure. "I need to work to keep from going nuts."

Kendall understood completely. Chaotic thoughts of work were better than idle thoughts of a marriage gone bad. "You know, when I was going through my divorce I surrounded myself with things that made me happy. I worked crazy hours, went to the spa almost daily, and listened to classical music."

Jami laughed. "These days, it's Dylan for me and having good friends."

"I hope that includes me," Kendall said hopefully. "I want you and Keerya to look at me as the slightly older sister and know that you can always come to me."

"You don't know what those words mean to me, Kendall. Especially now."

Jami's phone rang and Kendall listened to the one-sided conversation. She could easily tell it was Max. The biggest giveaway was that larger-than-life smile plastered on Jami's face.

"No, I'm fine. Kendall is here right now. No, you don't have to have come back to the hospital. I promise I'll call you if any trouble starts."

Feeling dismissed, Kendall rose and left Jami to her phone call. She walked to her car and headed home. Now she was really drained. She didn't even feel like putting together a salad, and turned into her favorite Chinese restaurant and ordered some stir-fried rice.

After getting her food, she resumed her journey home. When she let herself in her house, Jordan met her at the door. He was barking loudly and demanding attention. Kendall snickered. "I know I've been a bad mommy. I promise you're my main focus tonight." She walked to the back door and let him out.

While Jordan was enjoying the outdoors, Kendall dashed upstairs for a quick shower. After pulling on shorts and a T-shirt, she headed back downstairs.

She poured some food in his bowl and let him back inside the house. "I know you're ready to come back inside." Kendall watched him as he ambled to his dinner. While he chomped on his meal, Kendall emptied the container of rice on a plate and heated it in the microwave. She had just sat down at her formal dining room table with her meal and a glass of wine when the doorbell rang. "This had better be good," she mumbled, throwing her linen napkin on the table. She stomped to the front door and looked through the peephole. "This man has a lot of nerve." She opened the door. "Can I help you?"

Cole stood in her doorway dressed in casual slacks and a silk shirt, looking like a million bucks. "As a matter of fact you can." He walked past her and entered her house without so much as an invitation.

Kendall stood slack-jawed, as her mother would say. That wasn't the answer she was expecting, especially since they'd shared so much the previous weekend. She expected . . . well, she didn't know what she expected, but that wasn't it.

"Are you going to close the door?"

She closed the door before she answered. "Why are you here?"

"Something smells good." Cole walked to the dining room and took a seat at her table. "That looks good. Where's the meat?"

"I don't think I invited you," Kendall said, reclaiming her seat opposite Cole. "Besides, I thought you had a manuscript to finish."

Cole nodded. "Plate?"

Kendall was confused. "What?"

"Can I have a plate? Or do I have to eat with my hands?"

Kendall rose and retrieved a plate for him. She placed it in front of him. "You know that's my dinner?"

Cole scooped some rice on his plate. "Oh, we can go out for some real food later. We need to talk."

Kendall couldn't believe he was acting as if he lived there or something. "What are we talking about?"

Cole ate the rice in a few quick bites and drank her glass of wine. "That was good."

"You ate my dinner," Kendall complained. "Let's get that talk over with so I can find something else."

Cole smiled, irritating Kendall all the more. "Two things. The first, last night was amazing. I hope there will be many more to come. The second is that your board wants us to do a public service announcement to get more donations for your hospital."

That killed her appetite in a hurry. "This is just as I feared. The board wants to capitalize on the fact that a famous writer donated the money. I don't like this. The whole idea of the hospital is anonymity. I don't want to publicize the fact that people need to visit a charity hospital."

Cole nodded. "I know, but we can work around that. We could film general areas and without patients. If they need to see people, we could always hire actors."

"That's dishonest," Kendall said, but she thought his idea could work.

"It's not dishonest. It satisfied everyone involved. CNT wants to do the story, and it will be on national television. You could get a lot of money that way. You could have all the money you need for that cancer center you want to build."

She could also hire the appropriate personnel for the job. The possibilities would be endless with a larger budget. She could help even more people. Maybe it was worth a little smoke screen. "So what's in it for you?"

"Basking in your beauty." He rose and headed for the living room.

Kendall sighed and followed him. "Look, Cole, I'm not some starstruck fan. I know what's what." She wanted to beat him to the punch.

"Obviously you don't know." He sat on the couch and motioned for her to join him.

Kendall hesitated, not wanting him to think he had an upper hand, mainly because he did. In the end, she sat beside him. "Okay, Cole, tell me what I don't know."

He took a deep breath. "You have your little speech all ready because you think I'm going to break your heart. I have no intention of breaking anything. I have every intention of making love to you tonight."

Kendall didn't think her body could take another round of lovemaking with this man. Her brain would definitely turn to mush. "Cole, I thought you wanted to talk."

He leaned back on the couch, looking very at home on her suede sofa. "I can multitask. I can do a lot of things while I'm making love to you."

His voice had taken on that sexy timbre that sent shivers down her spine. He could he make her feel that way without even touching her! "You said you wanted to talk." She had to do something to get her mind off making love with this man or she would be in a world of trouble.

Cole smiled and enjoyed his moment of triumph. He'd actually caught Kendall off guard. "Why don't you move closer?"

"I think I can hear you just fine from here." Kendall grabbed a pillow and placed it between them. "Now what were we talking about? The PSA?"

"How about the fact we nearly used a box of condoms. I had to buy more today. Want to see how many we can use?"

"Cole, are you always like this? I think I liked you better when you were being an arrogant jerk that day you sprained your ankle. Horny Cole is not very becoming."

"You're just trying to find something non-sexual to focus on. Or at least that's what I'm trying to do, and it's just not working."

Kendall cleared her throat. "You were mentioning something about hiring actors if needed. How are we going to do that and the reporter not know and expose us as frauds?"

"We'll talk about the hospital and I'll talk about my new book, which happens to be set in a hospital much like Briarwood. We can get publicity for both, and it won't cost a dime."

"What am I supposed to say to this reporter?"

Cole shrugged. He had an idea, but didn't know how to present it to Kendall. He didn't want her thinking he was trying to take over the whole thing. "How about I come up with a little script and you can look it over. Say tomorrow night over dinner."

"Sounds like you're the one winning this deal," Kendall mumbled.

He moved the pillow from her iron grasp and tossed it on the floor. "Some would say so." He moved closer to her. "Some would say you're trying to play hard to get."

Her mouth hung open and Cole took full advantage. He kissed her slowly and hungrily, his mouth devouring hers, before he eased his tongue inside her mouth. He felt the surrender as she drew him closer.

But Kendall had a different plan for him. She broke the kiss, stood and straightened her shirt. "Don't just stare at me." She held her hand out. "I think you're trying to turn me into horny Kendall."

The next morning, Kendall heard the unmistakable sounds of a man in her bed. Her companion was snoring. Kendall pulled the sheet up to her neck and turned over slowly.

Cole lay on his side facing her, and had the nerve to wear a smug grin on his face. Kendall couldn't believe she'd succumbed to temptation again. She sighed and lightly tapped Cole on his shoulder. "Cole, get up."

"What time is it?" He never opened his eyes. "It can't be that late." He stretched his arms and reached for her.

Kendall yelped, but went into his embrace easily. "Cole, you have to leave." She didn't really mean it, but she had to say something.

He rolled on top of her, pinning her beneath him and his monster erection. Finally, he opened those beautiful hazel eyes and stared at her. "Okay, now that you have me up on all accounts, you have to do something about it."

"Cole, we don't have time for this, or at least I don't. You're a writer, so you make your own schedule, but I have patients to see."

Cole ignored her protests and kissed her. Kendall was lost in the feeling of his very experienced hands traveling her slender body, making her body sing for orgasmic penetration.

Her body wiggled as his long fingers entered her. She was trying to think of a reason to make him stop, but her brain wasn't working. Her legs were, as they parted to give him better access.

He reached for something under the pillow. A condom. "You were saying something about getting to work on time." He opened the packet with his mouth and slipped it on with the urgency of a horny teenager.

Kendall stared at him. "What?"

Cole smiled. "Now let's stop talking, at least with our mouths, and let our bodies continue this conversation." He withdrew his finger and entered her with one strong stroke.

Kendall gasped, wondering how many times the human body could experience an intense orgasm before totally collapsing. It could be an experiment worth researching. Cole would definitely be the perfect study.

He withdrew quickly and moved off her body. "Am I hurting you?"

Kendall reached for him. "Only if you stop."

Cole smiled and embraced her. He kissed her hard. "Well, I don't think I can. Want to find out?"

Kendall nodded, and for the first time didn't give a thought to the patients she had waiting. Her only thought was that Cole definitely knew how to take her mind off work.

When Kendall finally made it to work it was almost eleven. Thanks to Cole and his stamina, she was well on her way to finding out the answer to her research problem. They had made love until she cried uncle.

Thank goodness she didn't have any morning appointments. She was supposed to research costs for the hospital, but she could still do that later. Staci was her first afternoon appointment, so she had a little recoup time. In only a few days, she'd had more sex with Cole than she'd probably had in her entire adult life. She glanced at her clock; it was just before noon. She could take a little nap on her couch, and no one would know she and Cole had gotten their "freak on," as her nephew called it, again. Yes, thirty minutes of sleep should recharge her batteries, she thought as she walked to the couch.

The last thing she remembered was kicking off her stilettos.

"Kendall, wake up." A cold hand shook her.

But she didn't want to open her eyes. She had just closed them. Wasn't she allowed a little catnap doing the day?

"Kendall."

It was Staci's voice, she finally realized. But that appointment wasn't until one. "Staci, you're early. Come back at one."

Staci laughed. "Girl, you better check your watch."

Kendall finally pried her eyes opened and gazed at her friend. "It's barely twelve. Why are you here so early?"

Staci sat in the chair next to the desk and let out a tired breath. "First of all, Ms. Thing, I'm about an hour and a half late. It's two-thirty. I left you about five messages explaining I had an emergency and would be late."

Kendall sat up slowly. "I didn't hear the phone ring."

"I know. Jami thought you were trying to take a nap, so she took the messages. But I called your cell and you still didn't pick up."

"I would have heard the phone. I must have had it on silent or something," Kendall said. "I couldn't have been that tired."

"Don't tell me you and Cole have been bouncing around on the sheets again?"

Kendall couldn't hide the look. At least not from Staci. "I don't know what you're talking about."

"Nice try, Kendall. But the next time you're trying to feign innocence, make sure that you don't have a hickey on your neck." She started laughing. "I crack myself up!"

Kendall wanted to be mad. But soon she found herself laughing as well. "You got me."

"Okay, can I have some details?"

"Why on earth would you want details?"

"Hey, my very frigid friend is getting laid more times than an intern at the nation's capitol. Of course I must have details."

Kendall nodded. When Staci wanted to know something, there was no stopping until she was satisfied. She was much like Cole in that respect. "All right."

Staci leaned back in the chair and sighed. "If I wasn't pregnant, I'd need a cigarette after that story." She rubbed her stomach and laughed. "I can't believe two forty-year-old people used an entire box of condoms!"

Kendall couldn't either. "Actually Cole is forty-five," she said with feminine pride. "He's in pretty good shape."

Staci hoisted herself up from her chair. "Don't think I don't see you grinning like a Cheshire cat. I know you're proud of your man and I'm proud that you got some. I think Cole is going to give your hormones a run for your money, not to mention your heart."

"Oh, I don't think that will happen. I know it was because I confessed about the crush I had on him when I was a teenager." She opened the office door so that they could finally get started on Staci's test.

Staci walked to the door and slammed it shut. "Okay, start from the beginning."

Kendall shrugged, not wanting to remember that particular part of that magical evening. "Not much to tell. Remember after my divorce you thought I was depressed about James?"

"Yes. You didn't date for at least two years. When you finally started dating it was sparingly, I might add."

"It wasn't because I missed James. It was because I didn't love James in the first place. I married him in hopes he'd give me closure over Cole, my teenage crush."

"I guess that didn't work, did it?"

Kendall shook her head. "I felt bad for ruining what could have been a good marriage."

"He did cheat on you."

"I drove him to it," Kendall admitted. "I never gave the marriage my all."

Staci planted her hands on Kendall's shoulders. "Now you look here, missy. So your marriage didn't work. Don't blame yourself. James had been cheating on you longer than you realize. So don't go thinking you failed him."

"What do you mean?" Kendall faced her friend.

"I mean that man has had just about every nurse at my hospital. The only ones he never approached were yours. They were too afraid to cross you. Thank goodness you scare the daylights out of people."

"I don't know if I should thank you for that compliment or wait until the baby's born and knock you silly for the insult."

Staci ignored her remark and headed out of the room. "Yeah, yeah, yeah. You like it."

Kendall laughed. "Yes, I do, but that is about to change. I don't want the nurses to be afraid of me. In fact, I don't want anyone afraid of me anymore." They walked down the hall to the examination room.

"I knew you would change one day. Power is great, but friends last longer."

Trust Staci to hit the nail on the head.

CHAPTER 10

Cole was in the zone. Everything he typed on his laptop computer screen sounded like gold to his ears as he read it out loud. His story was coming along nicely and he was way ahead of schedule, and could probably set up a date with Kendall very soon. The more he thought of their night together, the more he had to see her, and soon. Who would have thought a forty-five-year-old man could feel this horny?

He thought he heard the phone ringing, but kept typing anyway. Whoever it was would have to call back. His family knew when he was writing that everything was off limits and not to call.

But the phone kept ringing, forcing him to stop his flow of creative juices and answer the darn thing. He walked down the hall to the nearest phone and snatched it to his ear. "What?"

"Dad?"

"Taylor?" Cole silently cursed his bad luck. Of all the times for his estranged teenaged son to call, he mused. He'd only been waiting a year for this call.

"Yes, Dad. Did I catch you at a bad time?"

"No, no. What's up? How's school?"

"That's kind of what I want to talk to you about. Is it okay if I come to Texas for a visit now?"

"Sure, Taylor. You don't have to ask. I didn't think you'd want to visit me here. At least that what your mother said each and every time I've called to speak with you."

His son sighed. "Well, Mom told me that you didn't want to see me, and that you went back to Texas to get away from me."

"That's rubbish," Cole spat. "You know how much you mean to me, Taylor. How could she tell you such lies? Sure, it didn't work out between your mom and me, but that has nothing to do with you."

"She was mad at you, Dad," Taylor clarified for his father. "I just found out she was lying to me about you. I overheard her on the phone to Grandmother. She told Grandmother she doesn't want me to see you, ever, and would do whatever it took to make sure it didn't happen."

Cole was about to let a string of expletives fly out of his mouth, but stopped abruptly. Taylor was an innocent in all this, and besides, it wouldn't do any good to be as spiteful as his former wife. His ex-wife was using the one thing Cole valued most against him, his son. "I'll get your ticket and call you back with the information."

"Okay, call me at this number." Taylor quickly rattled the numbers to his father. "Mom will kill me if she knew I called you."

"How's she going to take you coming to Texas?" Cole already knew how his ex would take the news. She'd more than likely kick Taylor out on his butt.

"I'll most likely be living with you from now on, but I just can't take it living here with her anymore. I don't like being her showpiece to all her friends. She keeps telling people that I'm going to Harvard. I don't want to go to Harvard. I want to go to SMU. Mom said if I stepped one foot on Texas soil, I no longer existed in her eyes."

Cole's heart sank at how selfish one woman could be. "Well, welcome to Texas."

"Thanks, Dad."

He heard the catch in his son's voice as Taylor ended the call. A sixteen-year-old shouldn't have to go through this. Taylor should be concerned with dating and college prep exams, not afraid of getting tossed out by his mother. But Cole would make sure his transition would be as painless as possible. First thing he had to do was to book a ticket for his son.

Kendall rubbed her head in frustration. The board wasn't making this PSA nonsense any easier. Now they wanted her and Cole to do two spots instead of just one. The CNT reporter wanted to do a phone interview before she committed to flying down to do the real interview.

What happened to her safe, controlled world? She couldn't imagine working with Cole through two PSAs. She'd be a basket case by then. Or a nymphomaniac.

She looked through her desk for some aspirin just as Jami walked in unannounced, breaking Kendall's cardinal rule. But one look at her new friend's tear-stained face, and Kendall's heart instantly softened. "What is it,

Jami?" She rushed to meet her and guided the younger woman to the nearest chair.

At first Jami was quiet and shook her head. Kendall knew the move well. Keeping everyone at a distance. She'd done it herself, countless times. That was why everyone feared her now. But it was time to change all that. She hugged Jami and offered words of comfort. "Jami, I know this looks bad now, but things will clear up, I promise. My offer still stands. Whenever you need me, I'll be here."

Jami's body started to shake and the tears began to fall. "I-I- don't know what to do, Kendall. Karl tried to snatch Dylan from the daycare earlier today. Luckily they knew about the trouble I've been having with him and called me before they released Dylan to him. I can't live like this. I can't live every day wondering if this is the day Karl finally flips his lid. I have to do something." She cried uncontrollably.

Kendall was trying to let Jami make her own decision, but a much-needed push wouldn't hurt. "You're going to move into my house, that's what you're going to do," Kendall said in a voice she hoped no one would argue with. "Tonight you can stay with me and move your things in tomorrow. I don't want you going to your house alone."

"I'll move in, but tonight I'm staying with Keerya. Her brothers are going to help me get my stuff out of the house, bright and early. I'll be at your house in the morning. Is that okay?"

Kendall nodded. "That's fine, Jami. I'll have your room ready. Are you putting your things in storage?"

"Yes. Keerya's brother owns a storage company, so we have free run of the place. He said I could use as much space as I need and he's not going to charge me."

Kendall smiled. Her mother was right. Sometimes things may look their darkest, but there's always some sunshine just around the corner.

Cole felt a little more at ease after he purchased the airline ticket for Taylor. Until then he'd felt like a spy making secret arrangements with his son to pick him up at the airport the next day.

After he finished with the arrangements, he realized one little tiny inconsequential thing: He didn't have any furniture in any of the other bedrooms. He would definitely need help. He dialed the number to the hospital.

"Hello."

"Hey, Max," Cole said. "What are you doing later?"

Max grunted. "Not going home."

"Good. Want to go shopping for furniture?"

Max laughed. "What?"

Cole knew he had to explain the sudden change in his household. "My son will be coming to live with me. I need some furniture for his room."

"Have you told my boss that your son is coming to live with you and there will be no more sexual marathons?"

"Hey, there's always her place."

"I guess you haven't heard the latest," Max said quietly.

Cole couldn't begin to fathom what could possibly be worse timing than his son coming to live with him just as he finally got Kendall where he needed her. "Okay, I'll bite, Max."

"I'll tell you later. But I can tell you this. Kendall is going to have a houseguest for awhile."

Cole's world tilted just a little off that perfect axis he'd worked so hard to achieve. "Is it her ex?"

Max laughed. "I'll let you figure that out for yourself, man."

Cole knew how determined exes could be. But he could be more determined. "Still want to go shopping?"

"Of course. Actually I'm getting off in about another hour. Why don't I meet you at your house?"

"Sure." This would make his plan work even better. If Max was getting off early, maybe Kendall was, too. But Max was always one step ahead of him when it came to Kendall.

"Kendall's got a meeting with the board this afternoon. She should be home around six."

Cole snickered. "You think you know me?"

"I don't know you, but I do know Kendall. And I like the smile you put on her face." There was a slight hesitation in Max's usually gentle voice. "She's the most important person to me in this world. She's like a sister and I don't want to see her hurt, especially after what that ex-husband did to her. So if you cause her pain, you will answer to me."

"You'd have to get in line behind her brother Charlie," Cole said. "He's already given me the speech. So I already know the consequences of my actions."

"And?"

Cole didn't want to say the words. He wasn't sure of his emotional state at the moment. After all, it could just be really good sex and the fact that he finally found a woman that could keep up with him, for the most part, anyway.

"Cole?" Max prodded. "What's going on in that writer's brain of yours?"

He didn't want to say it, especially to Max. "Just pondering."

"Yeah, I'll bet," Max chuckled. "Sure, I'll go shopping with you. I love to watch people spend money."

Cole laughed, wondering when his life had gotten so strange. Never in a million years would he have imagined one of his closest friends would be a white physician assistant, not to mention that he'd fall in love with Kendall. Now how was he was supposed to manage that with his son underfoot?

A few hours later, Cole and Max toured the furniture store looking for furniture for a teenager. Cole had expected Max to pounce on him the minute he saw Cole, but Max played it cool.

Max gazed at the sea of beds. "So how tall is your son?"

Cole shrugged. "I think he might be an inch or two shorter than me." He looked at a king-sized bed. "You know, he's not through growing yet. My dad was six-four."

Max nodded. "Yeah, go for the king-sized bed." He waved for the salesperson. "So why is your tall teenaged son coming to live with you?"

Cole had to admit Max had style. It had been almost an hour before he asked the first question. "It's a long, horrid story involving my ex-wife and her selfish attitude."

"Been there, done that," Max said dryly. "She's been lying to him? Telling him you're a horrible father?"

Cole looked sideways at Max's tanned face. "Man, were you in the room with her or what?" He noticed the salesman approaching them.

"Yes, sir, how can I help you?"

Cole pointed to the large four-poster bed. "I want this in king-size with pillow-top mattresses."

The salesman instantly smiled, most likely tallying up his commission on the sale. "Yes, sir. When would you like this delivered?"

"Tomorrow."

The salesman swallowed and asked incredulously, "Tomorrow?"

Cole knew it would be next to impossible for such a quick delivery, but he had to try. He didn't want his son sleeping on the couch his first night home. "Yes, I need it delivered tomorrow. Is it doable?"

"I'll have to check. Where do you live?"

"Biscayne Meadows."

The salesman's eyes widened in surprise, but he rebounded quickly. With his calm, stoic face back in place, he said, "Oh, I'm sure something can be worked out. Pardon me," the salesman said as he walked away.

Max stepped closer to him. "He's going to up the delivery charge for tomorrow. Just watch. He's going to come back with a higher delivery charge for such a quick delivery time. We can do it ourselves. I can bring my truck and we can set it up tonight."

"You really think he'll do that?"

Max nodded. "Hell yeah. He's probably worked a deal with the delivery guys and they'll split the money. Just watch."

Sure enough the salesman returned with a saccharine smile on his face. "Well, sir, we can deliver it tomorrow, but there's going to be an express fee of an additional one hundred dollars."

Cole glanced at Max, then back at the salesman. "Okay."

The salesman beamed. "Okay. What time do you want it delivered?"

Cole shook his head. "Oh no, I'm taking it today, without the delivery charge."

"Oh." The salesman frowned.

Cole laughed. "And I'm going to need a nightstand, a dresser and an armoire."

The smile was back. "Yes, sir."

Max and Cole laughed as the salesman took off. "I can't believe he was going to rip me off like that."

Max shrugged. "Live and learn."

Kendall rubbed her neck as she sat at her desk. The board meeting had taken longer than she expected. All she wanted to do was to help the less fortunate and add a cancer wing to the hospital, but all these people brought her were more problems. She reflected on the previous meeting.

"Dr. Matthews, the nuclear machine is going to cost a million dollars itself. We're really going to need more donations to get all the machinery that you want at the hospital and remain a charity hospital."

But Kendall knew that. She had already run the numbers through her computer, and she needed at least four million dollars to keep the charity hospital charitable. She was going to have to go public. "Yes, I've been in touch with Holly Banton of CNT and she wants to do a phone interview first."

"She's still going to do it, right?" Marty Kleinman, director of cardiology, asked. "We really need the press."

"So you do want me to mention Briarwood?"

Marty nodded. "It would certainly be a win-win. You can get more donations, and we can get some free advertising for the wonderful work that's being done at the hospital. We also want you to mention your track record."

She hated tooting her own horn. Hated it with a heartfelt passion. It reminded her of that dreadful day Cole landed in the emergency room, spouting those horrid words, 'Don't you know who I am?'

"How about one of you guys listing my accolades? It sounds less cheesy that way. Holly wants to do a character study of me. She wants people who aren't camera shy and can give me glowing recommendations. I hope you guys don't mind, but I told her she could talk to you all."

Marty spoke for the other four men. "Sure, Kendall. What's good for you is good for Briarwood."

"Of course. I wouldn't do anything to harm Briarwood's name."

And she meant that. She would do anything within the law, as long as it was morally sound, to keep the name of the hospital as prestigious as it already was.

She rubbed her neck again. She could really use a massage right now. Where was Cole when she needed him? She didn't have the time to take that lusty thought back when the phone rang. It was after five, so Jami wasn't at her desk to screen Kendall's calls.

She reached for the phone. "Dr. Matthews."

"Hello, Dr. Matthews," Cole drawled. "How are you feeling today?"

"Fine." She wasn't giving in to temptation this time.

"Hungry?"

"No." Every time she had dinner with this man, they ended up in bed.

"Can you speak in more than one-word answers? I know I'm not a pregnant woman, but I think I deserve your complete attention."

Kendall wanted to say something cutting to him, but her tongue wasn't working and her heart was remembering the last time she was in his arms.

Cole took advantage and pressed on. "I was thinking you could come over for dinner. We need to talk."

Oh, that didn't bode well. "Just say it now."

"I don't want to do this over the phone. I'll even make you a simulated burger while I'm grilling my T-bone steak."

"Cole, I'd rather you just tell me now what's so all-fired important."

"Tonight," he promised and ended the call.

CHAPTER 11

A few hours later, and after much debating, Kendall finally arrived at Cole's. She'd decided to dress casual since this was probably the good-bye dinner and all. She wore a snug-fitting tank top, cotton shorts, and her favorite sandals. Might as well be comfortable when Cole handed her her walking papers.

She rang the doorbell and waited. Cole answered the door looking like a cover model for a fashion magazine. He was dressed in a silk shirt and shorts, showing off those sexy legs. It was so not fair, she thought. She glanced down and noticed he wasn't wearing any shoes. Even his long feet looked sexy. Life was really not fair.

"Kendall," he said, leaning forward for a kiss and making contact.

She was getting lost in the soft kiss when she remembered the reason for this meal. He was going to dump her. She freed herself from his arms. "You said you wanted to talk," she said as sternly as she could muster.

He looked down at her. "Yes, I did, and we will. Later." He motioned for her to enter the house. "First, we're going to sit down and eat my wonderful dinner."

Once she was inside, she smelled the aroma of meat. The steak smelled wonderful and, for the first time in ten years, she wanted to eat a piece of beef. "What exactly did you fix?" She followed him into the kitchen.

He stopped walking. "You're not allowed in my kitchen. Sit." He pointed at the dining table that had been elaborately set with candles, linen napkins, and gold trimmed plates. If her mother had taught her one thing, it was china. She could usually determine the brand of china by the weight of the plate. Most likely Wedgwood, she guessed, and there was only one way to find out for sure. She took a seat and waited for Cole to retreat to the kitchen.

"I'll be right back," he said as if on cue and left the room.

She nodded and quickly picked up the plate to cure her curiosity. She was right. Wedgwood. High-end Wedgwood. Was this a remnant of his marriage?

"My mom bought me those as a housewarming gift," he said as he brought in a large bowl of salad. "She claims they are the best money can buy. I guess I should ask you if they are, since you're checking out the label." He placed the bowl on the table.

Kendall's mind stumbled over a logical explanation and couldn't think of one, so she decided to go with the truth.

"I was curious."

He chuckled as he took a seat. "You're not even going to try to say that you weren't looking? I'm shocked." He handed her a salad plate.

She scooped up some of the rabbit food, as he called it, and shrugged. "You caught me. I admit it. I'm surprised you have fine china."

"Do you have fine china?"

"Yes. It was a gift from my mother."

He lifted his fork to her. "To our mothers."

She hated when he was smug. "What did you want to talk about?"

He shook his head. "After dinner." He took another bite of salad. After he chewed the correct amount of times, he said, "And before we make love."

Kendall choked on the romaine lettuce. "Oh, no. That ship has sailed. You can't call me over to break up with me and then still expect me to sleep with you."

It was Cole's turn to choke on his salad. "What are you yammering about?"

"The reason you wanted to have dinner in the first place." She vowed not to give into tears, but she was losing the battle fiercely.

Cole slowly understood. "Oh, you think I called you over here, set a romantic table, and cooked you dinner to kick you to the curb. Woman, have you totally lost it? Besides, I didn't think you wanted a relationship, being one of those independent women and all."

"Cole, I'm confused. Why did you invite me over?"

"Kendall, I invited you here to dinner because I like your company. Yes, we had some amazing sex, but that's not the only reason I invited you over. I do have something to discuss with you, but I think we need to discuss what I am to you first."

Now she'd gone and done it. She'd hurt his feelings. "Cole, I don't know the answer to that question."

He wadded up his napkin and threw it on the table, shoving his chair back. He rose and reached for her hand.

"Okay, dinner is postponed until we figure out what's going on."

He took her hand and led her to the living room. They sat on the couch. "Okay, Kendall, tell me what I am to you. Am I just your handy man, only good for sex and little else?"

She heard the angry undertones in his voice and didn't want to provide any more fuel. "No, Cole."

"Then what? I'm getting mixed signals here. You're telling me that I'm not your boy toy, but that's exactly how you're treating me. You never tell me what's going on with you. If Max wasn't so loose-lipped when he drank, I'd never know anything."

"Cole, you're asking me to give you something I can't. I can't be that open with anyone. I think of you as more than a human sex toy."

His hazel eyes glared at her. "No. Max told me what he had to do to get you to open up to him. Whose sin am I paying for?"

She couldn't admit it. It would sound childish and petty. She ducked her head. "No one."

In a very unCole-like manner, he grabbed her by her shoulder and turned her toward him. "Look, I think I've been pretty patient here, but I need some answers."

Kendall's teary eyes tried to focus on Cole, but it was useless. He kept going in and out of focus. "After my divorce, I channeled all my energy into work. There I have maintained certain distance from everyone. Now I realize I was wrong and can still have friends at the hospital and my integrity not be challenged. It's hard breaking down a wall I've tried so hard to build." She realized how incredibly selfish that sounded. "I'll try to do better." She wiped her eyes.

Cole nodded. "That's all I ask. Now that we have all that taken care of, I'll tell you why I invited you to dinner."

She wiped her eyes. "I'm listening."

"My son, Taylor, is arriving tomorrow. He's moving here."

She wasn't expecting that. "Why couldn't you just tell me that on the phone? I was worried for nothing. How old is your son?"

"He's sixteen. He wants to visit, but I know his mother. She's not going to let him back in the house once she finds out he's been here."

Kendall nodded.

"So I guess our dates will have to take place at your place."

She almost nodded. "You might want to rethink that little plan. Jami and Dylan are moving in tomorrow."

"In where?"

"My house, silly. Jami's having marital problems and I offered her my house for safety. Her husband is crazy, and I don't want her coming to harm."

"So you had your own little drama going on. Were you going to mention it to me?" Cole stood and began pacing the room. "I can't believe you. This is exactly what I'm talking about. This affects both of us."

"Oh Cole, calm down. You kind of blew my thought processes with your 'we need to talk' thing. I was scared."

He chuckled. "You, scared? I must be dreaming." Cole sat beside her and pulled her into his arms, kissing her as if there was no tomorrow.

Kendall felt the blood in her body boil with each thrust of Cole's tongue. She was drowning in passion, and this time she wasn't going down alone. She returned his kisses with even more ardor until they were both swept away.

"We're going upstairs," Cole said between kisses.

"Uh-huh," Kendall moaned. She unbuttoned his shirt and shoved it off his shoulders. "No more talk."

It was much later when Cole forced his eyes open. Kendall's naked body was snuggled next to him and she was snoring lightly, the sound of a contented woman.

His hands roamed her warm body, happy for the moment just to hear her moan in her sleep. One of those sultry moans jump-started his engine. He kissed her awake. Her arms instantly wrapped him in an embrace and returned his kisses. Neither spoke, knowing what they both needed. Knowing that nights like these were going to be a thing of the past, they let their bodies speak for them.

Kendall thought she heard the phone ring downstairs, but wasn't sure. "Was that the phone?"

Cole shook his head. "Let it ring. It's not Taylor. His flight doesn't land until tomorrow afternoon."

His kisses took away any other worries she might have had, including not using any protection.

Taylor Highpoint snapped his cell phone closed. Although it was past midnight and he was sure his mother wasn't in the house, he had to get out of there before all the walls closed in on him.

He wanted to tell his father he was coming earlier than expected since his mother had found out he'd called his father and, as expected, had hit the roof.

"Why are you calling that man? He doesn't want to see you. He wants nothing to do with you," she said with a straight face. She didn't mention that she'd scrolled through his cell phone to check his calls to get that information.

Taylor decided it was time for some real answers, which he knew he wouldn't get from his mother. "Mom, what do you have against Dad? I know he sends you child support every month and still you act like he's a deadbeat."

His mother stared at him. "How do you know about the child support?"

"It's the law, Mom. And I know if he hadn't you would have his name all over the newspapers."

His petite mother walked to him. "You don't understand what he's done to us." She gave him her best sorrowful face, the one that had won her an Oscar and an Emmy.

"To us?" Taylor asked incredulously. "Don't you mean to me? You divorced him, remember?"

She sighed. "You're too young to remember those horrid details. Don't let me see his number in your phone again or don't bother coming home." She made her dramatic exit and headed upstairs to her bedroom.

That was the moment Taylor decided to make his break, so to speak, to Arlington that night. He knew he couldn't live another night in this house.

Now he shoved his prized possessions into a duffel bag and tossed the keys to his Mustang on the bed. The car had been a bribe for him not to call his father. Taylor was tired of living a life of lies. His mother had fed him so many lies in the last ten years about his father and paternal grandmother, he didn't know what or who to believe anymore. He had to know the truth. And there was only one way to do that. He had to live with his father.

Taylor gave his room the once-over, then left the house for the last time. He'd cashed out his checking and savings account, so he had enough money for a cab to the airport. Soon he would be Texas-bound.

CHAPTER 12

Cole woke up the next morning feeling as if someone had taken his body out and run it over with a truck. A really big truck. He yawned, stretched, and rubbed his hand over his face. What had he been thinking the night before? These sex marathons with Kendall were going to have to stop soon or he'd definitely land in the hospital from exhaustion.

The woman in question shifted against him, mumbling something about Jordan needing to go out. But she hadn't brought Jordan with her the night before, which meant Kendall's mutt had to go to the bathroom with urgency. He threw back the covers to get out of bed and laughed at himself. Here he was ready to go walk someone else's dog. Was he that far gone? He had his own set of issues to deal with that day and he didn't have time to walk Jordan anyway. Taylor was arriving that afternoon and he hadn't finished furnishing the room yet.

Kendall's warm hand caressed his naked back. Lord, that woman could get him hard no matter what part of him she touched. "Where are you going?"

Cole gave up on all his thought processes and crawled back in bed with her. "Right here." He drew her into his arms and kissed her. "Good morning, baby."

Kendall smiled and hugged him. Her lips were swollen from all the kisses they'd shared through the night. She looked well loved and beautiful. "Morning, Cole. You wore me out last night. I'm going to have to ration you from now on."

"What?" He kissed her again and let his hands caress her slender hips. His hand dipped between her thighs and he smiled as he found her moist and ready. "I see someone has been thinking about me." He moved his fingers back and forth, Kendall could only moan her approval.

She grasped his upper arms as her eyes drifted closed. "I-I—. When you do that, I don't have a choice."

He increased the pressure, sending her over the edge. "You always have a choice, baby."

She shook her head, gasped and then screamed, "Cole?"

He was just beginning to think he was all that and a bag of chips when he heard the tone in her voice. It wasn't a scream of passion. It was a scream of fright. He finally followed her gaze. Oh, my God. "Taylor?"

"Yeah, Dad. I took an earlier flight. I got in a couple of hours ago and sacked out on the couch. I heard noises so I came up here and found you and . . ."

Kendall pulled the covers further over her body. She looked so cute when she was caught off guard. Cole had to focus on the issue of his son. "Taylor, give us a few minutes and we'll be downstairs."

Taylor nodded and left, closing the door behind him.

Cole took a deep breath. He hadn't intended for Taylor to find him like this. He really hadn't intended for

Taylor to find Kendall like this. He'd planned a quiet night out for him and his son, but now all those plans had changed.

"You didn't know someone else was in the house?" Kendall accused as she wrapped the sheet around her slender body and rose from the bed. "You think he heard us?"

Cole laughed, watching her pace the room frantically. The king-sized sheet dwarfed her body. She looked like she was headed to the nearest toga party. Kendall was quite a different person when she wasn't in control. She was nervous and let her guard down, appearing more human. He rather liked it. "Yes, I'm sure he did. I told you you were loud. People in Dallas County probably heard you, and that's thirty miles away." He reached for his discarded boxer shorts and slipped them on.

She ran a shaky hand through her hair. "He probably thinks I'm your bit of stuff," she mumbled.

"Bit of stuff?"

Kendall stopped her pacing and looked at him. "You know, your little *something something*."

Cole knew she was just rambling. "Oh, I thought you were getting all UK on me. I don't hear that term much outside of British television." He would have said more, but Kendall was staring at him as if he'd just grown another head.

"He probably thinks I'm a tart or something," she mumbled. "I need to get out of here." She glanced around the room for her clothes. "I can sneak out of here without him seeing me if you divert his attention."

Cole sat on the bed, trying to contain his temper. "No one is sneaking anywhere. We're not doing anything wrong. We're two adults who happen to enjoy each other's company." He took a deep breath and stood. "We're going to take a shower. Then we'll have breakfast with my son and I will introduce you officially." He walked to Kendall and grabbed her hand before she could take flight.

Still Kendall countered him. "Cole, the last thing you need is a third party here today. It's hard enough since you haven't seen your son in a year."

Cole shook his head as they entered the bathroom. "It's actually been about four years since I've seen him. We've only started talking by phone the last year. So the road is going to be rocky regardless of whether you're here or not. His mother has been feeding us both lies, so we're going to have to start somewhere." He turned on the shower, closed the bathroom door and discarded his shorts.

Kendall stood before him still wrapped in his bed sheet. With a gentle tug the sheet pooled around her feet. Cole smiled at his handiwork. She had marks all over her body.

Kendall glanced past him into the oversized mirror and noticed the marks. "Cole, look what you did. You're awful."

He offered his hand to help her in the shower. "You didn't say that last night or this morning. As a matter of fact, you were begging for it." He pulled her under the spray of water.

Kendall sputtered her reply. Whatever she said was lost under the waterfall. Just the effect he wanted. It took a few minutes, but the water worked its magic and she eventually calmed down. He moved closer to her body and began washing her as she leaned against him. It felt great to be this close. Wishing this moment could last forever, but knowing that it couldn't, Cole cherished every second.

An hour later, Kendall sat on Cole's bed waiting for him to finish getting dressed so they could get breakfast over with. Their shower had been wonderful and she wished she could do that every morning, but knew it was probably very unlikely.

He finally walked out of the bathroom, dressed casually in shorts and T-shirt. "Are you ready to eat?"

She was ready to get out of this house. "Sure."

Cole walked toward her and offered his hand. "Come on. Let's go see what Taylor is up to."

She took a deep breath and took his hand. "What if he hates me?"

Cole kissed her on the lips. "How could he hate you?"

"I wish I had your sunny disposition." Kendall hoped Cole was right, but she had a funny feeling the morning ahead was going to be nothing but trouble.

They entered the kitchen and Taylor greeted them with breakfast already prepared. Cole helped Kendall with her chair, then showered his son with praise, right after he made introductions.

"Wow, Taylor, this looks great." Cole cleared his throat. "Son, this is my friend, Dr. Kendall Matthews. Kendall, this is my son, Taylor."

Kendall extended her hand to Taylor. "It's nice to meet you, Taylor. Your father has told me so much about you." She could see a lot of Cole in his son. Taylor had his father's honey-brown complexion and hazel eyes. His curly hair was cut short. She couldn't tell if the boy had his father's smile, because he was wearing a scowl. Typical teenager, Kendall thought. He reminded her of her nephew, Trey. "Breakfast looks wonderful."

Taylor looked at his bounty and shrugged. "I just made eggs, bacon, and toast. I had to do something to kill the time."

She didn't miss the bite in his remark. Now Kendall was faced with a dilemma. Although she was a vegetarian, she'd have to eat bacon that morning.

They ate breakfast in silence. Kendall felt the walls closing in on her. The lack of conversation was beginning to get to her. "Taylor, how was your flight?"

He looked at her, hazel eyes cutting straight to her soul. "Long."

"Why didn't you call and let me know you were coming earlier? I could have met you at the airport," Cole said.

Taylor looked at Kendall again. "I tried to call last night before I got on the plane, but it just went to your voicemail. I guess you were busy or something," he accused, looking directly at Kendall.

If she could have run out of the room in a dramatic exit, she would have, but life had a funny way of spitting on her from time to time, like today. All she wanted to do was to go home, but here she was stuck in the breakfast from hell.

"We were probably out or something," Cole lied. He grabbed her hand and whispered to her. "Don't worry, honey. It will be fine."

Taylor stared at Kendall for an extremely long time. "What kind of doctor are you?"

"I'm a women's doctor," Kendall said.

Taylor nodded. "Oh, like an OB or a gynecologist?"

Kendall nodded. "Yes, I am. I deliver babies."

"Any lately?"

"No. I have one due next week." Kendall hoped she sounded calm. "What brings you to Arlington?"

"My dad."

Cole joined in the conversation. "Did you tell your mother you were coming here?"

Taylor shook his head. "No, I just couldn't take it anymore."

Cole threw the napkin on the table. "Damn, I was afraid of this. Call her right now and tell her where you are. I talked to my attorney yesterday, and we need to establish you came here on your own and I didn't coerce you, or I'll be up on kidnapping charges courtesy of your mother."

Taylor shot an angry glance at Kendall. "Dad, we can talk about it after she leaves."

"She, as you put it, is a part of my life. So she can hear what kind of trouble we're in," Cole said, darting a glance in Kendall's direction. "Got it?"

Taylor cut his eyes at her. "Got it."

Kendall felt the morning would only get worse. She needed to make her getaway as quickly as possible. The clock struck ten, increasing the tension at the table. She had patients that afternoon and she needed to prepare for them. It would give her the perfect excuse to get out of the line of fire without being a total wimp. She cleared her throat as she rose from the table. "I really need to get going," she told the men at the table. "I have patients this afternoon."

Cole nodded. "I'll call you later. Give Jordan a kiss for me." He winked at Kendall.

Kendall smiled back at him. "I sure will." She glanced at Taylor, who was frowning at her at the moment. "It was nice to meet you, Taylor."

"Where do you live?" Taylor asked.

"About four houses down." She started to the front door. She heard some hushed whispers, and then Taylor stopped her by stating he wanted to walk her home. The last thing she needed this morning was to be interrogated by some sullen teenager. But he was special to Cole, so that would make it bearable. "Thank you, Taylor."

"I'm ready when you are." Taylor didn't really want to walk this woman home, but his father had insisted and he wanted to please him, at least for now. He didn't like the way his father looked at her. His father had never looked at his mother like that.

Kendall gathered her purse and opened the front door. "Let's go."

They started walking in silence. "I have a nephew, Charlie III, who's eighteen. We call him Trey. He's going to Princeton in the fall. He's very excited about going. That's where Charlie, my oldest brother, attended. He's an attorney."

"Don't you ever shut up?"

If that shocked her, she didn't let it show. "I was only trying to keep up conversation. I don't remember Trey being so surly at sixteen."

"I'm sure he didn't catch his father getting busy, either."

"Your father is human," Kendall said.

"Yeah, but he's not supposed to be doing that. You guys were acting like teenagers. What does your son think about you spending the night with my dad?"

Kendall stopped walking and stared at him. "I don't have any children."

They resumed their journey. "Well, who's Jordan? And what kind of mother would leave her son alone?"

Kendall laughed. "Oh, I get it. I'm sorry, Taylor, Jordan is my dog. Your father was being sarcastic. He thinks I spoil him."

They stopped in front of a large townhouse. Kendall walked to the front door and unlocked it. They entered the house and Kendall disarmed the alarm. She glanced around the room. "Jordi, Mommy's home."

Taylor listened as Kendall's voice became more frantic each time she called for her dog and he didn't come. He watched as she ran upstairs, slammed doors, and ran back downstairs. She had tears streaking down her face. "I can't find him! Help me!"

Taylor didn't know what to do. He had no idea what kind of dog he was looking for. "Where else can I look?" He just wanted to go back home.

"Check the garage." She pointed to the door to his left.

He did as he was told. He noticed the doggy door, and thought maybe Jordan was just napping in the garage. He opened the door and laid eyes on the coolest car he'd seen. It was a top-of-the-line Jaguar, the sports model. Endless nights on the Internet told him that car was very expensive. He also noticed a small dog napping under the car. "Kendall, I found him."

Kendall was in the garage in an instant. In a fit of celebration, she hugged Taylor. Jordan woke at the sound of Kendall's voice and scampered out. "Thank you so much for finding him." Kendall leaned down and picked Jordan up, hugging him fiercely. "I was so worried."

Jordan kissed Kendall, but he growled at Taylor. Instinctively, Taylor stepped back, fearing the little mutt knew his agenda.

"It's okay, Taylor. He just doesn't know you. Let him smell your hand."

Taylor tentatively held his hand out and the dog sniffed it, then licked it. Kendall smiled. "See, he does like you."

"Yeah, he does." Taylor only hoped his father would take to him as quickly as the dog did. He'd gotten on the wrong side this morning with his harsh treatment of Kendall, but watching her and the dog changed his attitude about her. In all his years, his mother had never worried about his absence and probably never loved him, her son, the way Kendall loved her dog.

CHAPTER 13

Cole paced the living room waiting for Taylor to return to the house. The walk to Kendall's house and back shouldn't have taken more than ten minutes at the most. It was now riding on an hour and Taylor still wasn't back.

Was forcing Kendall's company on his son the right thing to do? Had he put Kendall in harm's way trying to force a relationship between her and Taylor? How well did he really know his son?

He didn't really know his son at all. He grabbed his keys and headed for the front door just as it opened. Taylor walked inside and closed the door.

"Where are you going?" Taylor stared at his father.

Cole didn't want to start off lying to his son, and also didn't want to hurt his feelings. "Oh, I was just going to get the paper." It wasn't a total lie.

"Dad," his son pleaded. "The paper is on the coffee table. I set it there this morning. You were worried about her, weren't you?"

"I was also worried about you," Cole pointed out. He wanted Taylor's transition into his life to be as smooth as humanly possible. "I know I was asking a lot of you, but I wanted you to get to know Kendall."

Taylor plopped down on the couch. "I got to know her all right. I saw a side to her I wasn't quite expecting. She was acting all hard at breakfast like nothing could break her, but I found her breaking point."

Cole's blood chilled at the calmness in his son's voice. Was Kendall lying on her living room floor gasping her last breath? He walked to his son and grabbed him up by his shirt, pulling him up so that they were face to face. "What did you do to her?"

Taylor's eyes reflected the hurt that question raised. "You think I'm some kind of monster? I'm not like the kids on TV, Dad. I'm not as coldhearted as Mom, either. When we got to her place, she couldn't find her dog. She actually started crying."

Cole released his son slowly. "Oh, God, I'm sorry, Taylor. I didn't mean to imply anything. We don't know each other, so it's going to take some time for us to trust each other."

Taylor shrugged and smoothed out the wrinkles on his T-shirt. "You love her, don't you?"

Cole stared at his son. "What on earth would make you ask me such a thing?"

"I've never seen you ready to defend Mom like that. You were ready to kick my ass, I mean, butt, across the room. You probably should call her. She was pretty upset."

"Did you find Jordan?"

Taylor nodded. "Yeah, he was in the garage. He was sleeping under her car. Did you know Kendall had a Jag? A top-of-the-line model?"

Cole nodded. "Was Jordan okay?"

"Yeah, I think he was a little ticked she was gone so long." Taylor smiled at his father. "I'm sorry I was so rude to her this morning, but you never mentioned you were seeing anyone. It was a shock seeing you guys like that, and I guess I took it out on her. But once I got to know her, she was cool."

"It's going to take time, son. Don't worry. It's just you and me. So why don't we spend the day getting you settled?"

Taylor's eyes lit up like a Christmas tree. "You mean that, Dad? Just you and me, and no one else?"

That happy expression on his son's face told Cole everything he needed to know. His son had been neglected emotionally. He had all the material things a teenager could want. He just didn't have his mother's love, or his father's, for that matter. "Just you and me, kid. First, I need to make a few calls and then we'll go out and finish furnishing your room."

Taylor nodded and headed for the stairs. "I'll go shower and change while you're doing that."

Cole smiled as he picked up the phone. The first call was to Kendall. "Hey, how are you feeling?"

She sighed. "Much better now. Jordi gave me such a fright. If it hadn't been for Taylor, I think I would have lost my mind."

"What did Taylor do?" Cole feigned ignorance of the situation. He was very proud of his son.

"He found him."

Jami woke up that morning, exhausted. She'd spent most of the previous night moving her belongings into storage. Thank goodness her soon to be ex-husband was out drinking all night. She was able to make her getaway, thanks to Keerya and her brothers.

Now came the incredibly hard part. She had to move in with Kendall. She still had misgivings about it, but it would be the best thing for her and Dylan. Kendall lived in a gated community and they would be safe. Jami just hoped that Dylan didn't break anything expensive in Kendall's house.

She quietly got out of bed and hurried down the hall to take a shower and get dressed before waking Dylan. She met Keerya in the hallway. Keerya was already dressed for a day of moving in old jeans and an oversized T-shirt.

"Hey, are you ready for the big day ahead?"

Jami shrugged. "I don't know. I tossed and turned all night. I keep dreaming that Dylan is going to break a vase at Kendall's that costs a year's salary."

Keerya laughed. "Stop worrying. It's going to be fine. Kendall has mellowed out since she's been getting some. If I knew that was all it took, I would have set her up with one of my brothers years ago."

"Stop it, girl. You know she started changing before she and Cole started hitting the sheets. I think it started at Nurses' Night Out."

"I still think Cole has a lot to do with it. You probably should thank him when you see him walking through the house one morning." She winked one of her unmade-up eyes at Jami.

Jami inhaled. "I don't think I'll be seeing him. Max said something about Cole's son moving in."

"Oh, I just love a good story," Keerya said with a sly grin. "When's Max going to finally make his move?"

Jami didn't try to deny it. "He kissed me the other day."

"It's about time. You know I don't advocate the whole married man thing, but I know Max just has to realize how important you are to him and divorce that cow of a wife and pledge his undying love for you."

"I don't know if I have that kind of time," Jami said honestly. She didn't want to be one of those women waiting out a marriage. "Max has his own set of issues he needs to deal with," Jami said, more for herself than for Keerya. "By the time he works all that out he might not find me interesting anymore."

"Yeah, I'll believe that right after the Texas Rangers win the pennant."

"It's possible," Jami said.

Keerya placed her hand on Jami's shoulder. "We both know once Max decides on his divorce, it will be all downhill from there."

Kendall didn't know if she had the strength to continue. All she wanted to do was sit on her bed, hold Jordan in her arms and have a good old cry. She was afraid she'd lost him earlier, didn't know how she would live without her canine friend, but in the end he was okay.

She had to get hold of herself emotionally. Jami would be arriving shortly to move in, and Kendall had to at least appear in control of her world.

While Jordan ate his third helping of breakfast, Kendall went upstairs to change clothes. She'd just struggled into a pair of jeans and a T-shirt when the doorbell rang. "That's probably Jami," she muttered. "Time to slap on a happy face." She went downstairs and opened the front door.

Jami looked as frazzled as Kendall felt. "Hi, Kendall, I hope I didn't catch you at a bad time." She shifted her weight from foot to foot. "This is my son, Dylan."

Kendall looked at the little boy with his baby suitcase in his hand. He was the spitting image of his mother, with dark-chocolate skin and big brown eyes. She bent down and took the little boy's bag and then shook his hand. "It's nice to meet you, Dylan." She motioned them inside. "Come on."

"Keerya and her brothers are going to bring a few of my things over."

Kendall smiled. She was going to have to do something to make Jami feel more at ease or this wasn't going to work. "That's fine, Jami. This is your home, too. Why don't we sit on the couch where we can talk?"

Jami nodded and walked to the living room. "This is such a beautiful home, Kendall. Max was right, this is one gorgeous place." She sat down on the couch with Dylan in her lap.

"Thank you, Jami." Kendall glanced around the room. Her brothers often called it a showplace. She shook her head. Every piece of furniture had been perfectly placed, and yet it looked empty. In the years she'd lived there, this was the first time anyone other than her family had stayed there. "And while you're here, this is your home, so feel free to do whatever it takes to make you comfortable." She took the envelope she'd placed on the coffee table earlier and handed it to her new roommate. "Here are the keys to the house. My mom says if you need a babysitter, she'll be happy to help out. I think she's given up on me giving her grandchildren and thinks this is as close as she'll get."

Jami nodded. "I'll definitely need to take her up on that. I won't be able to leave Dylan at that daycare now. I just don't know what Karl will do."

"You're safe here. Mom can even come here if you like." Kendall took a deep breath. "You should file a restraining order for him not to come near you or Dylan. That way it's on record that he's threatening you."

Jami sighed and hugged Dylan closer to her. "Thank you, again, Kendall. My brain doesn't seem to be working. I'll file a report today."

"I have some patients this afternoon, but I could go with you later, if you like." Kendall glanced at the wall clock. She'd lost most of the morning to Jordan, and she barely had time to get dressed and get to work before her first patient was due.

"Keerya will go with me after we finish unloading stuff. How about I fix dinner to celebrate you taking me in?"

"You don't have to, Jami. You have enough on your mind already. Don't worry about me. I just want you to relax and get yourself together."

"Thank you, Kendall."

Kendall didn't think she could take it anymore. "Please quit thanking me. I should be thanking you. You and Dylan showed me I was missing something. You make my house a home."

"I don't understand," Jami said. "You have a lovely house, and I can't imagine you thinking your house isn't a home."

"It's not about the furniture, Jami. It's about the feeling of a home." Dylan slid out of Jami's lap and moved closer to Kendall. She picked him up and placed him in her lap. Dylan studied her for a moment, then hugged her. "This is what it's all about." She hugged the little boy, fighting back her tears.

Dylan raised his head and looked at him. "Hungry."

Kendall didn't give another thought to her work schedule and led the little tyke to the kitchen and made him breakfast.

CHAPTER 14

Kendall made it to work just minutes before her first afternoon appointment. Max met her at the employee entrance of the hospital, grinning. Not even his smart-aleck attitude would get to her today. Despite his grin, she knew her friend's mind was on something serious.

"Did Jami get moved in okay?"

"Yes, she did." Kendall wanted to know how Max was handling all the changes in his life, but the hospital was not the place to have that kind of conversation. She didn't want either of her friends to get hurt, but knew it was more than likely, considering they were both married to other people.

Max lowered his voice as they entered the hospital. "It was really nice of you to let her bunk with you. I was worried for her and Dylan's safety. I offered to help her find a place but she refused me."

That made Kendall proud. Jami refusing Max's help showed her character. "She refused me too, at first. I think Keerya talked her into it." Kendall walked to her office door. "I'll go put on my jacket and meet you in the lab."

Max nodded. "I'll go warm up the machine. By the way, you're working that dress. Too bad Cole isn't coming in the hospital today. I think he'd flip his literary lid."

"Says you." Kendall had picked out a bold olive green dress that morning with Cole in mind, even though she knew he was preoccupied with his new responsibilities as a full-time father. The dress hugged her curves and did wonderful things for her dark complexion. Her matching satin stilettos completed the ensemble.

Max shrugged his broad shoulders. "Hey, I might have to keep an eye on you for Cole. I heard a certain pharmaceutical salesman is back in town."

She looked back at him and tilted her head. "Oh, yeah, I heard that, too. My mom thinks he'll try to get in touch with me. I doubt my ex would want to even look at me."

"I think he will. In fact he already called once this morning." He sauntered off in the direction of the lab.

"Damn," Kendall muttered as she opened her door and retrieved her lab coat. The last thing she wanted to do was talk to that excuse of an ex-husband. But James Matthews could be a force to be reckoned with when he wanted to be. Kendall hoped his move back from the West Coast wasn't for her.

Cole sat in his attorney's office with his son by his side. He was concerned about the ramifications of his son coming to Texas without his mother's consent. Cole didn't want to be on the wrong side of kidnapping charges. Luckily, his attorney was also his close friend and Kendall's brother, Charlie.

Charlie listened as Taylor explained why he came to Texas in the middle of the night. He nodded at the appropriate times and made notes. He looked from Taylor to Cole. "Our first course of action will be to file for custody. Taylor needs to call his mother and let her know exactly where he is. The sooner the better."

Cole nodded. "He called her before we came here."

"And?" Charlie jotted more notes.

Cole recounted the brief conversation Taylor had with his mother. "She told him not to return."

"Her exact words?" Charlie looked at Cole with sympathy in his brown eyes.

"Unfortunately," Cole said. "She's transferred the hatred she had for me to Taylor."

Charlie shook his head. "Women. Some days it just doesn't pay to know one."

Cole laughed. "True. Some days. Other days, I'm glad I do." He instantly thought of Kendall and how he was glad he knew her. He hoped she adapted to the changes in his life quickly.

Charlie cleared his throat, beckoning Cole out of his daydream. "I have enough to get started with Taylor's deposition. I'll have the custody change filed with New York County by tomorrow. I'm sure I'll be hearing from her attorney within a few hours of the filing and we'll go from there." Charlie stood and shook Cole's hand. "I'll be in touch if I hear from her attorney."

"Great, Charlie. I just wanted to get something on paper," Cole stated. "You know how it is. I don't need another scandal attached to my name. I also don't want

reporters descending on Taylor in the quest for a story."
Cole wrapped a protective arm around his son and led
him out of the office.

Once outside, Cole tried to judge his son's mood. So
much had happened in the span of twenty-four hours; he
wondered how Taylor's teenaged brain was processing all
the changes.

Like all teenagers, his son was quiet.

"How about some lunch?"

Taylor nodded and started walking toward Cole's
Range Rover. "Dad, is that stuff really true? Could Mom
actually charge you with kidnapping just because I
wanted to visit you?"

Cole disarmed the car alarm. "Well, yes and no.
Legally, I do have a right to see you, being that I'm your
legal parent and I do pay child support. But I don't know
if the courts know about my address change back to
Texas." Cole didn't want to go into the legal ramifications
with his son. "But don't worry, son. Charlie will sort it all
out. Not only is he one of my oldest friends, but he's one
of the best attorneys in Texas." He opened the door and
slid behind the wheel.

"I always wondered why Charlie was your attorney even
though he lived in Texas while you lived in New York."

"He's the best," Cole said.

After Taylor was belted in, Cole started the car. "How
about the Olive Garden?"

Taylor nodded. "Sounds fine. I didn't mean to get
you into trouble, Dad. I just wanted to know the truth
about you, and coming here was my only option."

Cole started down busy Cooper Street, heading for the Italian restaurant. When his son's words hit home, he asked, "What truth?"

Taylor sighed, looking out of the tinted window. "Ever since the divorce Mom has been singing this song about how you didn't want anything to do with us, namely me. Why did you move here?"

Cole knew this was going to be a lengthy conversation and probably should take place at home, but he didn't want his son to think he didn't want to be seen in public with him, either. "I moved back because nothing seemed to be holding me in New York. You refused to see me. I had broken up with my last girlfriend and wanted to be near people who loved me. New York had lost its charm."

"Mom was playing us against each other. She told me you didn't want to see me."

The bitterness in his son's voice told him it was the truth. Did his ex hate him that much? Enough to deny her own son a healthy relationship with his father? Charlie was right, he mused. Some days it didn't pay to know women.

James Matthews entered Briarwood Hospital unnoticed, which was something with his movie star looks. Being six feet, four inches tall, he stood out like crazy. If his memory served him correctly, Kendall's office was down this corridor. It had been five years since she'd tossed him out on his ass. Surely she was over the whole cheating thing.

"James?" a male voice called.

He turned around, wanting to know who had breached his incognito thing. His eyes rested on a pale form and he sighed. He should have known. Max was better than any guard dog. "Hey, Max. Long time no see." He extended his hand in greeting.

"Yeah, man, what's it been? Like five years since Kendall caught you cheating on her for the millionth time?" Max took his hand.

"Something like that." James wished he could have said something to wipe that smug grin off Max's face, but the truth was the truth. "You know, it's been some time. Maybe she's ready to forgive me and take me back."

"Is that why you're back in Texas?" Max's grin told him not to count on winning Kendall back.

"Partly. I got a promotion. I'm the sales manager for the Dallas area. Right now I'm just touching base with the local hospitals and doctors, trying to get a feel for what's needed."

Max nodded. "And Kendall is the go-to person for not only Briarwood, but also InfaCare, so why not seduce two birds with one kiss, right?"

"Harsh."

"Sorry, James, I just call it like I see it. You forget who had the chore of telling Kendall you were cheating with the head nurse in cardiac care, the nurse in geriatrics, the surgical nurse at the new hospital, and we won't even talk about the ones at Arlington General."

He was a dog and he'd screwed up royally. But everyone deserved a second chance, right? James held up his hand in surrender. "Okay, man, I get it. You're still pissed. You're worse than her momma and her brothers. Is she around?"

Max hesitated. It was clear he didn't want James within spitting distance of Kendall, but he relented and said, "Yeah, she's in her office. She's got an appointment in ten minutes. Don't make her late." Max walked off without another word.

"Yeah, it was nice seeing you, too," James muttered at Max's retreating back. If he didn't know how professional Kendall was, and that she didn't believe in mingling with co-workers, he'd swear Max had a thing for her.

James headed down the hall and encountered another familiar face. It felt like a homecoming, seeing all these familiar faces, he thought. "Hello, Keerya. You're looking as beautiful as ever."

"She's in her office, Mr. Matthews." Keerya continued working.

Being dismissed, James walked the few feet to Kendall's corner office and knocked on the closed door. He waited an eternity before she invited him in. Like a condemned man on the last mile, he took a deep breath, hoping the warden would be kind, and entered.

He almost didn't recognize her. The woman he divorced would never have had her feet propped up on the desk, actually relaxing. What had happened to the workaholic he was married to? He liked the dress she was almost wearing. She always did have great legs. She was still a little thin for his taste, but overall the picture was quite enticing. "Hello, Kendall. Nice to see you." He meant that, no matter how trite it sounded. "I really like that dress."

She took her feet off the desk and rose, straightening her dress in the process. "James, what brings you by? I have an appointment."

"I know. In ten minutes. I met Max in the hall. I just wanted to say hello and maybe ask you out to dinner. How about it? Got a spare dinner for an ex-husband?"

"Why do you want to have dinner with me? I was only married to you for eight years."

"Look, baby, I know I cheated on you. I'm sorry. I was lonely. You were working all the time. What was I supposed to do?"

She stalked over to where he stood. "You were supposed to be supportive, not use my very expensive bed for your extracurricular activities."

James held up his hand. "I didn't come into this damn hospital to fight with every employee here. All I wanted to do was have dinner with my ex."

"And tell me that the hospital is your new territory," Kendall said.

"You already knew and you're reading me the riot act?" James asked incredulously. "This is so typical of your controlling ways. That's why I cheated. I wanted to do something you couldn't control. I was tired of sleeping with an ice cube. When we did have sex, all you did was lay there like a frozen lake." He wished he could take back every word he'd said. He hadn't meant to lash out at her. He'd wanted to soften her up, not prepare her for war. Instead of the old Kendall spouting how worthless he was, she laughed.

"Well, James, tell me how you really feel." She walked back to her chair and sat down. "Dinner will be fine. Check with Keerya on your way out to see when I'm free. I'm tied up the next few days, so anytime after that should be doable."

James didn't want to press his luck. He didn't know what alien had come and taken over his ex-wife's body, but he was going to get out while the getting was good. "I'll be in touch." He hurried out of her office.

Kendall giggled at her ex-husband's retreating back. In the old days James's accusations would have started an all-out war, with her taking no prisoners. But Cole Highpoint had changed all that. In the few short days she'd been intimate with him, she'd realized she was no longer an ice cube, but a simmering inferno. Too bad she couldn't thank him in person. Why couldn't she? She reached for the phone just as Keerya knocked and entered her office at the same time. "Yes, Keerya."

Keerya took a seat in one of the leather chairs after she closed the door. "Kendall, it's not my place to say anything."

She knew exactly what the young woman was going to say. "I appreciate your input, Keerya. I know you think I've lost my mind, but trust me, I know what I'm doing." And for the first time in four years, Kendall knew exactly what she was doing. She was getting closure.

CHAPTER 15

Later that afternoon, Cole unlocked the door to his house to let Taylor inside. His brain still whirled on the information his son had revealed at lunch.

Cole's ex-wife had done a mental number on their son just so he wouldn't come near his father. Taylor was more shell-shocked than a war veteran straight from the combat zone. He was cautious when he spoke. Taylor reminded Cole of some of the politicians on the hot seat, making sure not to let anything slip out.

Cole could strangle his ex for what she'd done in the name of revenge. He hadn't had any real communication with his son in four years, so they had a lot of ground to cover. But they needed a go-between, someone they both trusted, and someone who could ferret out the truth. There was only one unbiased person he knew who was right for this job: Kendall.

He watched his son plop onto the sofa and reach for the remote control. Taylor, being a healthy male teenager, channel-surfed until he found a music video channel. Cole shook his head in wonder as he watched the young women gyrate and Lord knows what else on screen. Seeing the concentration on Taylor's face, Cole knew better than to start the father-son bonding. He'd wait for a time they could concentrate on each other.

Cole went to the kitchen to call Kendall. Not being able to talk to her all day was beginning to wear on him. He'd noticed another car parked in front of her house when he and Taylor arrived home. He could be a good neighbor and call her just to make sure everything was all right.

Cole quickly dialed the hospital.

"Dr. Matthews," Kendall said after he was finally put through to her.

"Hey, baby," Cole said. "I was wondering if you'd fix something for me."

Kendall laughed. "I'm sorry, sir. You must have misdialed. This is not the help hotline."

Cole laughed as well. She sounded wonderful to his ears. "I was kind of hoping you were the help hotline. I need someone to listen objectively to both me and Taylor. My ex has fed each of us so many lies, we don't know quite where to begin. So I was hoping you could maybe join us for dinner."

"As wonderful as that may sound, Cole, I can't have dinner tonight. It's Jami's first night at my house. I want to make sure she and Dylan are settled in."

"How about tomorrow night?" Cole knew he sounded pitiful and Max would probably ask for his man card back for it.

"Now that sounds doable."

Cole relaxed. "I'll even make a vegetarian meal just for you. Of course, Taylor and I will probably eat steaks while you're munching on your salad."

"You know, I think I would like a steak, too. It's been ages since I had a good piece of beef."

"Are you playing with me?" He hoped so. "Are you using euphemisms for sex? All you have to do is ask, baby."

"If I were, and I'm not saying that I am, where would we have this sex?"

And there was the problem. Her place was definitely out of the question with her new houseguests and his place was definitely out. "How about the lake house?"

"How about you focus on your son?" Kendall giggled.

Cole shook his head. That woman had him seeing condoms when he should have been concentrating on his son and their fragile new relationship. "You're right, as usual. Guess I'll have to rein in those hormones until a more appropriate time."

"I didn't realize you were such a chicken. The Coltrane Highpoint I know would have figured out a way," Kendall hinted. "But I guess you're preoccupied."

She was actually daring him! He hated to be challenged, and this woman had just crossed the line. "I'm going to get you for that."

"What?" she asked innocently.

"You know what, woman, and you're going to pay for what you've done to me," Cole teased. She had him hard as rock with just a little innuendo.

"I have no idea what you're referring to, Cole."

Oh, she was good. "I'll refresh your memory," he promised. "Tomorrow."

"I'd like to see you try it."

"You will."

Kendall laughed as she replaced the phone in its cradle. She was definitely losing it. Cole had her thinking naughty thoughts, knowing very well that they wouldn't be able to act on those thoughts. Darn that man!

Max entered her office with a scowl marring his handsome face. He plopped down in one of the chairs reserved for her patients and let out the most dramatic sigh she'd ever heard. He was dressed in navy scrubs, and his short blond hair looked as if he'd been running his fingers through it in frustration all afternoon.

Something was wrong. This wasn't the happy-go-lucky man who'd bulldozed his way onto her staff and into her life. "Okay, Max, give." They'd been friends too long to dabble in pleasantries neither of them were feeling.

"Oh, it's nothing. Just my life is in the toilet and I have no idea how to fix it." He gazed at her with those penetrating blue eyes.

"Am I the black version of Dr. Laura?"

"No, but you're as close as I've got. And if I don't talk to someone soon I think I might just explode." He let out another sigh.

This wasn't going to be a boss-and-employee talk; this would be a friend-to-friend talk, she realized. She stood and walked to the vacant chair next to her friend and sat down. "Why don't you start from the beginning?" Kendall said softly. "It always helps me to solve a problem if I look at it from all angles."

"You know Caitlin and I have been having serious problems for about the last two years."

Kendall nodded. "You guys were going to counseling."

Max gave her a short laugh. "Yeah, that lasted about two months. I kept going for a while because I honestly wanted to try to make it work for Carson's sake, but now even that isn't enough."

Kendall knew what it was to be the only one in a marriage. "Have you guys thought about a trial separation to see what each of you really wants?"

"Okay, that was last year. We tried it for about three months. Caitlin claimed she was ready to make it work, so I, like the idiot that I am, believed her and moved back home."

Kendall shook her head. She didn't remember any of this. Was she so self-involved that she hadn't noticed her best friend was in a crisis? "I take it she didn't want to make it work."

"No, she didn't. But with her being from the Campbells of Dallas, divorce is not an option. She claims a divorce would kill her parents and they would disinherit her for disgracing the family name."

Kendall also knew all about image. Max's wife was from a very affluent family. Harold and Elizabeth Campbell could never hold their heads up at the country club if their only daughter was divorced. Poor Max. "So what are you going to do?"

"I wish I knew. Then there's Jami. I didn't mean to fall in love with her, but I have. She's everything Caitlin isn't. Jami is a good mother, a caring soul, and a great listener. I get goose bumps every time she smiles at me."

Kendall saw the train wreck ahead. "Max, both you guys are married to other people. You need to take care of one problem first before you try to tackle another. First, you need to decide what to do about Caitlin and your marriage."

Max sighed again. "This is where it gets real sticky."

"Give it to me," Kendall said, not keeping the dread out of her voice.

"You know, you sound like my mom when you say it like that." Max laughed. "Last weekend I told Caitlin I wanted a divorce. Her dad offered me a million dollars not to pursue it."

Kendall was stunned. A million dollars? "What did you tell him?"

"To take a hike."

"Good for you. Show that billionaire you're not for sale."

Max lowered his head, running his fingers through his hair. "No, not good for me. Caitlin still refuses to go to counseling and refuses to talk about the marriage. We don't even sleep in the same room anymore. My only bright spot in all this besides my son is coming to work and seeing Jami."

"Max, focus. If you guys aren't sleeping in the same room, what good is the marriage?"

"Exactly. I'm tired of living like that. Caitlin is never home. She's always out, most of the time with her socialite friends. She leaves Carson with the nanny constantly. I've been in a sham of a marriage for ten years, and it's time to get off the marriage-go-round."

Kendall felt her friend's sorrow. She picked up his hand and held it. "Max, there's not going to be an easy solution. You need to figure out what you really want. Do you want Jami because she's the total opposite of Caitlin in every way, or are you truly attracted to her? You guys both have a lot a baggage to work through before you can even think about being together."

Max nodded, listening to her every word. "Yeah, but we're not the only ones with baggage around here. What are you going to do about Cole and his son?"

Kendall dropped his hand and shrugged. "I don't really know. We had a rocky beginning, but he helped me locate Jordan the other morning. Cole wants me to act as an arbitrator for them. It seems his ex did a number on both of them."

Max shook his head. "Women. I wonder why we even try to love them. They only hurt us in the end."

"Not all women. There are still some good ones out there. And if you ever get out of this mess, you'll see that I'm right."

A few hours later, Kendall pulled up in front of her mother's house. She'd been summoned just minutes after her talk with Max to have dinner with her parents. Being the youngest, the only girl, and single, there was no way she could refuse.

She slid from behind the wheel of her car and headed into the house. She spotted her stepfather, Evan Duncan, reclining in his favorite chair, his eyes glued to the television. Evan watched CNN, the cable news network, faithfully. He was dressed in a polo shirt and slacks. "Hey, Dad. How's it going? Play any golf today?" She walked to him and planted a kiss on his cheek.

Evan snickered. "Yeah, took your mother out there on the links. I just hope I haven't been banned. Your momma caused a scene today."

"Not my sweet, docile mother," Kendall said sarcastically. She could easily imagine her petite mother causing a commotion at the Arlington Hills Country Club.

"She was defending your honor."

Kendall sat down on the nearby sofa. This was going to be good. Her parents had been members of that country club for the last thirty years. Zenora and Evan were one of the first African-American couples to join the formerly segregated club. "Okay, what happened?"

Evan smiled, revealing his white teeth, which at the age of sixty-eight were all his own. His smooth pecan skin glowed as his laughter lit up his face. "We were on the ninth hole and things were going well. I was letting her win."

"Wise man."

"We ran into Cole's mother, Martha, and her sister-in-law."

Kendall gasped. "Uh-oh."

"Yeah, uh-oh is right, young lady."

"How was she defending my honor?"

Evan turned toward her, leaving CNN's commentators to fend for themselves. "Martha hinted you were trying to snag Cole so he'd make another big donation to the hospital, just to keep you happy."

Kendall shook her head. "Oh dear."

Evan nodded and returned to watching CNN. Some young correspondent was reciting some horrible news about the war front with a smile on her face. "Yep, she put that woman in her place, but good. Before I knew it they were yelling at each other like you wouldn't believe. I was getting ready to stop the shouting match when the club manager appeared out of nowhere, telling all of us to leave the club."

Kendall took a deep breath. It didn't sound like her parents' membership was threatened, thank goodness. Arlington Hills had one of best golf courses in Tarrant County. "I'm seeing Cole, but not for his money. And for the record, Cole volunteered the donation. I didn't ask him for it. When he initially offered it to me, I refused it."

"I know, honey. And your momma told Martha so."

Kendall groaned and leaned back on the sofa. "How bad is it?" Her mother and Martha Highpoint had been friends since before Kendall was born. "Are they speaking?"

"Here's the funny part."

"Is there one?"

"Yes, there is. While we were being escorted to our cars, your mother mentioned Charlie catching you two the other week on the couch. The next thing I know Zenora and Martha are planning the wedding and how many kids you and Cole are going to have. So it all turned out fine. The women are speaking again and my life is as quiet as it should be."

Kendall sat up straight. "Except the fact that my mother will have a bee in her bonnet about Cole."

"Don't you like him?"

Kendall evaded the question. "Dad, that's really not the issue."

"And that answers my question. So have you guys set a date? How do you get along with his son? Martha said he arrived unannounced."

Kendall shook her head. Evan was her last hope for nipping this in the bud, but he was as bad as her mother. "Daddy, please. There's no date, we're just having a good time."

"Oh well, that explains everything."

Kendall was in too deep now. She'd have to tell her father something a little more concrete just to reassure him. "Dad, Cole and I are seeing each other, just not exclusively and now that his son is here, we're kind of on hiatus."

"So?"

"So what?"

"So when's the big day?"

Kendall sighed. Parents were the same no matter what. Her stepfather heard what he wanted to hear and that was it. She'd never convince him or her mother there was no wedding to be planned until they were ready to hear it.

"I'm going to the kitchen to see if Mom needs help," she announced to her stepfather.

"Okay, baby girl." He turned back to the television.

Kendall knew she was about to be interrogated by a fierce force named Zenora Stone-Duncan. It would take all of her diplomatic skills as a doctor to convince her mother there would be no wedding. She squared her shoulders and entered the kitchen.

Her mother was in her element. She loved to cook. Although her mother tried to abide by Kendall's vegetarian lifestyle as much as she could, she didn't believe in a meal without meat. In honor of Kendall, they were having roast chicken, mashed potatoes, corn on the cob, and salad. Looking up from one of her pots, she noticed Kendall in the doorway. "Hi, honey."

"Hey Mom. Dad told me about the country club. Thanks."

Zenora shook her head as she placed the silver lid on the blue boiler, a Christmas present from Charlie. "No need to thank me. I told Martha you didn't have to ask Cole for the donation. Charlie told me about catching you guys on the couch like teenagers in heat."

"Mom, I'm forty, you know. I can have male company without consulting you. As a matter of fact, I've had several dates."

"With Cole?"

"No."

"Baby, I just want you to be happy. After Martha and I talked we decided we just want our children to be happy. Cole is very successful and he's got a good future in writing. Martha said he just signed at multimillion-dollar book deal a few months back. You could do a lot worse than a millionaire."

Kendall should have known her mother would find out every detail of Cole's life. It was as if she were sixteen again and her mother was looking over a prospective beau. Her mother could ferret out information better than any reporter on CNN.

"Martha said his son showed up last night." Her mother immediately proved her worth to the gossip community. "She said she hasn't even seen him, but Cole promised her very soon. Can you believe he's sixteen years old and Martha has never met the boy? Cole said he just appeared in his bedroom doorway."

Was that just yesterday when the bottom dropped out of her world? "Yes, Cole didn't realize he was in the house until we woke up." Kendall realized her mistake, but it was too late. She'd just told her mother that she'd slept with Cole. She could only hope that her mother was too occupied with dinner to notice.

Zenora smiled at her daughter. "Well, I guess if you're waking up with him that's a good sign." She held up a slender, bejeweled hand. "Before you get all stuffy on me, it's perfectly fine for two adults to talk about sex, and we are two adults. We just happen to be mother and daughter. Now, I don't need details. That smile says everything. So I guess he knows what he's doing."

Kendall just wanted this evening to be over. It was only going to get worse as her mother started pumping her for more information.

"Mmm, I think the chicken is ready. Want me to call Dad for dinner?"

Zenora walked to the large wooden table and took a seat. She motioned for Kendall to do the same. After she did, her mother looked at her with a serious look in the brown eyes. "No, you're going to tell me just how many times Cole has awakened beside you."

CHAPTER 16

It was nearly ten when Kendall opened her door to her house. Her mother hadn't been satisfied until Kendall filled her in on most of the details of her relationship with Cole, not that there was much to tell.

She entered her house with a sigh and braced herself for what she thought she'd find in her living room. She had expected to see Dylan's toys scattered all over the place, but there was no visible evidence there was even a child in the house.

In fact, there wasn't any evidence that anybody was in the house.

Kendall noticed her mail was on the counter in a very neat pile. A yellow notepad bearing the logo of Briarwood Hospital sat next to the stack of letters. She glanced at the message and did a double take. She picked it up and read the message again. Cole had left a not-so-cryptic message about meeting him at "their" spot for some hot sex on a platter!

"That man has a lot of nerve," she muttered, as she wadded up the note and threw it in a nearby wastebasket. She grabbed her mail and took a seat in her favorite over-sized leather chair.

She was opening the electric bill when Jami entered the room dressed in bright red silk pajamas with a matching red robe. Jami took a seat on the couch and crossed her legs. "Hi, Kendall. Would you like me to get you something? Dylan and I had McDonald's this evening, and I got you a salad just in case you were hungry when you came home."

"Jami, you don't have to do that. I had dinner at my mom's tonight. I hadn't intended to stay as late as I did, because I wanted to make sure you guys were settled. But my mother found out about Cole, so I had to explain. Between his mom and mine, I'm going to have a crapload of trouble. They're already planning a wedding." She shook her head.

Jami nodded. "Kendall, you've been such a help to me when I had virtually nowhere else to turn. Max wanted to help, but he's in a dodgy situation himself. Besides, I couldn't take money from him. I just want to show my appreciation to you."

Kendall sighed and placed the unopened mail aside. "Jami, you've shown me appreciation for the last five years. Let me do this for you." She wanted Jami to feel at home, not like a visitor. "For now, this is your home, too. You don't have to fix me dinner, you don't have to get my mail, and it's okay if Dylan's toys are around the house."

Jami studied her, letting Kendall's statement filter through her brain. She toyed with the belt on her robe as she thought. "Thank you, Kendall, but I don't mind doing those things for you. Did you get your phone message from Cole? He told me to call him that," Jami quickly explained.

"That's fine, Jami. What time did he call?" Kendall fought the urge to get the note out of the trash.

Jami smiled slyly. "About an hour ago."

Kendall tried for a little levity. "Don't you look at me like that. I'm not going to meet him. His son just arrived today, so he needs to spend time with him."

"So that's who that was." She cleared her throat. "I saw Cole and a young man walking around the area earlier this evening."

"Yes, that's Cole's son, Taylor. He's going to be living with Cole."

Jami nodded. "Oh, my. That's going to take some adjustment for you guys. So that explains what he said."

Kendall was almost afraid to ask. "What did he say?"

Jami stood and readjusted her sash. "He asked me if I knew any good books for teenagers."

Kendall was relieved, envisioning Cole saying something off the mark to Jami. Thank goodness she was wrong. "Oh, I'll have to call my nephew and ask him tomorrow. Speaking of tomorrow, James will probably call. He wants to do dinner one day this week."

Jami nodded, but said nothing.

"Yes, I remember what he did to me," Kendall said. "He thinks he's going to worm his way back into my life. Like I'm going to forget about all his cheating."

"I'm glad you're cautious, Kendall. I don't want him to hurt you again. No one should have to live through a hurt like that a second time. I understand about revenge and closure, as long as you know which is which."

Kendall took in her new friend's advice. "That's very true, Jami. But I know what I'm doing. I need to know for myself that it's finally over. And today while he was in my office, I knew that it is over. He hurt me one time too many, and I'm not going to relive that. Unfortunately, both Briarwood and InfaCare are in his sales territory, so I have to deal with him on a professional level."

"I understand. It's for the hospital."

She didn't understand, Kendall knew, but it would take more than a night to explain it. For so long the hospital had been the only thing in her life, but now that was different. But how could she put those emotions into words? Kendall was living it, and she didn't know if she understood it. "Partly, but close enough for tonight."

"I'm going to bed," Jami said as she left the room. "Good night, Kendall."

"Good night, Jami," Kendall called as she decided that salad didn't sound too bad after all and headed to the kitchen.

After Kendall devoured the salad, she went upstairs to find her skating companion. Any other time, Jordan would have been at her heels the minute she walked inside the house, but tonight he was nowhere to be seen.

She went to her bedroom because that was where she'd assumed he'd be, stretched out on her king-sized bed and waiting for her. But he wasn't there. She knew he wasn't in the garage. As she started for the spare bedroom, she heard a bark. She heard another bark and Dylan's laughter. Then more barking, more laughter, and finally Jami telling Dylan to be quiet. The barking and laughter only increased.

"Come on, guys, you're going to wake Kendall, and then you're going to be in trouble," Jami threatened.

Kendall didn't know if she liked being the bargaining chip with Dylan. Besides, it didn't work anyway. Dylan and Jordan were bonding, much to her dismay. She knocked on Jami's door, and for a moment all Kendall heard were hushed whispers between mother and son. "Come in, Kendall," Jami said hesitantly.

Kendall plastered a smile on her face, so Jami and Dylan would feel comfortable with her. Jami was perched on the end of the bed, ready to defend her child, no doubt. She worried needlessly because the picture before her captured Kendall's heart. Dylan and Jordan were lying side by side facing each other, sharing the same pillow. One of Jordan's paws rested lightly on Dylan's T-shirt-covered chest. It was a Kodak moment that warmed her heart.

"Hey, guys, I was just wondering if I could borrow Jordan for a little run."

Dylan looked at her with his big brown eyes. "Are you going to bring him back? We promise to be quiet from now on," he said honestly.

"Yes, honey. You can play with him whenever you want."

His big brown eyes were going to be her undoing. Kendall sat on the bed next to Dylan.

He sat up and crawled into her lap and hugged her.

"Dylan, get out of Kendall's lap," Jami scolded. "How many times have I told you that you have to ask first?" She looked at Kendall with pleading eyes. "I'm sorry. He does that with Keerya and Max."

Kendall wrapped her arms around the child and squeezed him gently. "You can crawl into my lap anytime, Dylan."

"Can I go skating with you and Jordan?" He slid off her lap and stood on the floor. "I can change clothes."

"No, baby," Kendall said. "I think it's too late for little boys to be up. You need all your rest."

"Why?" Jami and Dylan asked simultaneously.

Why indeed? Think, Kendall, think. It was summer. What did kids do in the summer? "We have to go shopping for you some new toys."

"Why?" mother and son queried again.

Kendall had to get a lot better at this. "Because it's my housewarming present to you."

Dylan seemed satisfied with that answer, but not Jami.

"Kendall, you don't have—"

"Any toys here," Kendall circumvented. "I know. We're going to remedy that tomorrow, right after work."

That answer satisfied both mother and son, or either Jami didn't want to jeopardize her job. Either way, Kendall finally won. "Good. We'll go shopping right after work. I'm having dinner with Cole and Taylor tomorrow night," Kendall explained for no reason. "So do we have a date, Dylan?"

He nodded.

Kendall looked at Jami, who also agreed. She felt very satisfied. "Good, tomorrow at five." Kendall rose and whistled for Jordan to join her. She didn't actually think he'd leave Dylan's side, but if Jordan was anything, he was loyal. He knew where his gourmet dog food came from. He followed Kendall out of the room and down the hall.

Cole watched Kendall from his bedroom window. On the pretext of trying to get some work done, he had gone to his room earlier that evening. But now, watching her skating with total abandon, he knew where he needed to be. He wanted to see her so badly he didn't think he could last another day. He imagined his hands all over her slender body. He needed to show his son the love he needed, but his son was in his room playing on the new laptop computer Cole had purchased for him earlier that day. Surely Taylor would be okay for a few minutes while he took a short walk.

He walked down the hall and knocked on his son's door. When he was invited inside, he opened the door. Taylor was sitting at the ultra-modern computer desk, also purchased that day, in a leather high-back chair. "Hey, Dad."

Cole cleared his throat. "I'm going to take a walk. You'll be okay for about thirty minutes on your own?"

Taylor turned around and faced his father. "How about I go with you?"

Cole hadn't planned on that. But he should have known Taylor would want to accompany him. "Sure, if you really want to."

Taylor laughed. "No, Dad, I was just messing with you. I saw Kendall skating earlier. She's really hot, Dad. I couldn't imagine Mom or Holly skating just for fun. You better make your move. I thought I saw some other dude following her."

"Really?"

"Yeah, I don't think she knows he's behind her."

That was all Cole needed to hear. He had to find out what was going on. Kendall might be in grave danger. "Be back in thirty."

Kendall breathed in the night air as she skated. Exercise always helped her to clear her head. Jordan was a few steps ahead of her, jogging merrily and looking for prey, when he suddenly stopped. Kendall started at his attack growl.

"Calm down, Jordan. There's no way a prowler could get by security, baby. We're safe." She hoped the assurance would be enough for him to resume jogging.

But Jordan was on high alert and barking furiously even though she couldn't see anyone. Suddenly, Jordan took off for the large oak tree in the middle of the park and barked at it. Kendall skated toward the tree and spotted a figure in black jeans and black shirt. "James?"

"Call off your dog."

197

"Jordan, it's okay. It's just a two-legged dog." She patted her leg twice and called him again with just a little attitude in her voice, so he'd know she meant business. Jordan trotted over to her and James descended from the tree.

He walked over to her and stopped just short of Jordan. "Hey, he looks like he's going to take a bite out of me. Why don't you tether him or something?"

Kendall looked from tiny Jordan to her taller-than-average ex-husband. Jordan could probably take James in one bite. "He won't bite his own kind."

"I see you can't let that go." He brushed leaves and dirt from his pants. "I came by to see you, but the security guard said he had to announce me. So I took matters into my own hands," he said confidently.

"So who do you know in this subdivision?"

He didn't even try to deny it for one second. "A charming lady named Eileen Chambers. She invited me back to her place for a drink."

Kendall didn't know which infuriated her more: The fact that he'd willingly used another female to get inside her complex, or that Eileen was a sweet person and probably thought James was genuine.

"You're the same selfish bastard you were when I divorced you." She started to skate away, but James caught her by her arm. Kendall fell facedown on the concrete.

"Oh, baby, I'm sorry," James said as he helped her up. "You know I wouldn't hurt you for the world. I just want you to know what I'm willing to do to see you."

Kendall sat down on the grass and surveyed the damage. There were a few scratches on her left leg, but her right knee was bleeding and was beginning to throb like hell. "Why don't you just leave? And if you're on this property again, I'm calling the police."

"Baby, you don't understand. I really wanted to see you."

"And I think you didn't hear what the lady said," a deep male voice said.

Kendall knew that voice. "Cole, what are you doing here?"

"Watching this man attack you." He looked at Kendall's bleeding knee. "He did that to you?" He slipped his T-shirt off and kneeled down next to her. Not waiting for an answer he already knew, he began cleaning up her injury the best he could.

"Look man, there's no need for all that. It was an accident, that's all. No need to stick your pretty little nose into our business," James said sarcastically.

The rest happened too fast to stop. Cole stood up and knocked James out with one blow. By the time James hit the ground, Cole was back tending to her knee.

"Can you stand?" He was already helping her upright.

"Cole, I'm perfectly okay. I can walk on my own," Kendall protested.

He shrugged. "I hate hardheaded women, and I see you are one." He let go of her.

Kendall tried her darnedest to stand straight, but her leg would not support her. She crumpled, and Cole caught her just in time.

"Looks like you're going to have to depend on me." Cole lifted her in his arms. "Now, my place or yours?"

"You're thinking about sex now?" Kendall stretched the injured leg out to ease the pain. "My leg is killing me, and you're thinking about sex."

"No, my place is closer and I can clean your wound up a little better. Sex hadn't entered my mind. Until now."

Kendall lowered her head. "Your place." She didn't want Jami to see her like this anyway. She hated being weak.

CHAPTER 17

Taylor watched his father as he carried Kendall across the courtyard in his arms. Was he nuts? Why was he carrying her when she could walk? He hurried downstairs to open the front door and give that woman a piece of his mind. His father might not be thinking clearly, but he sure was.

Taylor snatched the door open just as his father rang the doorbell. "Dad, have you lost it? You could hurt your back."

Cole looked at his son sideways as he stepped inside the house. Kendall had a sick look on her face. "No, son. Kendall had an accident." He sat her on the couch so that she was sitting on one end and her legs were stretched out.

Taylor noticed her wincing in pain and finally looked at her legs. One of her legs was bleeding. "Wow, you took a nasty fall."

Kendall looked up at him and said sarcastically, "Yeah, I had a little help."

Taylor wondered if his father had actually gone nuts and beaten that guy to a bloody pulp, getting Kendall caught in the middle. "Dad?"

Cole looked at his son. "No, I didn't. It was someone else. I just came up after the fact."

Taylor sighed. "Sorry, Dad."

His father tended to Kendall's leg. "You have nothing to apologize for. We haven't been around each other for over four years, and you don't know me."

"Yes, sir."

"Run upstairs and get the first aid kit I showed you this morning."

Needing some space and grateful to his father for suggesting it, Taylor ran upstairs.

"Cole, maybe you should call Max. You might need some assistance. My knee is pretty banged up."

He shook his head and raised her injured knee. "Nonsense, it's not swelling. It just looks a lot worse than it actually is." He tried to make light of the situation. Her knee was scraped pretty bad, and her leg was bruised up.

"Well, it sure does hurt," Kendall said. "I could really use some aspirin."

Taylor made his entrance into the room carrying a red box the size of a small tool kit.

"What should I do?" his son asked, eager to help.

That made Cole smile. That had to mean something. "How about getting Kendall some water and aspirin?" He watched his son and Jordan run into the kitchen, then turned his attention to his patient. "I seem to remember a few months ago when this situation was reversed." He reached inside the kit for the antiseptic and a cloth. After he dampened the cloth with antiseptic, he cleared his throat. If he were a spiteful man this would be fun, but he cared for this woman and the last thing he wanted to do was to cause her pain. He cleared his throat. "This is going to bite, babe."

"I know," she whispered. "But you've got to clean out the wound."

Cole inhaled and applied the damp cloth to the wound and, as gently as he could, he cleansed it. Kendall didn't yell out in pain, which is what he probably would have done. She simply flinched. "You know, it's okay to admit you're in pain. I promise not to tell anyone if you shed a few tears."

"I'm perfectly capable of handling a little pain," she said calmly. "Just hurry up."

"My, we get an attitude when the bandage is on the other leg, huh?"

"I do not get an attitude, Coltrane Xavier High-point."

No one dared use his middle name. Only his mother used it when she was upset with him or he'd done something stupid. He didn't think anyone knew it. "How long have you known my middle name?"

"Since I was sixteen. Your mother told me."

At least she was honest. "Figures. Mom can't hold water. I guess you know about the golf course today?"

She bowed her head in embarrassment and nodded. "Yes. I also know they were planning our wedding, thanks to big-mouth Charlie."

He finished cleaning the wound and inspected his handiwork. It still looked pretty bad, but she didn't need stitches. Maybe a day or so off her pretty feet, he thought. That was probably as likely as him getting lucky any time soon.

"Cole, did you hear what I said?" Kendall groaned as she attempted to move her injured leg. "Damn, I can't believe it hurts so bad."

"It's supposed to hurt. That was more than a scrape. It's like a cement burn, only about ten times worse. And yes, I heard every word you said. I find if I don't fight my mother on some things she gets bored and moves on to something else."

"Apparently you don't know my mother," Kendall said. "Ignoring the problem just adds more fuel to the fire."

Cole nodded. "So where do you want to go on the honeymoon?"

"Cole, this isn't funny."

"Yes, it is. Our mothers almost come to blows on the golf course over us dating. I think it's hilarious."

Taylor entered the room carrying a tray with a glass of water, a glass of fruit juice, and small bottles of aspirin and ibuprofen. Cole thought it showed ingenuity on Taylor's part to cover all the bases. He placed the tray on the table in front of Kendall and looked nervously at his father. "Is she going to be okay?"

"Yes, son. Now that I've cleaned the wound, we just have to bandage her knee and see if she can stand on it."

Kendall looked at Cole with murder in her brown eyes. "What does that have to do with anything?"

Cole took out the large bandage he had in the first aid kit and taped it over the wound. "Well, Doctor, if you can't apply any weight to your leg, that means I'm going to have to carry you home or you're staying here."

"I'm sure it's fine." She glanced at Taylor, trying to reassure the teenager. "It's probably just a little stiff. Your father over-exaggerates." She attempted to stand. Cole tried to help her, but she brushed his hands away. "I can do this by myself."

Cole realized she was going to have to fall to understand she was actually injured. And that was exactly what she did. Flat on her face. She screamed bloody murder.

"You bastard! I can't believe you let me fall like that!"

Cole laughed as he helped her up. "Now will you listen to reason? You need to be still, so you're staying here." He handed her a tissue to wipe her tears. "Is that okay with you, Taylor?"

"Sure, Dad. You'll probably want to watch her to make sure she doesn't do anything stupid like try to walk home."

Cole smiled at his son. "You're right, Taylor."

"Can I say something?" Kendall crossed her arms across her chest. "You two talk like I'm not even here. What about Jordan?"

"He can stay, too," Taylor said. "I think we have some food he could eat."

Kendall closed her eyes and leaned back on the couch. "Fine. Could you call Jami and let her know I won't be home?"

Being victorious with Kendall was always an exhilarating feeling for Cole, but not while she was like this.

The painkillers must have kicked in, because now she was snoring lightly.

After Cole made the necessary phone call and Taylor went to bed, he settled in the loveseat across from Kendall and watched her sleep. An hour later, they both seemed uncomfortable. Cole thought about his actions and decided Kendall would just have to be mad in the morning, but for tonight they were going to sleep in his bed.

CHAPTER 18

Cole woke up first the next morning. Kendall was lying on her side and snoring happily. He imagined her leg would give her a lot of pain today, but that was where he came in. He'd make sure she stayed off her feet and, hopefully, in his bed.

He slipped out of bed and headed for the shower. The hot water cascading down his body fully woke him, and Taylor came to mind. What was he going to do about his son?

Cole slipped on a pair of jeans and a T-shirt as quietly as he could. He didn't want to wake Kendall. She needed all the rest she could get. He left the room smiling at her soft snores.

Smells of breakfast wafted up the stairs. He immediately knew where his son was. Taylor was making breakfast. He hurried downstairs and into the kitchen, then stopped dead in his tracks. Taylor wasn't cooking. He was in the kitchen sitting at the table with Jordan at his feet. Cole couldn't form the obvious question that stuck in his throat.

"You can't say good morning to your mother?" she asked, scrambling eggs in a skillet. "Is Kendall coming down? Taylor said she hurt her leg."

Cole walked to the coffee pot. He needed to be alert dealing with his mother, especially since Taylor had already ratted him out. He poured a mug of coffee and gulped a few swallows. "Good morning, Mom. When did you get here?" He walked to his mother and kissed her on her cheek.

"I got here about an hour ago. I wanted to see my grandson, and I couldn't wait for you to decide when the time was right." She emptied the fluffy eggs only she could make onto a plate.

"Mom, it's not that. It's just I wanted everything to be perfect. And how did you get in, anyway?"

"I do have a key to your house. Taylor did look at me strangely when he and Jordan came into the kitchen. That wouldn't have happened had he known what his paternal grandmother looked like."

Cole knew he'd gone about it all wrong, and now his mother was reading him the riot act. "Okay, Mom, it was my bad. Sorry. I was just doing what I thought was right at the time." He took a seat at the table across from his son. "So, Taylor, what do you think of your grandmother? Are you going to call her Grandma?"

Before Taylor could speak, Cole's mother did.

"He wouldn't dare. Grandma sounds like I should be sitting in a rocker and knitting. Since he's my only grandson, I think he should call me Gigi."

Cole shook his head. "That sounds like a topless dancer. How about Grandmother? That sounds very cosmopolitan."

"No," she said as she brought breakfast to the table. "I'll let him pick out a suitable name." She looked at Taylor as she placed a plate loaded with eggs, bacon, toast, and hash browns in front of him.

Cole laughed. "Uh-oh, you're in trouble now," he teased his son as his mother placed a plate in front of him.

Taylor smiled and started eating his breakfast. "How about Gram?" He shoveled the food in his mouth as if it were his last meal.

She sat down at the table with the men and nodded. "I like that. What do you call your other grandmother?"

Taylor looked up from his half-eaten breakfast and said, "Grandmother."

An hour later Cole took a tray up to Kendall. His mother had drilled him like an interrogation specialist about Kendall's injury. It took all his persuasive skills for her to go home without inspecting Kendall personally.

He couldn't explain Kendall's food preference to his mother, so he fixed a plate for Kendall and bade his mother good-bye. She took Taylor with her, claiming they needed some grandmother-grandson bonding time.

He could imagine his mother spoiling Taylor like crazy, which is what he planned to do with Kendall.

Cole entered his bedroom, surprised to see Kendall still asleep. It was after nine in the morning. He'd expected her to be up and ranting about being late for work. But she was buried underneath the bedclothes and snoring. He sat the tray on the bedside table and shook her awake.

"No, I don't want to get up," she murmured and turned over on her stomach.

He laughed and caressed her back gently. "Come on, I brought you breakfast. Plenty of eggs, toast, and hash browns."

"Bacon."

"What?"

"Bacon," she said into the pillow. "I want some bacon with my eggs."

"But you're a veggie. You don't eat meat," Cole reminded his overnight guest.

"Bacon."

"Okay, babe. I'll be right back." Cole went downstairs and got the forbidden meat. His mother had told him Kendall would probably want a little something extra with breakfast, and she'd been absolutely right. Must be a girly thing, he thought.

When he returned, Kendall was sitting up in bed. She looked like a vision nestled against the pillows. She smiled as he entered the room. "Well, it's about time you got back." She reached for the tray.

Cole placed the tray on her lap and sat on the bed. "Sorry, babe." He took the lid off the plate and presented her with the breakfast. "You should eat. I called Max and told him you were injured last night."

"You did what? It was just a scrape on my knee."

He thought it was more than a scrape, but maybe he was overreacting. Apparently Kendall thought he had overstepped his boundaries in calling Max. "Before you get all 'how could you do that' on me, I did it because I knew walking wouldn't be easy for you. Max said he could push the appointments back until you became ambulatory."

She sighed. "If I try to say that you're trying to take over my life, I'm going to sound like one of those selfish independent women. So I would like to say thank you."

Cole relaxed. "Wow. A female actually saying thank you and not reading me the riot act."

Kendall laughed and began eating her breakfast. "I'm already eating your breakfast. Are you going to feed me some humble pie, too? You know I'm injured. You need to cut me some kind of slack."

Martha watched as her grandson picked out a pair of tennis shoes at Parks Mall. They had originally gone to the mall to pick out Kendall a get-well gift, but somehow they'd ended up at the athletic store.

"Gram, are you sure?" He looked at her with hazel eyes just like his father's.

She'd been waiting for this moment for sixteen years. She wanted to spoil him, but knew his mother had probably already done that. "Yes, baby, I'm quite sure."

Taylor nodded. "I think Dad wants to beat that guy up."

"What guy?"

"I was watching from my window. Some guy snuck up on Kendall and tried to grab her, but she skated away. Then he knocked her down and fell on top of her. Then Dad showed up and the guy left."

Martha didn't like the sound of that. Kendall's mother had told her Kendall's ex was back in town wanting to get back with her. "What did your father do?"

Taylor picked up another pair of sneakers and shrugged his slight shoulders. "Dad was taking care of Kendall. Probably if her leg hadn't been bleeding so bad he would have kicked that guy's butt."

"Well, at least he took care of her."

"Yeah, I was kind of scared last night. I thought we were going to have to take her to the hospital, but once Dad started cleaning it up and stuff, it didn't look so bad. She just couldn't walk on it."

"Oh, my goodness."

Taylor smiled at her. "Don't worry, Gram."

Martha returned her grandson's smile. "I'm going to have a long talk with your father."

He dropped the expensive tennis shoes and walked to her. "No, Gram, it's okay now."

"All right, I won't say anything yet. I'm hoping they get together. So why don't we work on getting them together?"

Taylor's eyes gleamed with hope. "Yeah. After what Mom and Holly have done to him, I think he needs some happiness in his life."

Jami stared at the clock on the wall. Kendall had called her an hour ago, telling her she was on her way to work and evading the issue of why she hadn't come home last night. Had Jami and Dylan run Kendall from her home in just one night?

She glanced at the clock again. Where was she? Not that Jami believed that story Cole called with last night.

No way would Kendall would have stayed with him while his son was in the house. No way in hell.

"Hello, Jami."

When she heard the masculine voice, her internal alarm instantly buzzed. She greeted him because it was part of her job. Otherwise she'd tell him where to go. "Hello, James. Kendall isn't here." She turned her attention to the computer, dismissing him.

He leaned over the counter, invading her personal space. His cologne permeated her senses. James Matthews might be a jerk of the highest order for cheating on Kendall, but he always smelled great. That, coupled with charm and good looks, meant an unsuspecting woman didn't have a chance.

"Look Jami," he said in that sexy voice, "you and I both know Kendall is always at work promptly at eight. So don't tell me that she's not here."

"She's not here."

"Nice try," James said. "I'm not leaving until I see her."

Jami looked at him. "James, I told you she's not here. She's coming in later this afternoon. Something about falling last night."

James frowned, marring that handsome face. He didn't believe that any more than Jami had. "She wasn't hurt that bad. It was an accident."

"What?"

James sighed. "I wanted to talk to her, and I met her while she was skating. We had a little disagreement and we kind of fell over each other. She might have skinned her knee a little."

Jami felt awful for doubting her boss. "You mean you didn't stay to see if she was okay?"

"I would have, but some light-skinned brother appeared out of nowhere telling me to get lost. So I left before he called the cops."

Typical James. It was always all about him. "Nice to know you haven't changed. She's still not here."

"Well, I'll just wait. If she shows up, tell her I'm in the lobby." He walked down the hall to the main lobby.

Jami shook her head as he left. Kendall really had been hurt, and that jackass of an ex-husband hadn't even stayed to see if she was all right. She didn't know who she was more disappointed in, James for not helping Kendall, or herself for not believing her in the first place.

Kendall looked sideways at her driver. He was as stubborn as a mule and then some. "You know, Cole, I could have driven my own car. It's my left leg that's injured."

"I'm well aware which leg is injured, Kendall. You still don't need to be driving. You shouldn't even be trying to go to work. You should be horizontal in my bed." He turned toward her and winked mischievously.

She had no response, not that he was giving her room for any. "Cole, it's not that bad. It's a scraped knee. I'm a doctor, I know when it's serious, and this isn't. Besides, you should be getting acquainted with your son, not chauffeuring me around like I'm some invalid. I'm a grown woman with my own car, and I feel just fine."

"Blah, blah, blah. You might as well save your breath for tonight, 'cause I'm not hearing it. I'm taking you to work and I'm picking you up tonight. And we'll have dinner at my house."

She didn't take kindly to Cole thinking he was running her life when he clearly wasn't. "I can ride home with Jami."

He shook his head. "Jami drives a Beetle. I don't think you'd be very comfortable. The Range Rover has plenty of room for you to stretch those long legs out."

"But Cole," she started. "I can manage."

"You might as well save it for someone who'll listen, because this discussion is so closed."

Kendall thought it was sweet, but she could never let it show. So in the true spirit of independent women everywhere, she crossed her arms across her chest and huffed.

"You don't know how that turns me on."

"Sick."

"Yeah, and you know you like it," Cole said. "Hey, about a delicious hamburger before I drop you at the hospital?"

After such a huge breakfast, Kendall couldn't eat another thing. "No, thank you. What did you mean about dinner tonight?"

"You promised yesterday you'd listen to Taylor and me and be an arbitrator. We both have issues with his mother. It seems she was trying to turn each of us against the other. She told Taylor I didn't want to be part of his life, and she told me Taylor didn't want to see me."

Kendall was shocked that anyone could be that hateful toward another human being, especially hurting her own child in the process. "Cole, I'm sorry." She reached across the console and rubbed his hand in comfort. "That's awful."

He shrugged. "Yeah, what can you do? We just have to go from here. We have to build our trust with each other. Right now he's with my mother, so I can just imagine what she's telling him about his mother."

Kendall didn't have any bright words of wisdom, having never been in the situation. The only thing she had that was remotely close was her womanizing ex. "It's hard when someone lets you down. But Taylor is here with you now, so that has to mean something."

"Yeah, I guess I didn't look at it that way." He leaned over the console and gave her a peck on the cheek. "Thanks, Doc."

Kendall blushed. The temperature in the SUV had just increased about twenty degrees with Cole's gesture. Was he trying to butter her up for something? "Okay, what gives?"

"Can't I give you a compliment without you ripping it to shreds? I'm having problems relating to the son I haven't seen in four years and you offered a few words of comfort. I was just saying thank you. But if it's too much emotional attachment for you, I rescind the thank-you."

"I'm sorry, Cole. You have to admit you usually have an ulterior motive for everything."

He laughed. "Gotcha!"

Kendall gasped. "You bastard! How could you bait me like that?"

"You make it too easy." He leaned over and kissed her again. "Now how about that hamburger?"

"How about a salad? I'm still paying for breakfast."

"Okay, rabbit food for you, and a greasy burger for me."

Kendall nodded, knowing that was about as good as she was going to get.

About two hours later, Kendall limped into the hospital with Cole on her heels. She'd thought he'd just drop her off and leave, but he had to escort her to her office.

Both Jami and Max ran to her side. "Dr. Matthews, how are you? You should have gotten a wheelchair," Jami scolded her. "You probably shouldn't be at work." She looked at Max. "Get a wheelchair for her. She shouldn't be walking."

Kendall appreciated the concern, but it was a little unnerving to have people fussing over her. "Jami, I'm fine. Max, if you value your life, don't you dare get a chair."

Jami stared at her with big, disappointed eyes. "Sorry, Dr. Matthews, I was just trying to help." Jami started to walk down the hall back to the nurses' corner.

Both Max and Cole stared daggers at Kendall. Cole leaned down and whispered in her ear, "You need to fix this."

She already knew that. "Jami," she called. But Jami kept walking. "Jami, please don't make me come after you."

Jami stopped walking, but didn't turn around. "Yes, Dr. Matthews?"

"Please look at me."

She did and walked back to Kendall. "You wanted me, Dr. Matthews?"

"Yes, Jami. I'm very sorry for snapping at you and Max. I appreciate you guys caring so much, but this is still a little new to me. You're going to have to give me some wiggle room on being thankful. Okay?"

Jami smiled and wrapped her arms around Kendall, almost knocking her off balance. "Oh, I'm sorry." Jami stepped back. "I'm just glad you're all right. I'll get you some tea."

"No, I'm fine. Cole stopped for lunch before he brought me here." All at once, her knee began to throb with a vengeance and the hallway went dark.

When she woke again, she was lying horizontal on her couch. Cole and Max were sitting in the leather chairs and staring at her. "How long was I out?" She struggled to sit up.

Cole glanced at his watch. "About thirty minutes. Now do you still doubt my infinite wisdom? I told you you needed to stay off your leg, at least for today. But no, you didn't want to listen to me." Cole continued his martyr speech. "I'm just a mere man, so I have no idea what I'm talking about."

"Oh, will you please stop it. I feel like they should be carrying you on the cross." She took a deep breath. "I thought I could handle it."

Cole smiled at her. "So does that mean you're ready to go home?" He stood and reached for her hand.

"Whose home?" Kendall smelled a rat, and his name was Cole.

"Mine, of course. Jordan is there, you know."

Kendall was too exhausted to argue. The little outing had zapped her energy; she was totally drained. "Only to pick up my dog. Then you're taking me home, right?"

"Sure, babe. Your wish is my command. Whatever you tell me you want to do, then that's the agenda for the evening. Just remember that tonight when you're begging for it."

"Coltrane Highpoint, I'm going to kill you."

Cole laughed. "Oh, you know you want me."

The truth was she did, but she couldn't let Cole know that. "Just take me home."

CHAPTER 19

Kendall wasn't sure what she was expecting when Cole parked in front of his house, but her mother's Lexus parked in the driveway wasn't it. She wasn't quite ready to face her fireball of a mother. "What's my mom doing here?"

Cole shrugged, shutting off the engine. "Mom said something about running into Zenora at the mall and inviting her for tea. I thought she meant her house, not mine."

Something in the way he said it made her mistrust him. She knew he was up to something. "Cole, what's going on?"

He got out of the SUV and walked to the door and helped her down. "I told you I don't know. You know how our mothers are when they get together."

She did know. They were holy terrors. "You don't think they're here to tell us we need to get married?" She didn't need this right now. She needed aspirin, and lots of it. The thought of what her mother had in store for them overwhelmed the slight pain in her knee.

Cole scooped her up in his arms and carried her to the front door. "I think my mom told your mom that you hurt your leg and she wants to see if you're really okay."

Kendall groaned. She'd forgotten about her mother. Not an easy feat, but somehow Kendall had managed it. "Quick, Cole, just take me home. My house. Now."

He laughed and shook his head. The knob started to turn and the door opened. "Too late," he said. "Hello, Zenora," he said to her mother.

Zenora smiled at him. "Hello, Cole. Thank you for taking care of my headstrong daughter." She opened the door wider and motioned them inside.

Cole walked to the couch and deposited her. As if on cue, Taylor walked in with a tray that held a bottle of water and a large bottle of Tylenol. She took out two pills, mumbled thanks to Taylor, and swallowed them. After she drank the water, she turned to her mother and tried to explain.

Zenora, seated in the loveseat with Cole's mother, listened to her feeble excuses like a good mother and nodded on occasion. "I quite understand, dear."

Now that didn't sound like her mother. "Mom, I really am sorry for not calling," Kendall said. Cole put a pillow under her knee and sat at the opposite end of the couch.

Zenora nodded. "It's okay. I'm just happy Cole was there to rescue you from that horrible James. Max said he was at the hospital this morning looking for you, but Jami got rid of him."

Kendall exhaled. "Thank goodness. I really don't want to deal with him right now. This is all his fault, anyway."

The women nodded, so Kendall knew they knew the story of how she'd hurt her leg. The much larger question was the identity of the rat who'd told. She stared at Cole until he finally looked in her direction. "You told?"

Cole didn't answer her. Zenora did. "He didn't have to tell me. I knew something was wrong, so I called the hospital."

"Jami didn't tell me you called."

"That's because I didn't talk to Jami. I talked to my own personal spy, who shall remain nameless. This person told me you weren't in. The rest was easy."

"Max?" Kendall doubted it could have been Max, since he didn't know of her accident until she arrived at the hospital. Now this was going to eat at her until she found out who the snitch was. She hated not being in total control.

"Nope." Zenora chuckled and elbowed Martha in the side.

Kendall really didn't like the fact that these two women were in cahoots and that she was the intended victim.

After they ate a meal prepared by both mothers, Kendall settled down for a nap on the couch. Taylor took Jordan for his evening constitutional, so that left Cole to contend with Martha and Zenora and their quest for a wedding.

And contend was putting it lightly. Cole sat in his home office listening to the women as they chattered endlessly.

"I think you should have a holiday wedding," Zenora offered. "I think around Labor Day. You know, it's not too hot, it's not too cool."

Cole wanted nothing better, but knew it would take more than that to convince Kendall that he truly loved her. "Zenora, I think you're way ahead of the game. We're fine for now. When the time is right, we'll see."

His mother grunted her disapproval. "Sounds like a bunch of rubbish to me. In a few weeks it'll be the Fourth of July. I say let's aim for that."

He had two stubborn women on his hands. "You know I appreciate the help, but if the two of you want a wedding, I suggest you convince Kendall that I'm very sincere. Because her first husband was—is—a first-class jackass, my work is cut out for me."

"Not just you. I see the scars of your ex, too," Zenora said. "You both have some trust issues to work through first. Don't get me wrong, I do want you to marry Kendall, but I don't want either of you going into this for the wrong reasons."

Cole shook his head. "I don't believe you for one second, Zenora. What a load of crap. You want the same thing as Mom, and if you two start meddling it's just going to make her dig her heels in against getting married."

Zenora poured a cup of tea. "Do you love my daughter? Or is it because she is a challenge and you find that fascinating?"

Cole knew the answer to the question, but didn't want to voice his feelings to anyone but Kendall. Besides, the choice to marry would ultimately be theirs, not their parents'. "I care for her a great deal."

"Is this that man-protecting-his-woman thing?"

"Partly, Zenora. But I do see a future with her." Now if Kendall saw that same future, everything would be great.

"You know you could always get her pregnant on purpose. People do that all the time," Zenora hinted.

Martha also nodded in agreement.

Cole knew that. That was how he'd ended up being married the first time. He'd been living with his ex, Gabriella, for over four years when she became pregnant. "I'm like the guy in those romance novels. I want to marry for love."

Zenora looked at him with happy eyes. "That's good in theory. But you know you have your work cut out for you. I can do a lot, but I can't make my headstrong daughter love you if she doesn't."

"And I wouldn't want you to. It's just going to take a little time, that's all. But first things first. I need to make sure my son is comfortable with all this before I can move forward with my plan."

Martha spoke up this time. "Oh, we've already covered that territory. He wants you to be happy. I got the feeling he's not certain of your feelings concerning him 'cause of what his mother told him over the last few years."

Cole could strangle his ex for what she'd done to Taylor. But at least he knew where to start. "I have a plan to work on Kendall, but it's going to take some time and maybe a little help from you guys. My son, however, is my first priority. Are you game?"

"Of course." Zenora winked at him. "You haven't had a vasectomy, have you?"

He wasn't shocked she asked, but thought she could have been more subtle. "No, I haven't. Don't worry, Zenora, we use protection." Almost every time, he thought. His memory quickly floated to the time when passion had overtaken good sense and they had had unprotected sex. He smiled at the memory.

"I know that look," Zenora said. "Am I going to be a grandmother sooner than I expect?"

Cole shook his head. "Afraid not." He hoped with all his heart it wasn't a lie. The last thing he needed was another kid.

"Cole, I demand you take me home this instant!" Kendall insisted a few hours later. He was carrying her up the stairs to his bedroom. "I feel perfectly capable of taking care of myself and besides, Jami is there."

He ignored her protest and entered his bedroom, depositing her on the bed. "Why?"

Kendall crossed her arms over her chest. "Because I need to be there. Jami is there all alone and this will be the second night. It'll look like I don't want to sleep in my own house 'cause she's there, and I don't want her thinking that."

"She's not alone."

"I know that. Dylan is there."

Cole shook his head. "No, Max is there."

"What?"

"He needed to talk to Jami."

"Cole, he needs to stay away from Jami until he decides what he's going to do about his wife. I don't want either of them to get hurt. They need some space."

"Is that your prescription for their problem? Space? I think they need to tackle the problem head-on. See if what they have will last."

"And put Jami and Dylan in the line of fire? You don't understand what's at stake here. Caitlin is from one of the wealthiest families in Dallas. They've already offered Max a load of money not to pursue the divorce. If they find out there's a woman involved who's not only married herself but also is black, what do you think will happen?"

Cole sat next to her on the bed. "I'm sorry, I didn't know. He called while you were asleep and he was crying. Actually crying. I didn't know what else to tell him. He needs to sort his feelings out for Jami before he can go any further. I thought if he talked to her, he'd see how happy he could be and ask for a divorce. I didn't realize I'd be putting Jami in harm's way."

Kendall sighed. There was no easy way out. "I know you didn't mean to, but now we've got to fix this."

"What do you mean, *we*?"

"I mean you, me, and your big mouth," Kendall said softly. "Come on. Help me downstairs so we can drive to my place."

Cole muttered something under his breath, stood and walked to his bedroom door. "Taylor, Kendall and I have to go out for a little bit."

"Okay, Dad."

Cole looked at her long and hard, marched to her, and scooped her up in his arms. "Ready?"

Kendall nodded, not believing the chain of events. The next thing she knew, they were in the garage and Cole was settling her in the passenger seat.

After he made sure she was belted in, he stalked to the driver's side and slid behind the steering wheel. Without another word he started the Range Rover and opened the garage door. He put the SUV in gear. "Okay, I hope you have your speech ready. You have about two minutes." He backed out onto the street, closed the garage door, and headed for her house.

In much less than two minutes, they arrived. Kendall had no idea what she was going to say. She spotted Max's truck in her driveway and hoped she wasn't too late.

Cole parked the SUV, got out, and helped her out. "Cole, you don't have to carry me inside," Kendall said. It would look too much like a romance novel entrance. She needed a level head when she talked to Jami and Max.

Cole helped her to stand and put a protective arm around her waist. "I could have carried you. You don't weigh that much."

He was being polite, she told herself. Why did the remark about her slight weight hurt so much? "I'm not that skinny," she muttered.

Cole chuckled as they walked slowly to the front door. "I don't get women. They complain if you say they're too heavy, and they complain if you don't. A guy just can't win."

She realized he was right. "Sorry, Cole. It has nothing to do with you."

He grunted, and without another word, he scooped her up in his arms and continued walking to the door. "The ex, I'm betting. But we'll deal with that later." He stopped at the front door. "Where's your key?"

"At your house. In my purse." She pushed the door-bell. "You didn't give me a chance to get it."

Before Cole could respond, the front door opened and a very shocked Jami let them inside.

"Kendall, are you okay? I didn't think you'd be home tonight," Jami said. "Dylan wanted to see you and Jordan, but I told him he'd have to wait until tomorrow."

Kendall knew Dylan was probably more concerned about Jordan than her. Then she remembered. "Oh no, I promised him a trip to the toy store. I totally forgot."

Jami shook her head. "Oh, that's okay. I told him you hurt your leg. Is everything okay?"

"Hey Jami, who was at the—Kendall?" Max stood beside Jami. "I didn't figure you'd be here tonight."

"I wanted to talk to you guys," Kendall said, realizing they were standing in the entryway to her house and she was still in Cole's arms. They probably did look like the cover of a romance novel. "Cole, put me down."

"Not until we get to the couch." He walked into the living room and placed her on the sofa. "Now we're all going to talk like adults and figure a way out of this mess you let me get involved in." He sat at the opposite end.

"I got you in?" said Kendall in a tight voice. "You got your own behind in this mess, giving out horrible advice for a situation you know nothing about." She crossed her arms over her chest. "I can't believe you're trying to blame me!" Just like a man to shift the blame, Kendall thought. If her leg didn't hurt so much, she'd give him a good swift kick in that very muscular ass.

"You know how much I get turned on when you get all hot and bothered." He moved closer to her and pulled her into his arms. He kissed her gently at first, then added power as she joined in.

Max chuckled. "Now that's what I called a power struggle."

Kendall eased out of Cole's embrace and cleared her throat. So much for decorum, she thought. "Sorry about that. I got lost in the moment."

Jami smiled at her. "I hope you don't mind that Max dropped by." She sat down in the loveseat next to Max. "We were talking."

Kendall nodded. "That's what I wanted to talk to you guys about. Jami, as you know, Max and I have been friends a long time, so he has told me his side of things. I want both of you to know I'll be here for both of you, but I want you to think about the consequences before you act on impulse."

"Thank you, Kendall. Those are the same words I just told Max. I want forever. I want someone supportive, caring, and nurturing, not manipulative and a bully. Max can't make a decision about his future, so I just did. He was getting ready to leave."

Kendall wasn't expecting Jami to be so rational and practical. "Jami, are you sure about this?" Kendall looked at Max, but his expression broke her heart. He was truly a man with a dilemma.

"Yes, I'm sure. Dylan and I deserve it. And I want to make sure this is what Max wants. He has a lot of issues he needs to work through, and so do I. I don't want Dylan caught up in a bad decision. So we're friends, right, Max?"

Max sighed. "If you say so."

Kendall didn't know who had her sympathy more: Jami for making a difficult decision, or Max, who still had a difficult decision to make. "My offer still stands. When either of you need to talk, my ears are always open."

"You mean our ears are open," Cole said. "I'm in this mess too, and I want to see you guys end up happy."

Jami laughed. "I could say the same." She nodded at Kendall.

"Only my knee is banged up, not my hearing. I'm sitting right here. And I take offense to that statement, Jami."

Max laughed. "What else is new? She's going to be a tough nut to crack, Cole." Max winked at Kendall, then to Jami he said, "I'd better go. See you tomorrow." He kissed her on the cheek and rose. "I won't see you tomorrow, right?" He looked directly at Kendall. "I can reschedule anything you have that's pressing."

Kendall hated everyone telling her what she needed to do. "I'll be there. What if someone goes into labor?" It would be a good argument if her patients hadn't predominantly decided on Caesareans.

Max took out his PDA and turned it on. After he touched the screen several times, he turned the small computer off. "You only have two appointments tomorrow, and I can reschedule them. So you can stay at home and nurse that leg. Besides, it's Friday and you have the whole weekend to . . ." he cleared his throat, ". . . sleep."

Kendall didn't like the insinuation, however true. "I'll be in my bed alone, and Cole will be bonding with his son. So I'll be resting all weekend and will be back at work on Monday."

She saw the look that passed between the men and hated it. "Sure, anything you say, boss." Max kissed Jami again, then left the house without another word.

CHAPTER 20

Monday morning Kendall walked into the hospital under her own steam. Two days of being in bed had been more than enough time for her knee to heal. She could walk almost normally. Between Cole calling her every hour on the hour and Jami, Max, Dylan, Kendall's mother, and Cole's mother waiting on her hand and foot, Kendall had never felt more loved than she had that weekend. And to think she had that miserable ex-husband to thank for it all.

She walked into her office and immediately put her feet up on her desk. She might have been recovering from her injury, but the journey from her car to her office had been a long one. She was just about to pop some Tylenol when Jami buzzed her office.

"Dr. Matthews, James Matthews is here. Should I tell him you're busy for the rest of the day?"

Kendall wanted to say yes, but knew she was only putting off the inevitable. "No, send him in." She washed down the pills.

A few minutes later, James walked inside her office and closed the door. "Hey, glad to know you're up and about." He took a seat in one of the leather chairs.

Kendall took a long sip from her water. She was actually tempering her anger before she spoke to him. "Yes, my fall wasn't too bad."

"That wasn't my fault."

"Nothing is ever your fault. When I caught you with that nurse from Arlington General, that wasn't your fault, either. It was mine for coming home early and catching her in my bathroom in my bathrobe." She took a deep breath, not wanting to relive that awful day. "You know, James, I'm not going to relive the past with you. What do you want?"

He studied her carefully before he spoke. "To put it in a nutshell, I want another chance with you. I've changed a lot over the four years we've been apart, and want to show you how much you mean to me."

She wanted to yawn to show him how little those words affected her, but that would have been rude. But sometimes rude was good. She opened her mouth, but closed it quickly when she noticed the serious expression on his face. "James, it's too little, too late. Just as I told you the night you knocked me down."

He nodded, letting the words sink into his thick skull. "Look, baby, you know how it is. Those nurses were always throwing themselves at me. It was hard to resist."

"Apparently. Why are you here?"

"I told you."

Kendall shook her head. "No, you told me your motive for seeing me. Why are you back in Arlington? The last I heard you were in Milwaukee."

"After our divorce, I headed to Seattle for a district vice-president promotion. After two years of getting rained on constantly, I moved to Boston."

"Why did you come back?"

He smiled the smile that had been the way to her heart. "My family is here, too, you know. Mom has just been diagnosed with breast cancer, and I needed to be here for her."

She gasped, not wanting to believe. She loved James's mother with all her heart. Janet Matthews was a good soul, unlike her player-player son. "I didn't know Janet was ill."

"Yeah, she was diagnosed about four months ago, but only told me last month. I had to call in some pretty big favors to get this territory again."

"I'm glad you've started using the larger brain for thinking."

He laughed. "Okay, I probably deserved that barb," he said good-naturedly. "I told you I've changed."

"Please don't tell me that you're channeling the artist Matisse, or some kind of Zen thing."

"I said I was in Boston, not LA." He sobered. "I've changed emotionally, but I've not taken up talking to things that aren't there. I know how you hate that whole artistic, free-spirit thing."

She instantly thought of Cole and how he had burst into her very predictable life and refused to leave her alone until she succumbed to his charms. She was so glad he was as stubborn as she was.

"You know, with that giddy look on your face, I'd say you were hiding something. Speaking of which, who was that guy? I think he would have kicked my ass if you hadn't been bleeding so badly."

"Thanks to you. That was my neighbor."

"He looked like more than a neighbor to me. The way he was tending to your leg, he seemed more like a lover to me."

She knew that. That night she'd seen a very different Cole. If she hadn't fallen in love him already, she would have fallen in love with him that night. "He's a good friend."

"I should smack your tight butt for lying," James said. "That is, when you're more ambulatory. Now it wouldn't be any fun. I like a challenge."

Kendall was shocked at the remark. "There'll be no butt-smacking here. Now back to your mother. Tell her I'll come by soon to see her."

He shrugged and rose. "Sure. I hear your dream of the cancer wing is underway."

"Not exactly. Just in the planning stage. I'm trying to keep the cost down so the hospital can remain a free hospital."

"You know, you should think about getting on the Net. A website could increase the public's knowledge about what you're doing."

"James, what a sensible idea, but the board has beat you to it. Some reporter from some cable news network is supposed to come down in a few weeks and do a full-scale interview."

"Wow, I'm impressed. Mom told me some big-time writer donated a million bucks to the hospital, but I didn't know of anyone like that in Arlington, not a male one anyway. I know there are a few female authors in the metroplex that could afford a donation like that, but I don't know of any black male authors. Most of them live in New York."

"That's stereotyping. Authors live everywhere. Since I know you're going to badger me until I tell you, the man who helped me the night you knocked me down was Coltrane Highpoint, the author. He's also the same man who made the million-dollar donation."

For once in his forty-two years, James Alexander Matthews was shocked into silence. Not able to make a comeback, he simply bowed to Kendall and left her office without another word.

Kendall laughed so hard she started to cry. No matter what all those new age spiritual people said, revenge did feel good.

Jami watched James walked down the hall and to the elevator. She glanced at Keerya, waiting for some kind of sign from Kendall's office.

Keerya stood and walked to the counter. "What do you think, Jami? You think we should go in there and console her?"

Jami shook her head. "No, I don't think that's necessary. Cole is in her life now, and James couldn't compare to him."

"Well, look who's on the Cole Highpoint bandwagon," Keerya drawled. "If I didn't know you're in love with Max, I'd say you have a crush on Cole."

"I'm not in love with Max, Keerya. And that's supposed to be a secret, big mouth," she chided her friend. "I just think Cole is perfect for Kendall. He's brightened her life these last few months. You have to admit she's been a lot easier to get along with since he stumbled into her life."

Keerya shook her head. "Very true. Okay, I'm on his side, too."

"Now if we could just get Kendall to see it our way, everything would be great." Jami glanced at her watch. It had been at least ten minutes since James walked past the nurses' station. She should really check on Kendall. "I'll go check on her."

Keerya nodded. "Yeah, she likes you best. She won't toss you out on your ear. Yell if you need me to call my brothers."

"What on earth for?"

Keerya snorted. "Girl, don't you know nothing? I'm from a large Hispanic family. I'm the only girl. All I have to do is tell my brothers and James Matthews will be a thing of the past."

"I'll keep that in mind." Jami knew Keerya was being very truthful. When she was having problems with Karl, Javier, Keerya's oldest brother, offered to have a little talk with Jami's husband. Thank goodness she'd refused his kind offer or Karl would probably be at the bottom of the Trinity River. Jami walked down the hall to Kendall's office and knocked timidly on the closed door.

"Come in."

Jami took a deep breath, whispered a prayer, and entered the office. To her surprise, Kendall wasn't crying her eyes out. She was leaning back in her chair with her leg propped up on her desk and she was smiling.

"Did you need something, Jami?"

"No, Dr. Matthews. I was just making sure you were all right. You know, since your ex just left."

"I told you it was only Dr. Matthews out on the floor. I'm fine. I finally got closure from the idiot."

Jami nodded, but didn't understand.

"I know you think I'm nuts, but that man used to have quite a hold on me. I always thought the dissolution of my marriage was my fault. James constantly told me I was frigid, and I had begun to believe him and doubt myself."

Jami didn't believe that for one second. Kendall was the most put-together person she knew. "I'm sorry."

"There's nothing to be sorry for. Actually, if Cole hadn't burst into my life, I probably still would have gone on thinking James was right. Since I've been seeing Cole, I realize that I'm worthy of a lot of things, including love."

"You love him?"

"Unfortunately."

"Huh?"

"I hadn't planned on falling in love with Cole. I was looking for anything but love. A little fun, yes. I hadn't planned on it going this far."

"Kendall, I'm sure this makes sense, but I'm just too thick to get it right now."

"You're not thick-headed, Jami. You're very smart. Let me explain. You see, I like being in control of every aspect of my life, professionally and personally. With Cole there's no such thing as control. It's his way or no way. When I hurt my leg, I wanted to come home, but he wouldn't hear of it."

"He just wanted to look after you." Jami thought it was very sweet.

Kendall smiled. "He just wanted me to stay in his bed. When he kisses me, something happens to my brain and I find myself agreeing to whatever he suggests."

Jami thought it was the cutest thing. Kendall would fight love with all her might, but it was useless. She'd already lost the battle. "So what do you plan on doing?"

"I have no idea." Kendall took a deep breath. "How is the situation with Max? I know what you did the other night wasn't easy, especially since you both work at the same place, but I applaud your decision."

Jami felt as if her heart was breaking, but she had to deal with the small battles before she could actually handle the war. "It's been hard, but it had to be done, or one of us was going to end up getting hurt. I'm dealing with enough stress with Karl and my impending divorce."

"You know my brother is an attorney," Kendall offered. "He doesn't handle divorces as a rule, but he'd do it for me."

Jami was shocked. "Wow, thanks, Kendall. I'm not ready to start proceedings yet, but it's nice to know there's an attorney waiting."

"Jami, I want you to know that any way I can help you, I will." Kendall did something Jami wasn't quite used to her doing. She stood and hugged her.

Jami hugged her back. "Thank you, Kendall. I appreciate your support."

Kendall glanced at her wall clock. "Oh, God, is that really the time?" It was past two in the afternoon. "I have a meeting with the medical board in an hour."

Jami nodded, knowing Kendall's schedule to the last minute of her day. "Yes, you're supposed to discuss the publicity options. Personally, I think the interview with the cable person will reach more people. Is it true she used to date Cole?"

"What?"

Crap. Jami wished she could take back the question, but it wasn't like it was a secret. Keerya had found the information on the Internet. "I'm sorry, Kendall. I thought you knew."

"No, we've never really talked about past loves or anything. We're doing good just to make it through an evening without getting into an argument."

Jami knew that was Kendall's pride talking. She also knew that those arguments were something she looked forward to. This woman was fighting love every freaking step of the way. "Actually, I saw her name in the headlines about a story she did about a year or so ago. Remember that congressman from New Jersey who got caught in that bribery scandal?"

"Yes, the story kept alluding to some famous writers being behind it all, but later they found that wasn't true. She claimed she was misinformed."

Jami nodded. "Yes, after she had tarnished the reputation of those writers. The network had to offer them a public apology plus a monetary settlement. This is supposed to be her way to get back in good with the network. It's her first assignment since then."

"I guess you got all this from the Internet?"

"Guilty. It was quite a juicy story."

"So I'm her redemption story?"

Jami smiled. "Pretty much. This is do or die for her."

"That explains her eagerness for the interview."

"Yeah. Just wait until she finds out you're seeing Cole," Jami said.

"Let's hope she doesn't find out."

An hour later Kendall entered the medical building a few minutes late for the board of director's meeting. Although she detested tardiness with a passion, there was a good reason for hers. Her accountant had called at the last minute with a reprieve for the new wing. Through some palm greasing on his part, he'd worked out a deal, saving InfaCare over a million dollars.

She walked inside the large room expecting to see ten faces. There were eleven. The extra face belonged to Cole. What was he doing there? She took a deep breath and took the last empty seat, which was next to him.

"Gentleman," she said calmly. "Please excuse my tardiness. I was on the phone with InfaCare's accountant."

"Good news, I hope," Philippe Wynn, the chairman of the board, said.

Kendall nodded. "Yes. It could save over a million dollars."

"Wonderful."

Kendall thought so, too. "Yes, we can use that money to update the office equipment," Kendall said.

"That's what I love about you, Kendall," Philippe said. "You're always thinking ahead. Have you heard from the network person yet?"

She darted a glance at Cole. "Actually yes, but I was on my way here, so I told her I'd call her back."

Philippe nodded. "Who's doing the interview?"

"Holly Banton."

Cole cleared his throat. "Did you say Holly Banton of Cable News Tonight out of New York?"

"Yes, I believe she did say she was from CNT," Kendall said. "Do you know her?"

He nodded. "We'll talk later," he whispered.

Philippe picked up the conversation. "Make sure you get back to her as soon as possible. We need that to happen during sweeps week."

Kendall already knew that. An interview on a national news network during sweeps week would mean maximum exposure for the hospital for minimum cost. "She wants to do a telephone interview first."

Philippe snapped his chubby fingers. "I just had a great idea. Why don't you and Cole both do the interview? I think it would work great. We could capitalize on his celebrity status and he could explain about the hospital and it wouldn't sound so cheesy."

"I'll bring it up when I talk to her." Out of the corner of her eye, Kendall could see all this Holly talk was making Cole quite uncomfortable. But Kendall couldn't do anything to ease his pain at the moment, because it sounded like a good idea.

"How are the plans coming for the cancer wing?"

"Still on the drawing board at this time. I'm looking at several designs for the wing. My accountant is crunching numbers as we speak."

Harold Bryant, public relations director for the hospital, asked, "When are the PSAs scheduled?"

"Actually," Cole started, "I've had a recent family situation arise and haven't been able to work on them, but I think if Kendall and I get together over the next couple of days we should be ready to go next week."

Kendall stared at him. Was he nuts? "Cole, are you certain? You do realize that's not that far away."

"Trust me. I thrive under pressure." He winked at her.

Kendall just bet. She didn't want to trust him. She'd already given him her heart. Did he want her brain, too? "Then we'd better get busy."

"Why don't we start tonight?"

That was definitely trouble, Kendall thought. And it was a challenge of the highest degree. The hospital hung in the balance if she didn't complete this task, and that sealed her decision. "Of course, Cole."

"I'll come by later and we can discuss it," he said for the sake of the others listening.

"We'll schedule the first PSA filming for Monday afternoon. How's that work for you guys?"

"I'm pretty flexible," Cole volunteered. "I can create anytime."

"Monday isn't going to work for me," Kendall said. "I have a Caesarean Monday afternoon. Perhaps later that evening."

Harold nodded. "That may be better. Less traffic and less chance of you being paged for an emergency, hopefully."

Kendall laughed. No matter how much a Caesarean birth was planned, babies still entered the world when they wanted to. "You can always hope."

CHAPTER 21

Holly Banton answered the ringing telephone on her desk. Hopefully this was the call she'd been waiting for all afternoon. Dr. Kendall Matthews was going to be her ticket back to prime time. "Holly Banton."

"This is Dr. Kendall Matthews returning your call," a very businesslike but feminine voice said.

"Yes, Dr. Matthews. I wanted to set up a time for a phone interview," Holly said. "I'm very flexible, and I know how busy your schedule is."

"Please call me Kendall. Actually the board wanted the phone interview to include one of the donors if that's possible."

Holly would have agreed to walk on hot coals to get the interview process going. This woman had been impossible to get any real dirt on. Her professional record was beyond reproach. Holly hated that. "Sure, who's the benefactor?"

"Coltrane Highpoint, the author," Kendall said.

So that was where the elusive bum was, she mused. After the debacle with the senator, Cole had disappeared from Holly's life like a thief in the night. Granted, she was at fault, but he didn't even give her time to explain. Not that she could have ever told him the truth. Maybe this was her chance.

Cole knew he had a lot to discuss with Kendall later that evening. The script for the PSA was minor. Besides, he had already completed it. He needed to tell Kendall about Holly.

The breakup hadn't been amicable by any means. Her betrayal had been the last straw. Spilled milk, he reminded himself. It didn't matter anymore. He loved Kendall.

Kendall arrived wearing tight jeans and a crop top blouse. She'd worn the low-cut blouse on purpose, he thought, no doubt trying to distract him. But they had much to discuss. He kissed her softly on the lips before allowing her to enter his house. "You look good, baby."

"Right back at you." She walked to the living room and sat on the couch. "Where's Taylor?"

"He's spending the night with my mom. She's spoiling him rotten, you know. She says she's making up for lost time." He sat beside her on the couch. "Tonight isn't about anyone but you and me."

Kendall nodded. "Do you have any ideas on the PSA?"

"I told you I had it under control. I wrote a script out this afternoon. It's only a thirty-second spot, so it didn't take long. You can look it over and tell me what you think. I thought we could do a few shots of the hospital, maybe a doctor, the facilities, and then we beg for money."

"Wow, Cole, that actually sounds pretty good." She leaned over and kissed him. "Now you want to tell me about Holly?"

She didn't waste time beating around the bush. That was one of the things he loved about her. Might as well get it over with, he mused. "Remember when I finish this horror story that you asked me."

"Yes, and I'll tell you about James."

He agreed and began his story. "I met Holly about five years ago at a party in Manhattan. She'd just been named prime-time anchor at CNT. She was pretty and knew all the right things to say." He saw the disappointment in Kendall's brown eyes. "Hey, I'm a man. She built up my ego when I thought I was a loser."

She sighed. "You know, you sound just like James did when I caught him with the night nurse in our bed. Continue."

"Before I knew it, we were a couple. I was just looking for something to smooth out the rough edges, but she'd all but moved in with me. People were calling leaving messages for her on my phone. Her mail was coming to my house."

"She was establishing residency. How could you be so thick-headed?" Kendall folded her arms across her chest.

"I realized that and soon put a stop to it, but that took another year. The final straw came about three years ago. She announced she wanted a baby. She was nearing forty and thought we'd have a very intelligent child. She didn't mention anything about loving me or the child. She felt it would help her career. I didn't want a kid under those circumstances."

"So how did you get out of donating to the cause?" Kendall laughed at her play on words.

"After a conversation with your brother, I started using protection even though she said she was on the pill. Holly can be very determined when she wants something, and I can be very crafty when I have to be. Eventually, I stopped having sex with her."

Kendall laughed in disbelief. "A man refusing to have sex? Yeah, right."

Cole was offended. "I beg your pardon, Dr. Matthews. Before you seduced me that night of the charity ball, I hadn't had sex in about two years."

"No wonder you lasted so long," Kendall mumbled. "I thought I was just out of practice, but it was you trying to make up for lost time."

"Partly." He smiled at her, wanting to dispense with all these confessions and go upstairs and take advantage of the fact that Taylor wasn't home. "Mostly because it was you. I've never been so amorous with anyone else." He moved closer to her and kissed her.

"Finish the story," she said against his lips. "What happened next?"

"Holly figured out what I was doing and started her own plan of attack. She tried everything to get me to cave and have sex with her, but I held firm."

"I just bet you did."

"Yes, I did. I won't bore you with the sordid details of her escapades, but after about a year she finally gave up. Then the real trouble started."

"What kind of trouble?" Kendall sat up straight. "And is it going to affect the hospital?"

Typical Kendall. The hospital was first in her life. Everything else was a distant second. "I don't think so. I'll do everything in my power to make sure it doesn't come anywhere near you."

He took a deep breath and got to the juicy part. "About two and half years ago, I decided I was tired of the big city and was ready to come back home. So, on the DL, I put my condo up for sale and started cleaning out my office. By this time Holly had the rep of being a hard-hitting investigative reporter. Then I found some information that didn't quite jibe with the report she gave on TV."

"So she was lying when she got two senators indicted for political fraud and sent to prison?"

Cole nodded, remembering those next few months. "Yeah. Then I made the mistake of confronting her. In her next story I was named as a chief donor to their political campaigns, along with a few other celebrities. My book contract was cancelled."

She nodded. "I'm sorry, Cole."

"You knew about that, didn't you? Did my mother tell you?"

Kendall stared at him, wondering how much to admit to, if anything at all. "Parts of the story, yes, but not from your mother. Jami told me she found it on the Internet. The information is out there, and I know you overcame that glitch in your career. Mom said you just landed a big contract last year."

He smiled at her. "So you do like me, huh? Searching for me on the Internet is the equivalent of driving by my house to see if I'm home." He kissed her soundly on the mouth. "You like me, admit it."

Kendall saw what he was doing and refused to be challenged about something this important. Besides, he should say it first. "No." She kissed him back. Two could play at this game, and this time Cole was going to lose.

"Why not? You admit looking my name up on the Web. That says it all."

"That only says that Jami looked you up." Kendall tried to keep the sarcasm out of her voice, but it was useless. "Finish your story."

He shrugged. "Not much else to tell. It took some killer PR, and I moved back to Arlington sooner than I anticipated, but I got a better contract. So everything did work out for the best. I haven't spoken to Holly since that fiasco."

"So how do you plan on getting through the interview?" Kendall wondered if the situation was salvageable. "Maybe Max could take your place."

He shook his head. "No. I gave my word to do it, and I will. I don't feel anything for Holly but disappointment. I just want to get through it and get you lots of donations for the cancer wing."

"For the Coltrane Highpoint Cancer Wing," Kendall said.

"Baby, you'd name your wing after me? I'm touched, or at least I'd like to be." He winked his eye at her.

"Is sex the only thing on your mind these days? I mean, you're not a young man." She tossed out the dare.

He pulled her onto his lap. "You think I'm going to forget about you telling me about the ex. Well, I haven't.

I've seen your ex. What on earth could make you marry such a moron?"

She weighed her options. They weren't good. "I could say that in a small way he reminded me of you and it was a way of getting you out of my system, but that would be lying."

"Okay, I'll bite. Why did you marry him? I remember parts of it. Charles said it was kind of sudden. You didn't even have a wedding. You got married at the courthouse."

She remembered it well. A small chapter in her life she wished had never occurred, but that was life. "Yeah, I was pregnant. No one knew. Not even Mom. I was about four weeks along when I found out. We got married the next week."

"You had a miscarriage," Cole surmised.

Kendall could feel a tear escape down her cheek. She nodded. "It was one of those quirky things. I started cramping, and that was that."

Cole embraced her. "I'm sorry, Kendall. What did James do?"

"We were both hurt by it, but we dealt with it differently. I cried at work a lot, behind closed doors of course, but James refused to talk about it. That's when his affairs started. I didn't really care about his affairs in the beginning because I knew he would never change and was too immature to handle the responsibility of having a family. The final straw was about four years ago when I caught him in bed with a nurse from Arlington Memorial. I'd found out I was pregnant again, but this time I did something about it."

"You didn't?"

"Yes, I did. The day before I caught him cheating the last time, I'd flown to Ontario and had an abortion. I never told James I was pregnant. I wasn't showing, so he had no idea. I just threw him and the nurse out of my house. You know, that cow had the nerve to walk around my house in my bathrobe."

Cole chuckled and stroked her arm. "I've never heard you use such a term as 'cow.' James didn't deserve you. I'm sorry you had to go through that. No one else knows, do they?"

"Only Staci. It feels good to get rid of the secret. Thank you for letting me vent."

"It's okay, baby. So why is he back in town?" Cole kissed her forehead.

Kendall relished Cole's embrace. It felt good leaning on someone else for a change. "His mother is sick. He claims he's changed. I don't believe that for one second."

"That makes two of us." He kissed her. "Now that we've discussed the important matters of the night, how about a quickie before we order something to eat?"

"You mean you didn't cook?"

"Well, no. I was working on the script." Cole rose and reached for her. "I think we could order some Chinese food and have a short lovemaking session while we wait for the food."

Kendall smiled as she wrapped her arms around him. "I didn't think there was anything short about you."

CHAPTER 22

After much loving and dinner, Kendall went home to ensure she would get a restful night of sleep. She also had to be prepared for Holly's call the next morning. With all the history between Cole and Holly, Kendall had to make sure Holly didn't realize she was seeing Cole.

She entered the house to find Jami sitting on the couch shaking with fear and Dylan watching his mother intently. Kendall rushed to the sofa and wrapped her arms around Jami. "What's wrong?"

Dylan answered for his mother. "Daddy was chasing us."

Kendall knew exactly what that meant. "Oh, no. Are you guys okay?"

Dylan nodded. "The man wouldn't let Daddy inside."

"It's nice to know Kenneth is on the job at the gate," Kendall said of the security guard.

Jami slowly regained her composure, her breathing returning to normal. "Karl followed us to McDonald's, but I saw him in my rearview mirror. I floored it, and luckily Kenneth was on his toes and refused to let Karl inside the gate. I know this isn't over."

Kendall watched Dylan as he studied his mother. "Why don't I put Dylan to bed and then we can talk. That way you'll have a few minutes to collect your thoughts." She walked over to him and picked him up. "You don't mind if I read to you tonight?"

"No, Aunt Doll." Dylan couldn't say her whole name so he'd given her a new one. He wrapped his small arms around her neck and hugged her. "Will Mommy be okay?"

"Yes, honey, I promise." She looked at Jami, waiting for her approval. She gave a timid nod.

"I'm fine, baby. Mommy just needs a time-out." Jami leaned back and smiled at her son.

Kendall took Dylan upstairs to bed, wondering where her brain had gone. She knew very little about putting kids to bed. She kept her nieces and nephews only for a limited amount of time, usually daytime hours at that.

She helped him into his Superman pajamas and reached for the latest children's book. As she read him a story of perseverance, she found herself getting involved in the story. She wanted to make sure this was the best story Dylan had ever heard.

"You read just like Mommy," Dylan said, yawning.

Kendall took that for the compliment it was. "Thanks, Dylan."

She continued reading, and before the main character was triumphant Dylan was asleep. She placed his favorite stuffed animal next to him. Jordan was also nestled next to him. She'd lost her companion to a little boy.

With a sigh, she turned on the night-light, turned off the large overhead light, and left the room. When she returned downstairs Jami had prepared two cups of tea for them.

"Thank you, Kendall. I don't think I could have read to him tonight."

"Jami, if something like that happens again, call me. I would have come home sooner. I don't want you suffering through any of this alone."

Jami wiped her nonstop stream of tears. "I appreciate that. I think I just lost it tonight. I don't even know how long we sat on the couch. Thank goodness you came home when you did."

Kendall was glad she stuck to her original plans as well. Cole hadn't been happy about her leaving the one time they could have gotten their freak on, as he put it. "I hate to admit it, but I have an early call coming in the morning. That was the main reason I came home. Holly Banton is calling at seven our time."

"Does she know about you and Cole?" Jami took a sip of tea.

"No, and I don't intend for her to find out. The board wanted Cole in on the phone interview, but I think it would be better without him. He wants as little interaction with Holly as possible."

"Did he tell you about her?"

Kendall took a sip of her tea. It was perfect. Jami knew exactly how much cream and sugar to put in it. It was almost as good as having a man, she thought. She also realized she had no idea on earth as to how Jami took hers.

"Kendall? Is there something wrong?"

"No, everything is fine. Yes, Cole told me about their relationship and its demise." Kendall didn't want to betray Cole's confidence in her. "It sounded worse than my marriage."

"James didn't know how good he had it," Jami said, taking another sip. "You know he's looking for a place."

"As long as he's nowhere near here I'm fine." Kendall took another sip of tea, vowing to watch Jami closely when she next fixed her coffee and tea and make a mental note on how she took her hot drinks.

Jami put her mug of tea on the table. "That's just it. When I was running from Karl this evening, I noticed his Land Cruiser parked at the vacant house down the street. I think he was just looking, but still I thought you should know."

"Thanks, Jami, but tonight isn't about me or that idiot I married. This is about you. How are you feeling?"

Jami sighed. "Better. Max offered to follow me to McDonald's but I told him no. Now I wished I had taken him up on his offer."

"I know this is hard for you guys, but I'm sure it's for the best. One disaster at a time."

Jami laughed. "Yes, I can only handle so much stress. Max has to actually miss me and decide what he wants. I can't believe he's been married to her for ten years. I've only been married to Karl for five, and know it's time to end it."

"Are you ready for me to call my brother?" Kendall placed her mug on the table. "He's not going to charge you as a favor to me."

"Really?" Jami wiped her eyes. "You have been great through all this. I don't know what I would have done without you." She hugged Kendall.

Kendall feared what would have happened had she not intervened and offered Jami lodgings. "I'll be right here beside you. And with that little stunt he pulled tonight, I bet you'll be able to get total custody with no problem."

"I hope so. I don't want Dylan even going to visit him. I keep dreaming about those missing children. You know, when the parent takes off with them and they're missing for years on end."

"That's not going to happen," Kendall reassured her. "You're surrounded by people who love you and won't let Karl anywhere near you."

"I know. You guys have been wonderful." She stood. "I'm going to bed. You have a busy day tomorrow."

Kendall supposed she did. "Yes, and to top all that, I have to start working on that PSA for InfaCare. They want to shoot it in a week."

"I know you hate the idea of publicity for the hospital, but it would mean you could help so many more people who really need your help."

"When I came up with this idea it was because of my stepfather. He's the reason I'm a doctor. When I was growing up, he'd treat people all the time whether they had money or not. He always said sickness and disease didn't know financial barriers, and neither did he."

After a peaceful night's rest, Kendall awoke extra early to prepare for Holly's call. Knowing her reputation as an over-aggressive reporter, Kendall wanted to be on her toes. She was going over a few notes when the phone rang precisely at seven. "Hello."

"Dr. Matthews, this is Holly Banton," the caller announced.

"Yes, I was expecting your call."

"Good, you're alert and ready to go. Most times the interviewee isn't prepared, and it's a waste of my time."

Kendall decided not to trade barbs with the woman, especially when she didn't know anything about her. "Time is the one thing I don't have much of, so if we could get started . . ." Kendall pointed out.

Holly laughed. "I like a woman who knows what she wants. Okay, let's get down to business." She shuffled some papers in the background. "How about InfaCare?"

"What about it?"

"According to my sources, you started the hospital about eight years ago. The hospital is one of the few charitable hospitals in the Dallas/Fort Worth area, excluding the county hospitals. You keep the hospital in the black by persuading some of the more notable doctors to volunteer their time."

Kendall took a deep breath. She didn't want to blurt out something that would bite her in the butt later. "Yes, that's true. Doctors and nurses from the area hospitals volunteer their valuable free time. The only paid employees are the administrative staff."

"So why start InfaCare? You come from a middle-class family and attended college and medical school at Fort Worth University, a private college, without financial assistance, I might add."

"Yes, I was blessed with parents who could afford to send me to medical school. I wanted to give something back to the community. In a time where layoffs are more commonplace by the year, insurance is one of those luxuries some families can't afford. I'm sure you can appreciate that there is a place like this out there for people who need it."

"Good answer," Holly chimed. "I'm sure the donation you received from noted author Coltrane Highpoint was a blessing for you. How did that come about?"

"He also believes in giving back to the community where he grew up. He and my oldest brother were best friends in high school," Kendall said, hoping she didn't give too much away.

"Your brother is Charles Stone?"

"How do you know my brother's name?" Kendall asked, already knowing the answer.

Holly cleared her throat. "I know Coltrane. We dated a few years back. Cole mentioned his name a few times."

Kendall wanted to ask more probing questions about her relationship with Cole, but that would give away the game and she couldn't have that. "Small world, huh?"

Holly sighed. "You have no idea. I'm going to be straight with you, Kendall. This interview is very important to me. It means whether or not I can go back to being lead anchor."

"And that means what to me?" Kendall tried to keep the attitude out of her voice. It was a losing battle.

"I think we can help each other. With a little cooperation from you, I can line up some big donors for your hospital that will make Cole's million look like pennies. All I ask is that you give me Cole's home phone number. I need to talk to him."

Kendall knew Cole valued his privacy from the press, not to mention that Holly was persona non grata. "I'll have to get back to you on that. How about we just do the interview with no incentives? I'll give you the best interview possible."

Holly pondered the turn of events. "At this point, you're my best option, but once on-camera we will need Cole's input."

Kendall smiled to herself. "Not a problem." She hoped she was telling the truth.

CHAPTER 23

A week later, Kendall parked in front of InfaCare, hoping she hadn't made a drastic mistake. It was D-day, the day of filming the PSA for the hospital. She'd dressed in her best power outfit, a close-fitting black dress.

Actually Cole had picked out and purchased her dress.

The dress was tighter than she would have normally worn for the occasion. But Cole had that part covered, telling her the dress wouldn't look that tight.

She stepped out of her car and smiled as she saw Cole driving into the parking lot. He parked next to her and quickly got out of the Range Rover.

"Baby, you look like a million bucks." He took her in his arms and kissed her. "I could strip you right now."

Kendall laughed. This man would never change. "Thank you, Cole." She took a long drink of Cole. He wore a dark suit, his wavy hair was freshly cut, and his smile was dazzling. "I could say the same thing about you. In more subtle terms, of course." She inhaled his cologne. "My God, you smell great."

"Close enough for me." He leaned in for another kiss.

Kendall glanced around the parking lot, hoping there was no one looking at them. Since it was Sunday morning, there weren't many people about. She took advantage of the situation and began to kiss the stuffing out of him. When he enthusiastically joined in, she knew she was in trouble.

"You know I don't mind a public display of affection, baby." He pulled her flush against him. "But Philippe said he was going to drop by. Do you really want him seeing you trying to seduce me?"

Kendall put some space between them. "Seduce you? Are you out of your mind?" Leave it to Cole to ruin a moment.

He pulled her back to him. "Oh, you know I just love pushing your buttons."

"I know, but I can't be as cavalier as you. Kissing you in public like that is probably the wildest thing I've done in years. I'm more of a behind-the-scenes kind of girl."

Cole grinned, pulling her closer. "You're my little closet freak." He kissed her softly on the lips.

She giggled against his lips. "I'm not a freak, Mr. Highpoint. I'm an adventurous spirit." Neither statement would have been true if he hadn't stepped into her life.

"You know you're a tight ass, woman, but I like it." He stepped back from her and grabbed her hand. "Now come on, let's go make this commercial so we can find a place to celebrate."

"Cole, are you nuts? You need to get back to Taylor and I need to get back to Jami and Dylan. We're going to the movies later."

"Taylor and I could join you guys." He led her into the hospital.

"I know you're new at this fatherhood thing, but a teenager will not want to see a kiddie movie with three adults."

"Actually there would be two teenagers. Your nephew will also be joining us. I'm sure the guys won't mind. What time?"

She shook her head. Cole was going to be her Achilles heel. He was as stubborn as a mule. "Didn't you hear me? We're going to a kiddie movie. You know, one of those animated things."

"I heard you. What time?"

And that was that. "Six."

"I'll pick you guys up at five."

Before she could respond, a very tall, very slender red-haired man greeted them with a smile that was too large for her taste. "Mr. Highpoint," he gushed. "I'm Keith Hartley, from WJPR. I'm here to film the PSA with you and Dr. Matthews. My crew is ready when you are." He pointed to the three-man crew standing in the lobby.

Kendall was furious. The young twerp was totally ignoring her, and it was her hospital. She was just about to read the miserable excuse for a man the riot act when Cole spoke.

"Actually, Dr. Matthews is the person you need to talk to. I'm just here as support." He put his hand on Kendall's shoulder to stop her from tearing the man limb from limb.

"Oh, I'm sorry, ma'am. I didn't know. It's just that Mr. Highpoint is a celebrated author and I just assumed . . ." He stumbled over his words. "I can't apologize enough. This hospital has helped so many citizens of Arlington."

Personally, she loved it when a man gushed, but this kid was too much. "Forget it. Let's just get this over with. I want as little disruption to the patients and their treatment as possible."

"Yes, ma'am."

Cole watched his woman as she worked her magic on the three-man crew. A few words from her and she had the professional men bowing to her. He didn't, however, like the way those same men were checking her out and nodding to each other.

She began her spiel about the hospital and how it was formed, but Cole soon realized she hadn't kept to the script he wrote. Dr. Kendall Matthews was ad-libbing.

"InfaCare started as a dream," she said to the camera. "There needs to be a place where a person can bring their child to get the quality care they need without worry about finances. Besides health care, we offer counseling services for parents with financial and emotional needs."

Cole stood transfixed. So transfixed he missed his cue. Kendall cleared her throat, bringing him back to the present.

"I would like to introduce one of our benefactors, best-selling author Coltrane Highpoint."

Cole stepped before the camera and said his rehearsed lines flawlessly, or so he thought. The cameraman shook his head with laughter.

Kendall giggled and pulled Cole away from the counter. To the men she said, "Give us a minute and we'll re-shoot it."

"Yes, ma'am."

Cole was confused. "What's the problem? I delivered my lines right on cue. There's nothing wrong with the take."

"You called me baby," Kendall said softly. "I appreciate the term of endearment, but this is very important to me, Cole. I don't want anything to go wrong. This has to be professional. So stay focused." She beckoned the men back to their posts.

"I'm going to need an incentive for that," he whispered in her ear. "I'm going to need a lot of incentive."

She smiled at him. "If we have to shoot this again and I miss my play date with Dylan, you're going to need more than an incentive to remember the last time."

Cole didn't need a translator for that statement. "Message received." He knew he'd better concentrate on his lines, or making love or anything remotely close to that with Kendall would definitely be a thing of the past.

She nodded and began spouting orders to Keith. "I believe we're ready, Keith." She walked in front of the camera and looked directly at Cole. "Are you ready?"

Cole knew this was do or die. "Yes, I was born ready."

"That theory will have to be tested at a later time." She nodded to the camera. "Right now we have a job to do." She began her speech.

This time Cole was more than ready. He nailed it perfectly. He didn't miss his cue, and even threw in a few ad-libs of his own.

Keith turned off the camera and walked to them. "That was excellent, Dr. Matthews. I'll have it edited and ready for your viewing tomorrow morning."

Kendall nodded. "Good. I'll meet you at my office in the morning at nine."

Cole laughed as Keith readily agreed. Not that Kendall gave him much of an option. Keith and his crew packed up their gear and left the hospital.

Cole hugged Kendall. "That was great, baby. I just know the donations are going to start pouring in. When are they planning on airing it?"

"The board wants it to air starting this weekend. It's also going to be on the radio in an abbreviated version." She glanced at her watch.

Cole could see the wheels turning in her work-focused brain, but he wasn't having it. "How about a late lunch?"

She shook her head. "Since I'm here, I want to check in with the DIC to see how everything is going."

"Excuse me?" Cole must have been hearing things. "What did you just say?"

"It stands for Doctor in Charge," Kendall said dryly. "Get your filthy mind out of the gutter. Some people do have responsibilities." She started down the hall for the doctors' offices.

Cole was on her heels, ready to defend his career. "Just because I write for a living doesn't mean I have any fewer responsibilities than you."

Kendall sighed. "I wasn't trying to say that your job was any less noble or anything. I like to stay on top of things here, and I can't do that by letting other people handle things."

"I like you on top," Cole muttered. "It's okay to lean on someone else. The DIC here is just as capable of handling things on his or her own, or there would be no way in hell you'd let them near InfaCare."

Kendall stopped abruptly and faced him. He expected her to give him grief about what he'd said, but it was the truth. Instead, she kissed him. "You're right. I have to start leaning on other people. Why don't you take me to lunch and we can start that whole leaning thing today?"

Jami glanced at the clock as she fixed Dylan lunch. Kendall had been gone most of the day filming the PSA for the hospital. The day was actually quiet. She was preparing her son's favorite lunch since moving with Kendall. Dylan had taken to eating cheese sandwiches.

She called her son to the kitchen. "Dylan, time for lunch." She heard his footsteps before he entered the large room. "How many times have I told you not to run? Aunt Kendall is going to get you if you break anything."

He sat at the table. "Sorry, Mommy. We're going to the movies today with Aunt Doll?"

"Yes, baby, this evening, and then we're going to eat."

"Yeah!" Dylan clapped his hands.

It did her heart good to see him so happy. The events of the last few weeks were a distant memory, thank goodness. Now if she could just get through the divorce with no scars, everything would just be fine. "Now eat your lunch."

Dylan nodded and gobbled the sandwich in record time. Jami still didn't understand how he could eat a sandwich with no meat. The phone rang, interrupting her musing. She picked it up on the second ring. "Hello."

"Kendall?"

Jami recognized the voice of James Matthews, the snake. "I'm sorry, she's not in," she said in a short tone.

"Jami?"

"Yes."

"What are you doing there? Where's Kendall?"

"Neither of those questions are your concern, James. I will tell her that you called." Before he could utter a retort, she ended the call and smiled to herself. Kendall was right. Revenge did feel good.

CHAPTER 24

Two days after the first PSA ran, Kendall got her first phone call concerning a donation for InfaCare, which was remarkable in itself since it was Sunday. By the time she got to work Monday morning, her accountant was calling her with good news.

In just a few days the hospital had gotten over a hundred thousand dollars in donations. It was a far cry from the several million she needed for the cancer wing, but it was a step in the right direction.

She didn't have long to enjoy her celebratory moment. Jami walked into her office with excitement on her round brown face. "Kendall, the board wants to meet with you this afternoon. They want you to film another PSA with Cole, but this time they also want it with Holly."

"Are they serious?" Kendall rose and walked around her desk. The last thing Cole wanted was to be in the same room with Holly.

Jami nodded. "Yes. They think it would look better with her boasting of your accomplishments. And before you object to her, the board has already cleared it with her superiors."

"Cole is going to have a fit when he finds out." But if it would get more donations for the hospital, then the ends justified the means, or at least she hoped so.

Jami grinned. "Maybe not. If you can persuade him to do the PSA, the donations for the hospital will start pouring in like hail in Texas tornados and you can get the cancer wing built."

"And in what way do I have to persuade him?" Kendall stared at her friend. "Does this have anything to do with me dressing up in something slinky?"

"Could be. It would be for the hospital. Think of all the children you can help. And it would only cost you one night of incredible sex."

Kendall thought of the last encounter she'd had with Cole. He'd knocked her socks off, and then some. It took every ounce of her willpower not to admit how much she loved him. "That's a pretty high price tag." But she couldn't let the kids down. They were depending on her. "But you're right, the kids need me."

Jami patted her on the shoulder. "That's my girl. Take one for the team."

The two women looked at each other and thought of Jami's play on words. They laughed until they cried.

Holly Banton left the production meeting with a plan of action. She could kill two birds with one stone, so to speak. Maybe with Cole being forced to talk to her, she'd actually have a second chance at him.

She just needed a few minutes with him and he'd be begging her to come back. Rumor had it he'd bought a house in Arlington, but that could quickly be changed and he'd return to New York to be with her.

She walked into her office and sat at her desk. She was on her way back to the top, and this time nothing was going to stop her.

"Holly, got a minute?" Herb Kelly stood in her doorway with a small stack of papers in his chubby hands.

"Sure, Herb." She put away her notes on Dr. Kendall Matthews and motioned him inside.

He sat down in the oversized leather chair and exhaled. "It's about Dr. Matthews."

"What? Don't tell me she doesn't want to do the interview. I've already got her phone interview recorded. It's too late to get someone else." She placed a nervous hand over her chest, hoping her chance at reclaiming her fame hadn't been shot to hell.

Herb raised his chubby hand. "No, no, nothing like that. They've started running the PSAs on the hospital and so far have gotten some good results. They want to record another one and would like you to be in it and list Dr. Matthews's accomplishments. Apparently she doesn't like to talk about herself much. I've already agreed. I also thought you could interview Coltrane Highpoint to show there are no hard feelings between CNT and him. You two have mended fences, right?"

"Yes," she lied. "I told you all that is old news. Cole and I are friends."

"Good. Set everything up and give me your timetable. I want this to go on without a hiccup. I'm sending the film crew with you to document it."

Holly nodded, guessing what her boss didn't tell her. Word on the street was Cole had just inked a seven-figure book deal from the very publisher that gave him the push when her story broke two years earlier. "Of course. I'll make arrangements and get back to you."

He stood and prepared to leave her office. "I'd hate for anything to go wrong with that interview, Holly. Not only is your job riding on it, but so is mine. The network can't afford any more publicity about erroneous information. Make sure you get good, solid quotes." He opened the door and left.

Holly counted to ten, then fifteen, twenty. She counted all the way up to fifty before slamming her manicured hand against her desk. How dare that excuse for a boss talk to her like she was a rookie reporter on her first assignment. Granted, the network had taken a beating with lawsuits when the scandal broke about her stories. They were just covering their own backs, she reasoned.

She would just have to show them all. She would get perfect, reliable, and verifiable quotes. This was going to be the best story about a charity hospital since St. Jude's, she promised herself.

A few nights later, Max sat at his favorite bar drinking away his sorrows. Or maybe not. It could be viewed as a celebration of sorts. He'd finally done it. He'd made the decision, and this time he was sticking to his guns. Not even the lure of millions from Caitlin's dysfunctional family could stop it. This time he had proof.

"Hey, man." Cole slid on the barstool next to him. "I heard you're trying to break the state record for beer consumption. Kendall's really worried about you. Me, too. Jami was in tears tonight. Max, what's going on with you?"

He finished his beer and ordered another one. "Not much. I just decided to get a divorce from my wife of ten years. I know you've heard this before, but this time it's going to happen."

Cole gasped. "Max, are you sure?"

He took the folder the private detective had given him earlier that day, the folder that would free him from the marriage from hell. "Yeah, Cole. I'm real sure." He handed him the folder. "Take a look for yourself."

Cole squinted his eyes at Max, but opened it anyway. After coughing to cover his surprise at the subject matter of the pictures, he looked at Max. "I think you have a good case for alienation of affection. Who's the guy?"

Max shrugged. "Who cares? Probably someone from the country club, or maybe the pool guy. The point is, I can get out of the marriage and be with Jami, and there's nothing Harry Campbell can do about it."

"Whoa, big guy," Cole said. "You need to take care of this one step at a time. Believe me, the last thing you want is a scandal. And I know you don't want Jami's name dragged through the mud."

"I know. Caitlin's dad is notorious for fixing trials, getting people to take a hike, or paying people to lie on his behalf. This has to be clean. That's why I hired a private detective."

Cole nodded. "I get it. You received the pictures at work, didn't you?"

"Yes. I had always figured she was sleeping with someone, and now I have proof. She was actually cheating on me."

"That's why you were snapping at Kendall and Jami today?" Cole signaled the bartender for a beer. "You know, there are easier ways to deal with hurt than to take it out on the people you love."

"Big talk," Max shot back. "Have you told Kendall how you really feel about her?" Max took a long swig of beer. "You're going to mess around and let that no-account ex worm his way back in her life."

"Max, you don't know what you're talking about. Kendall doesn't have any feelings for James. There's no way that can happen."

"I know you don't think so, but stranger things have happened. I just don't want you to lose her. You guys are great for each other."

Cole shrugged. "This is about you, Max, not me. What are you going to do?"

Max often wondered if he were walking a tightrope without a net below. "I know I want to get out of this sham of a marriage. Caitlin doesn't love me."

"How do you know that?"

Max hated to admit this to another man, but he needed to get it off his chest. "She tells me so. Every day. She says she only stays married to me to keep her dad off her back."

"How did you guys meet?"

Max remembered the beautiful woman he'd met eleven years ago. Caitlin had been vibrant, full of life, and sexy as hell. But it had been an act. "Actually, we met in college. We were both mature students, and I guess we kind of bonded. We studied together, and before long the study sessions started to include breakfast. About six months later, her dad made me an offer I should have refused."

Cole snapped his fingers. "Let me guess, he offered to pay for you going to school if you married his daughter."

Max felt like a prostitute now. "Yeah. Back then, I was fresh out of the air force, and I had school covered. But I still needed a job. He made it possible for me to totally concentrate on school. The house was our wedding present, cars were birthday presents. Everything was taken care of. Credit cards, utilities, car insurance, all the bills went to him."

Cole shook his head. "Why did he feel the need to have to sell his daughter?"

Max laughed, remembering the past and hating himself for his moment of weakness. "Caitlin has a rebellious streak. She'd been through several less desirable men when I came along."

Cole patted him on the shoulder. "Max, that's awful. I now understand her father's motives. He's trying to preserve the family name. A divorce is going to rock the facade of the proper family and Dallas upper-crust society."

"This time money is not the answer. The next few months will be tricky, but I'm hoping those pictures will speed up the process."

"Did you sign a prenup?"

"No."

Cole laughed. "A man that on the ball didn't have you sign a prenuptial agreement before you married his wild daughter? You know you could get half of her estate."

Max grinned. "Caitlin doesn't have any money of her own. She's a daddy's girl to the bone. Why do you think we have a live-in nanny for Carson?"

"She only had the baby to make you happy?"

"Back then we were still trying to make it work. Foolishly we thought a baby would cure the problems in the marriage. Boy, were we stupid."

Cole thought he had had a great idea. Or at least it felt good at the time. After Kendall told him she'd never been to a professional baseball game, Cole decided he would take everyone. Little did he know that little gesture was like the firing of the starter pistol to his and Kendall's mothers.

His mother had nothing but one insane idea after another when she learned of the outing. The day of the game she came over to give him some last-minute advice. Cole was in his home office hoping to finish at least a chapter of his latest book before he and Taylor left to pick up Kendall, Jami, and Dylan. Max and Trey, Kendall's nephew, were meeting them at the ballpark.

Martha marched into the office and took a seat in a chair next to the desk. "Are you ready? This is your first real outing with Taylor and Kendall. How do you think Taylor is going to react with Jami and Dylan also being there? And who invites all these people on a date?"

"Mom, it's just a baseball game, not a date. There will be at least seven people there with us."

"See what I mean? Did you remember the car seat for Dylan? You know the law."

"Yes, Jami is going to switch the one in her car. There's plenty of room for him in the back. And yes, I have the tickets. And yes, they're near the bathrooms. We're sitting between home plate and first base, two rows back."

"Wow! Taylor is excited," his mother said. "That's all he talked about yesterday when he came over to the house. I can't tell you what a joy it's been having him visit us. I'm learning quite a bit about this hippy-hop thing. You know he wants more brothers and sisters."

Cole knew exactly what his mother was doing. He had, in fact, planned for this little moment. Martha wasn't going to miss one chance to tell him how he needed to be married and that he should marry Kendall. But this time he was going to beat her at her own game. He opened his desk drawer and extracted an envelope, handing it to his mother. "Just in case you wanted to have some fun this evening, here are tickets for Zenora and Evan, too."

His mother smiled. "I must be getting old. I didn't see that coming." She took the tickets. "You just might see me out there."

Cole watched his mother walk out of the room. Tonight was going to be something. He just hoped he lived through it to tell the story to his grandchildren.

Two hours later, Cole doubted if he would ever live through the night, let alone be able to tell his grandchildren how he'd outsmarted his parents. He hadn't really expected his senior citizen mother to show up, but as usual she'd outsmarted him.

Kendall laughed. "I guess you're going to have to move your hand or I'm going to tell your mama."

Cole had his hand planted on Kendall's thigh and had no intention of moving it. In fact, he moved closer to her. "My mama would applaud my efforts," he whispered in her ear. "I guess I should tell you I invited your folks, too."

She stared at him, mouth hanging open in surprise. "How could you invite that woman? Our mothers will be planning the wedding before the Rangers get another hit. I can't believe you didn't tell me."

He knew only one thing to do to shut up her tirade. He pulled her into his arms and kissed her. She laughed against his lips but didn't pull away. She increased the pressure and moaned against him. He heard clapping in the back of his mind, but ignored it, until he heard his son complain.

"Dad, this is so embarrassing. Could you guys please stop!"

Cole reluctantly pulled away from those soft lips and shot his son a baleful look. His son stared back at him, but pointed to the screen over right field. Cole finally looked at the screen and gasped. "Oh, my God." There was an instant replay of him and Kendall kissing like lustful teenagers for everyone at the baseball stadium to see, including Kendall. He was in the doghouse now, he knew. Kendall didn't go for public displays of kissing. "Sorry, babe." He moved away from her. "I had no idea they were filming."

Kendall smiled and pulled him closer to her. "It's a little late for that, Cole." She kissed him quickly on the lips. "Thank you."

Okay, he was totally confused. "Why are you thanking me?"

Kendall held his hand close to her body. "I thought I would be embarrassed by the whole kissing scenario, but I wasn't. I can actually laugh about it."

Cole was relieved. "Okay. But if you really want to thank me," he said, enjoying the slow smile adorning her face, "you could give me a more private kiss later."

"No, you invited my parents. You'd better hope they don't show up."

Cole didn't want to think about the "what if" of that threat. "Too late, baby. Here they come." He nodded to her parents being led to their seats by the usher.

Kendall bowed her head. "Thank goodness they didn't see that kiss."

Cole nodded, knowing the likelihood of them seeing that kiss was pretty good.

"Was that you guys kissing like Cole was going off to war?" Zenora asked as she sat in front of the now embarrassed couple. "You were really going at it. I was very proud."

Kendall looked at him with an unreadable expression on her pretty brown face. "Just great. You've got my own mother thinking I'm a freak."

"It was my fault, Zenora," Cole said. "We got a little carried away."

She waved away his comment. "Hey, you have one life. Live it. How many women can say their daughter was caught on the JumboTron screen smooching with a prominent author?"

Cole chuckled. Leave it to Zenora to make a moment of unbridled passion sound like an everyday occurrence.

After a grueling day of trying to get some background information on the charity hospital, Holly relaxed in front of her TV, hoping to catch the last of the baseball game. Baseball was her one vice. She loved the New York Yankees and followed them religiously. She attended the games when she could, and when they were on the road she was glued to her TV set.

She turned on the TV and quickly found the game. It was the bottom of the seventh and the Texas Rangers were leading by two runs. She picked up her notes on Dr. Kendall Matthews and began skimming them. The only blip in this woman's past was her no-account ex-husband who didn't know how to keep his pants zipped. Since the Rangers were at bat her attention wasn't on the game until she heard the kissing song. The cameras skimmed the crowds, catching couples in an awkward moment. She remembered the last time she'd attended a game with Cole. She'd tried to get him to kiss her, but he wouldn't.

She didn't know whether it was the music or the crowd making noises, but she looked up from the computer and her heart stopped. Cole was in a serious lip-lock with Dr. Kendall Matthews in public at the baseball game. She quickly hit the record option on her remote and viewed the scene again. Holly recognized Taylor instantly. When had his son come back into his life?

Her phone rang as she played the scene again. She picked up the phone. "What?"

"I guess you're watching the game?" the male voice asked.

She recognized her fellow reporter friend, Jason Carr, and knew he just wanted the dirt. "Yes, can you believe it? The nerve of that woman! I knew that stuff about his donating was more than him just trying to clean up that mess behind that scandal. I've got to get to the bottom of this."

"You think he's serious? I mean, he was caught on film with his tongue down her throat and then they were laughing about it. You know what a private person he became after the scandal."

Holly thought it about for a scant second. "You're saying that was my fault?"

"Yes. You didn't have to release his name to the public, but I know you were trying to save yourself when your story started falling apart. I'm not judging you, just stating the truth," Jason said.

Holly sometimes hated Jason and his very cut-to-the-chase personality. "You're right. After that hit the fan, Cole just kind of faded away."

ANYTHING BUT LOVE

"Looks like he's over the whole you-lied-on-him thing and has moved on to the good doctor," Jason said dryly. "So what's on your agenda? You still have to interview them for that story, if you plan on keeping your job. How are you going to handle that?"

She wished she knew. "I'll just be professional. So far Cole has refused to speak with me. But the board wants to do another PSA with me talking to him and naming Kendall's long list of accolades."

Jason sighed. "Holly, this is me, the man you cried to last week when Cole told you not to speak to him. He obviously is still holding on to what you did to him, and rightly so, but you guys need closure. Yeah, you did him wrong and almost ruined his literary career, but you gotta somehow find a way to talk to him."

Holly knew all that. What she really wanted to do was throw the phone across the room. "Any bright ideas? I could sure use one."

"How about I come with you next week when you fly down to Texas. That way I can be sure you won't do anything that will get you fired."

Holly wanted to refuse her friend, but knew he was probably right. He needed to be there to save her from herself. "All right, Jason. I'm flying out next Thursday morning. I'll even put your plane ticket and hotel on my expense account."

"Wow, thanks, Holly."

"I should be thanking you. I have a bad feeling about this. Somehow I think that interview is going to cost me something. I just don't know what."

James entered his hotel late that night. He'd been doing the good son thing by visiting his mother, who was in good health, though he'd told Kendall a different story. The short visit he had originally planned had gone by the wayside when she decided she wanted to go shopping. Not being able to deny his mother anything, he'd taken her to Parks Mall.

She had a lot of energy, he thought. He walked to the phone. He'd been trying to call Kendall for the last three hours but she wasn't home. He absently turned on the TV for the nightly news. Suddenly he heard the name Coltrane Highpoint and glanced up at the screen.

"Oh, my God. That's Kendall!" James was shocked to see his ex-wife kissing some guy on national television. He quickly turned up the volume.

"Bestselling author Coltrane Highpoint and Dr. Kendall Matthews, noted area doctor, have their own game going. I haven't seen kissing like that since my honeymoon," the announcer stated.

James shook his head, not believing his eyes for one second. That couldn't be his uptight ex being caught in such an embarrassing moment. The Kendall he was married to didn't believe in public smooching. The Kendall he knew was too uptight for anything spontaneous. She was always concerned about her image.

He watched the woman on the screen laughing as she realized they were being filmed. He almost fell out of his chair when he saw her kiss Coltrane again. Something was definitely wrong with this picture. He had to find out what exactly was going on, then get rid of Coltrane and work his way back into Kendall's heart.

"That was fun, Cole. We'll have to do that again before baseball season ends," Kendall announced as they headed home. Thanks to a home run by the newest Ranger acquisition, the Rangers had won the game by two points. She wasn't really a baseball fan but tonight had given her more insight into the game, as well as into Cole.

"I'm glad you liked it. The next home game is on the holiday. How about a replay?" Cole asked.

Kendall heard laughter from the second row of seats in the Range Rover. Jami and Taylor were laughing at them. That would have bothered the old uptight Kendall. But the contented Kendall who was in love with Cole thought it was funny. "Kiss included?"

"Of course." Cole came to a stoplight, leaned over and kissed her. "It will make the one tonight look like a good-bye peck on the lips."

More laughter from behind them. Kendall felt a shiver of excitement at Cole's promise. It was getting more and more difficult to deny her feelings for this man. To get her mind off the lustful fantasies forming in her mind, she turned to Taylor. "What did you think of the game?" She hadn't noticed him talking much during the game, but she hoped he'd enjoyed it. It was so difficult to tell whether a teenager was happy or not.

Cole resumed driving, darting a glance in the rearview mirror, waiting for his son's response.

"It was cool. I used to go see the Red Sox play all the time with my friend Justin. But this was way better."

"Why?" Something in the teenager's voice made her curious.

"Because all those years Justin's dad took us to the game when he could, and this time I got to go to a game with mine," Taylor said softly. "I wouldn't trade tonight for anything. Even you and Dad getting caught on camera kissing didn't ruin it. It was a MasterCard moment."

Kendall remembered those commercials about the credit card, but didn't know how that compared to a baseball game. Taylor soon put her out of her misery and explained.

"Priceless. Nothing could top this. Well, maybe the next game can, but I doubt it."

Kendall nodded in understanding, then looked at Cole. He was unusually silent. She noticed a lone tear streaking down his handsome face. She reached for his free hand and caressed it. Both and Taylor and Cole had so many issues they needed to work out, but tonight had cemented their relationship as father and son.

Cole cleared this throat, no doubt trying to rein in his emotions. "Looks like we're going to the Fourth of July game. I'll order the tickets tonight. You think I should invite the parents?"

Kendall laughed. "The more the merrier. Besides, I can't imagine them not being there." She felt so content at the moment that not even the thought of her mother at another baseball game could ruin the mood.

CHAPTER 25

The next day, Kendall went to work late. After Cole had dropped her, Jami, and Dylan at her house last night, sleep hadn't come so easily. Her mind was still on Cole and the events of the evening. It felt as if she'd just had her first date.

She walked into the hospital with a smile on her face. Nothing was going to ruin her day. All that changed when she turned the corner leading to her office. James was standing at the nurses' station, apparently waiting for her.

"Kendall," he called to her. "What on earth is going on with you?" He marched toward her with a determined gait.

"James, keep your voice down," she muttered, meeting him at her office door. "You do not own me, therefore I don't owe you an explanation." She knew he was referring to the kiss. She'd fielded many calls this morning about that very thing. Most couldn't believe she had been caught in a lip-lock with Cole on national television, but they were happy she was finally letting her hair down.

James sighed like the prima donna he was. He followed her inside her office and took a seat in front of her desk. "I saw you on TV last night, and you're on the front page of the paper this morning. Have you lost your mind? What about your image, or the image of the hospital?"

"You never cared about those things before, James, why now? What I do is my business, not yours. We're divorced, remember?"

He took another deep breath. "Sorry for tripping like that, but I know how much you're concerned with image. I know it's easy to let passion rule your actions. What is the board of directors going to say about Kendall going wild?"

"I don't know, and I don't care. It's my life, James. Why are you here?"

"I came to talk some sense into you. That guy is a writer, and you know how they are. They live for free publicity. He's just riding your coattails."

"Like you did," Kendall accused. She couldn't believe she'd said that, and out loud. "Look, James, I don't want to fight with you. My business is my business. Our past is just that."

He nodded, probably trying to think of something soothing to say to her. "It's cool. I probably deserve that for coming in here like I own you. Why don't we have lunch and talk like civilized people?"

"All right. How about one o'clock? I have meetings until then. I'll meet you in the cafeteria."

James rose from the chair, smiling. "I was thinking of something a little more private. How about Eduardo's? It's just down the street. I'll pick you up." He walked out of her office before she could reply.

Kendall sat back in her chair, laughing. She wondered what her ex was up to, but knew she'd find out at lunch. Max burst into her office a few minutes later.

"Please tell me you're not going out with James? What about my boy?" Max took a seat. "I just saw James talking on his cell phone. He was making reservations at that swanky place, Eduardo's. You know, just because he's spending a lot of money on lunch doesn't mean you have to give him some."

Kendall snorted with laughter. "You know that is not about to happen, Max. I don't feel anything for James. He's up to something, and lunch is the only way I'm going to find out what it is. Now what's up with you?"

"I had a meeting with Caitlin's dad this morning. He offered me two million dollars to not file for divorce. Kendall, I'm tired of being with someone who doesn't love me."

"I've been there, and you're right, it sucks. What did her father say?"

"He gave me a sob story about how no one in their family is divorced. Granted that's true, but he has a mistress, and Caitlin's mom is a depressed alcoholic. This is what he's holding up to me as a good family."

Kendall was well acquainted with Max's in-laws and the society set. It was all about appearances, not feelings or what was best for the family. "Max, you do know Harry is not going to let this happen. He's going to find a way to force you to stay married."

"I know. And here comes the hard part. I'm going to have to make sure I stay completely away from Jami, and you're going to have to help me. I don't want Harry getting his mitts into her."

"Don't worry, that's not going to happen on my watch. Jami has been through enough."

"You'll get no argument from me." Max left the office.

Kendall sat there thinking of all the trouble surrounding her when she should be focusing on the next PSA and her interview with Cole's ex. Could she help Jami and Max through this difficult time ahead while trying to maintain her relationship with Cole as he tried to establish one with his son? And there was always her mother to deal with, trying to deter her from planning Kendall's and Cole's nonexistent wedding.

Thursday morning, Holly arrived at Dallas-Fort Worth International Airport. She was glad Jason had decided to accompany her. It would make her time in Texas go by faster. She stood at the baggage carousel next to Jason, waiting for their luggage.

"Have you spoken with Cole yet?" Jason yawned. "I can't believe we left New York at four in the morning. You so owe me for this."

Holly reached for her large suitcase. "I know I owe you. Cole won't return any of my calls. I don't know how I'm supposed to interview him if he refuses to talk to me."

Jason reached for her bag and then grabbed his much smaller one. "You could always just show up at his place. That's always worked in the past."

She'd already thought of that. "Nice try, but he lives in a gated community with an armed security guard."

"Since when has a little thing like a gate or an armed guard stopped you?"

"Since the person is Cole. His lawyer contacted me yesterday and said if I come near him other than the interview, he was going to file charges against me."

Jason choked. "Ouch. I think he really means business. It's going to be kinda hard to interview him if you can't talk to him beforehand."

"You don't have to tell me." She snapped her fingers. "Hey, I have an idea."

Jason rolled his eyes toward the ceiling. "What? And how many years am I going to get for this?"

Holly laughed. "You're such a drama queen. It's not illegal, just a little misdirection. Tomorrow, you call Cole and ask for a quickie interview before we start filming at the hospital."

Jason put their luggage on a cart and started for the rental car area. "And you'll just happen to be hiding in a broom closet somewhere and jump out and scare the poor man to death, adding murder to your long list of foibles."

"You know, a little support would be nice." She walked alongside Jason. "I'm just trying to keep my job."

"I know, sweetie, but there has to be a better way than trying to trick him into conversation. Since he and the doctor are an item, why not go through her? I'm sure she'll do anything to help the interview, provided she doesn't know you're the ex."

"I think my plan would be so much easier," Holly said as they arrived at the rental car counter.

Kendall arrived at work early to find Max sleeping in his truck. She knocked on the window and smiled as he slowly came awake. Her heart went out to him for all the trouble he'd been having lately. She wished she could help.

He sat up, opened the door, and got out. "Hey, Kendall."

They were good enough friends that explanations weren't always necessary. He didn't have to spin her a story about why he was sleeping in his truck. "I bet you could use a good breakfast." She thought a moment. "Right after you shower. Why didn't you sleep in my office? The couch folds out."

Max stretched his long form. "Because I didn't want the cleaning crew to find me in there." He reached into his truck and retrieved a bag. "I'll meet you in the cafeteria in thirty minutes."

Kendall nodded. "Okay, don't make me come looking for you. You know I have no problem walking into the men's room." She joked in reference to her earlier mistake of catching a glimpse of Cole in the buff at the gym. "Besides, we have to go over the notes for the PSA tomorrow." She walked inside, ready to face the day of challenges.

Max met her later as promised. He looked refreshed and ready to face whatever life was going to throw at him. They joined the long line of customers. Kendall felt the need to keep a light banter between them. "I'm feeling really hungry today. You know I'll freak out the workers if I ask for bacon and eggs."

Max smiled. "You'll definitely freak me out. What's gotten into you?" He started laughing. "Oh, I forgot, Cole got into you."

"I'm not dignifying that remark with a response." She picked up a tray and moved down the line. After she gave her breakfast order and received it, she found a quiet corner so she and Max could talk.

"I still can't believe it. You've probably scared the cafeteria workers by ordering regular food." His order was identical to Kendall's.

"Everybody changes, Max. I'd been a vegetarian for the last ten years. Cole's been in my life for a few months and he's gotten me to try more things than I want to mention. But the occasional meat is okay."

"I'm glad you're giving Cole his props," Max said between bites. "That's what I want, someone to be in my corner no matter what. Caitlin threw me out of the house last night," he admitted. "She was having some kind of fit. I'm guessing her dad told her I turned down the two mil."

"Why didn't I see more clothes in your truck? I know you own more clothes than this."

"I could only leave with one bag, or she was going to call the police and tell them I'd threatened her and Carson."

"That bitch," Kendall muttered. "I hate when women take advantage of a situation. You need to call Charles. He said he'll take you on as a favor to me."

"You know I can't afford your brother. His retainer is probably half a year's salary."

Kendall smiled. Her brother was good at what he did. That's why he had such high-profile clients. But because he was so good, Kendall knew he was exactly who Max needed to represent him. At least she could do this for her friend. "Max, it'll be free. Consider it your Christmas gift for the next ten years."

"I do have *some* money, Kendall."

"And you're going to need it when you find a place of your own and start your life over. What about your SUV? Is it in your name?"

"Yes. I think that's why she hates it so much. It was the first thing I bought with my own money."

"Where are those pictures the private detective took?"

"In a safe place. With Cole."

Kendall knew the men had formed a bond over the last few months. She hadn't realized it was so strong that Max would trust Cole on that level. Max didn't trust easily. She knew Max needed a man to confide in, most likely due to some male code of bonding. But still, Kendall and Max had been friends for over six years. He could have given the pictures to her for safekeeping, but she also knew why he didn't ask her. "That was very smart, Max."

Max must have been reading her mind. "You know I couldn't leave them with you. I needed someone no one would think would have the pictures. I just know Harry is going to hire someone to steal them."

"You're right. Caitlin knows you house-sit for me on occasion, so I'm sure a visit from an unannounced repairman is coming."

Max nodded. "I'm surprised it hasn't happened already. You know Harry isn't going to let grass grow under his Italian loafers until he has me begging for mercy and taking whatever amount of money he throws at me to disappear."

Kendall knew the next few months were going to be tough for everyone involved. "What about Carson? Are you going to fight for custody?"

Max looked at her with big blue eyes. "I want to, but I don't want to subject him to more hurt. I probably should call Charles today and see what kind of chance I have at sole custody. Carson is Harry's only grandson and sole heir to the Campbell fortune, so you can imagine what I'm up against."

Kendall knew exactly what he was up against: a very rich and powerful mountain. Max was going to need a miracle.

Cole woke to a ringing phone. He didn't want to get up. He wanted to sleep as late as possible, but the phone wasn't going to let him. Reluctantly, he reached for it and pulled it to his ear. "What?"

He heard Charles chuckle. "And here I was thinking you were already up. My sweet, innocent baby sister isn't there, is she?"

Cole sat up, laughing with his friend. "You know I wouldn't tell you if she was. I'm not quite ready to die yet. What's going on?"

"I heard about the baseball game. I can't believe you didn't invite me. I'm hurt," he said. "I'm only your best friend, and you're sleeping with my sister, but you forgot about me. And I'm also your lawyer. Man, I feel an increase in fees coming on."

He knew Charles was only half kidding. No matter how good-natured Charles was, Cole knew he was deadly serious about Kendall. "All right, put away your violin. I plan on taking everyone to another game right after Kendall and I finish the last PSA."

"Yeah, Mom mentioned the interview coming up. I'm glad Kendall's going to realize her dream of InfaCare getting a cancer wing. I still can't believe you donated a million dollars. Was that just so Kendall would have to go out with you?"

Cole weighed his options. Charlie was in his lawyer mode and no doubt had good reason to continue his line of questioning. "Yes, it was. You know Holly, who's doing the interview, and I used to date."

"Who could forget! It took you almost two years to recover from what she did to you. She almost ruined your career. And now she has the nerve to want to interview you. Is she why Kendall didn't want to have anything to do with you?"

"Come on, Charlie. When I first ran into Kendall a few months ago, she treated me pretty bad in the beginning. She didn't want to have anything to do with me because I'm a writer."

"That wasn't the reason." Her brother didn't elaborate. "So you hit her below the belt and did the Godfather thing of an offer she couldn't refuse. I'm going to have to call the players' club and nominate you for player of the year," Charlie joked. "That's a rather expensive date."

"I did what I had to do," Cole said. "Besides, it's a tax write-off for me, and I needed some good press. It was kind of two for the price of one million," Cole said. "So did you get the restraining order done?"

"Yes, I did. I had it delivered to her yesterday. But when has a little thing like a court order stopped Holly Banton? I don't understand why you're going to all this trouble. Why not just refuse to do the interview?"

Cole sighed. So much was riding on the success of the PSA and interview for Kendall, he couldn't let her down. No matter how much he hadn't wanted to do it, he had to suck it up. "Because it's important to Kendall, so that makes it important to me."

"So Mom is right. You've fallen hard, my friend, and for my baby sister, no less."

"Yeah, tell me something I don't know, Charlie. As much as I don't want to see Holly, I have to endure it for

Kendall. Holly called me after she saw me and Kendall kissing on TV. She still has my New York cell phone number and I haven't changed the number to a Texas one yet," Cole explained. "I couldn't believe that aired all over the country. My agent even called me and congratulated me." Cole chuckled, remembering the calls he'd received the morning after.

"You know Mom has marked you and is planning the wedding already? She was looking at a bridal magazine the last time I was over there."

Cole knew that too. "Yeah, your mom and my mom put me and Kendall on notice. Kendall was a little upset about it. I thought it was funny. You know what our moms are like. The more you tell them no, the more they want it. I figure humor them for a little while and then they'll move onto something else."

"When my mom puts you on her agenda, you're as good as gone," Charlie said. "Hey, look at me. She did me the same way, over twenty years ago."

"Thanks for the warning." Cole knew his single days were over the first time he laid eyes on Kendall. He just needed to convince Kendall of that fact. "There's a lot we have to work through first."

"Namely, one Holly Banton."

"And James Matthews," Cole added. "He's been all but stalking Kendall since he got back."

"That scumbag is back in town?" Charlie yelled into the phone. "I thought he was still in Washington."

"Charlie, calm down. Max told me he's been hanging out at the hospital the last few days. He was supposed to have lunch with her a few days ago, but Kendall had some kind of emergency and had to cancel."

"Good," Charlie said in his protective brother voice. "I don't want him anywhere near her."

"You're too late for that."

"What?"

"He snuck into the subdivision a few weeks ago, but I took care of him." Cole didn't dare mention Kendall hurt her leg in the process, or Charlie would probably be gunning for James.

"Good. Thanks, man, I owe you one," Charlie said quietly. "I'll be your best man when you marry my sister."

Cole laughed. "You know that's so not funny, but you've got a deal." He heard a beep on his phone. "Hey, gotta go, another call is coming through. Later." He engaged the second call. "Hey, Max."

"No time for chitchat. Get down to the hospital as quick as you can."

Cole glanced at the bedside clock. It was barely nine in the morning. "Max, you're not making sense. Why am I coming to the hospital? Is Kendall all right?"

"She won't be if that no-account ex-husband of hers has his way. He just called and made arrangements for lunch."

"What?"

"I'm telling you to get down to the hospital as quick as you can. James is taking her out for lunch, so you'd better have some kind of master plan by the time you get here." He ended the call.

Cole threw the phone on the bed and headed for the shower. Hopefully the hot water would wake up his brain and he would come up with a plan that would get rid of James Matthews forever.

CHAPTER 26

Kendall was just finishing up a consultation with a new patient and her husband. As a rule, in just a few minutes of questions, Kendall could determine what direction to take. Russell Cagner was the newly elected mayor of Arlington. Both he and his wife, Melissa, were in their mid-forties. The Cagners had been trying to conceive for years. Now, at the age of forty-four, Kendall was Melissa's last hope.

After Melissa took a battery of tests, Kendall suggested a follow-up in a week to discuss their options and dismissed the couple.

Once she was in her office alone, she could actually close her eyes and relax. The room had started to spin counterclockwise again. It was probably just the stress of the interview, Cole, Max, Jami, and just about anything else she could think of going on in her life. How did her calm, collected, and very predictable life get like this?

All she wanted to do was curl up on the couch and take a quick nap, but knew that was impossible. Too many things required her attention. Her phone rang, interrupting her quiet time. "Yes, Jami?"

"James is here saying something about a lunch date," Jami said cautiously.

Kendall sighed. She'd forgotten about the arrangements she'd made with James, but that was before the Cagners. She didn't have the strength to deal with James and his game. "Tell him something has come up and I'll need an hour." Maybe a quick nap would regenerate her.

"Yes, Dr. Matthews," Jami said and ended the call.

Kendall walked to her couch with a tired smile on her face and took a well-deserved nap.

James didn't believe her one second. "She said what?" He knew Jami and Kendall had formed a bond, according to his hospital spies, but no way in hell did he have to believe anything that came out of the those full, pouty lips.

Jami replaced the phone in its cradle and smiled up at him. "She said something came up and she's going to need an hour."

James wondered if Coltrane Highpoint had anything to do with it. He had to talk to her, or his butt would definitely be in a major sling with his bosses. He probably shouldn't have promised he could get Briarwood and InfaCare's business, but he'd thought Kendall would be a piece of cake. That was before he knew about Coltrane Highpoint and the new Kendall Matthews. Now his task wasn't as easy as he once thought it might be.

"So what's it going to be, James?" Jami taunted him. "Shall I put you down for one o'clock?"

"Yeah. I'll be back." James stomped down the hall to do a little brainstorming.

He found a quiet corner and sat down. His mother was right; being good-looking was a curse. He'd always fallen back on his looks when nothing else worked. When he was married to Kendall, he took her for granted, had affairs right under her nose, and had paid the price.

There was a time Kendall would have dropped everything to do whatever he asked. What did Coltrane have that he didn't? He noticed Max walking down the hall. Max was the advantage that Coltrane had.

His hospital spies had informed him of how tight Max and Coltrane had become in just a matter of months. Talk about having the inside track, James mused. Max was the direct link to Kendall, and Cole had it.

"James, what are you doing here?" Max asked, walking directly to him. "I thought you had a lunch date with Kendall," he said, smiling.

"Yeah, me too. We had to push it back. Something came up."

Max's blue eyes expanded with shock. "What? An emergency and no one told me?" He whipped out his PDA and tapped on the screen. "That's funny." He turned off the handheld computer and shoved it in his pocket. "Nice to see you, James." He took off for Kendall's office.

James stared at Max's back. Something was definitely not right. Maybe Kendall was putting him off, but being evasive wasn't Kendall's style. Or was that Kendall's new attitude? Only one real way to find out. He took off for Kendall's office.

Kendall was having a dream to end all dreams. She and Cole were somewhere tropical and it was just the two of them. No kids, no problems, just them. And they were doing something very wicked.

Cole was working his magic on her when Kendall heard a knock. She turned over, hoping to keep the dream, and feigned sleep. Then the knock became louder, demanding her attention.

"Kendall," Max said, opening her door. He immediately turned on the lights. "What is with you lately? You're always tired. Are you and Cole hittin' it like that?"

She opened her eyes at her friend's questions. Leave it to Max to ruin her dream. "I'm under a lot of pressure right now, Max. It's just stress." She yawned and sat up. "I needed a little nap to face James. I know he's up to something, and he doesn't know that I know."

Max sat beside her. "And what could he want?"

"Briarwood and InfaCare."

"Oh, he needs you to get the pharmacy thing going?"

"Pretty much. James doesn't know, but I found out his true motive for moving back, and it has nothing do with the story he spun me. His mother isn't sick. He didn't get a promotion. In fact, he got a demotion. He didn't ask for this territory. It was this or nothing."

Max shook his head. "How did you find this out?"

"How else? His mother. I went to see Janet when he told me she had breast cancer. While I was there, she gave me the real story."

"I can't believe he did that," Max said. "Check that, yes I can. Now what are you going to do?"

Kendall shrugged. "I'll meet him for lunch." Her eyes met Max's scornful gaze. "Max, I was married to the man. I owe him lunch."

"You don't owe him squat," Max said. "Don't forget he knocked up a nurse, in your bed, I might add. So don't try to go all melancholy on me."

"Thanks for bringing me to my senses." Kendall rose from the couch, straightened her dress and walked to her desk to retrieve her purse. "Now I'm ready to face the idiot."

Max nodded, walking toward her. "That's my girl." He hugged her and left the office.

Kendall was about to leave her office when another knock came. "Come in," she called.

James walked inside and closed the door. "I was just wondering if you were going to be a no-show or what. Are you ready?"

She didn't want to trade barbs with James, but she wanted this lunch date over as quickly as possible. "Yes, I just need to check in with Jami and we can be on our way."

He smiled. "Good." He reached for her hand. "Shall we?"

Kendall moved past his outstretched hand. "Yes." She opened the door and walked down the hall, leaving James to close it.

He caught up with her by the time she reached Jami's desk. "I'll be out about an hour," Kendall told Jami unnecessarily. They'd already discussed her lunch appointment the minute James made it. "Any emergencies, please page me."

"Yes, Dr. Matthews." Jami handed her a message. "Phillip wanted to know about the shooting schedule for the PSA tomorrow."

Kendall looked at the small piece of paper with her most professional doctor look, hoping to fool James. The note said nothing about a PSA. Jami had scribbled a wager that James would probably want her to drive. Kendall smiled. "I'll call him when I get back." Kendall turned to James. "Where did you park?"

He cleared his throat. "I was hoping you'd drive."

Kendall heard Jami's soft chuckle. Same old James. "You invited me, remember? So I don't have to tell you what that means, right?"

James' sure, confident shoulders sagged in defeat. "Yes, I know. My car's out front."

Kendall wondered what she'd ever seen in James Matthews. Clearly she had been blinded by those classic good looks and slippery words. "Lead the way."

Cole was halfway out the front door when his good sense surfaced. If he got to the hospital, what was he going to do? How was he going to explain his presence to Kendall? If the shoe was on the other foot, how would he take this little maneuver if it had been Kendall spying on him?

He'd be livid, for sure. Pissed? Naturally. Kendall was a practical woman and knew what an ass James Matthews was. She just needed closure. With those thoughts, Cole relaxed and decided not to go to the hospital. He had to let Kendall handle James on her own terms.

An hour later, Cole was seated in his home office reading over his notes for his book. If he could knock out a chapter today and one over the weekend, he might just make his deadline with time to spare. The phone rang just as he was getting started. Since Taylor wasn't home, Cole took it for granted it was either Taylor or Kendall.

He was wrong on both counts. "Cole, it's nice to actually talk to you," Holly said softly.

"I talked to you the other day."

"I don't think 'leave me alone' and hanging up in my face constitutes a conversation."

Cole sighed. As if today didn't have enough problems with Kendall having lunch with her ex-husband and Max having a crisis, now this happened. "It does in my book. Is there a reason for this call?"

"I need to talk to you. Alone. Without the spectacular Dr. Kendall Matthews at your side."

"No. Whatever you have to say to me, you can say in front of her. We have no secrets."

"Does she know everything about you? I mean those years you abused me and made me have an abortion?"

In the four years he was with Holly, Cole had never raised a hand to her. When she ruined his life he'd felt like it, but his mother would have killed him. She was trying to bait him, draw him into a battle. He was ahead of the game for once, and it wasn't going to happen. "I never hit you and you never had an abortion."

"Yes, I did. I just never told you."

"What?" Cole slumped down into the nearest chair. That was the last thing he'd expected to come out of Holly's mouth.

She sighed. "Oh, don't be such a drama queen, Cole. It was years ago, back when we actually had sex. I knew you'd want to do something silly like get married, and I was the anchor at CNT. I wasn't about to go out on a maternity leave and possibly lose my job simply because I'd been stupid enough to get pregnant."

Cole thought his brain was going to explode. Why was he just now realizing Holly was no better than his ex-wife? Their careers came above anything else, especially family. At least Gabriella hadn't had an abortion. How could Holly be so cold and uncaring? "You killed my baby and didn't bother to tell me?"

"Cole, it was a long time ago. Five years ago, you were in a different place. You were riding on top of the world with your book on New York bestseller lists. Movie houses were courting you like crazy, and my career had just begun to flourish. Did either of us have time for that?"

I would have made time, Cole thought. "That's not the point," he said through gritted teeth. "You made the decision without me. Just like you always did. You decided since all your girlfriends were either living with someone or married, that you'd move in with me. You didn't ask. You just started moving all your stuff into my place."

"Cole, that's old news. Why did you move here and ruin everything?"

Now he was seeing red. Had she forgotten everything she'd done to him? "Holly, you almost ruined my career for the sake of yours. Let's leave it at that. Now, if you want to do that interview tomorrow, I suggest we end this conversation now."

She actually laughed. "You think you can get rid of me this easily? We still have some business to discuss, and we can do it now or in front of your little friend. How do you think she'd like it if we did it at the hospital?"

She'd hate it, and him, forever. Cole didn't want Kendall's hospital tainted with his baggage. "What business?"

CHAPTER 27

Kendall stared across the table at her lunch companion. She supposed James thought he was being romantic, pretending to care about anything important to her. Lunching at Simply Good would have been a grand idea when they were married. But now it wasn't so appealing.

Simply Good, known for its vegetarian cuisine, had been around Arlington for about twenty years. Kendall had frequented the establishment at least twice a week. That was before Cole entered her life and reintroduced her to meat.

Instead of her normal lunch of soup, salad, and mineral water, she wanted a cheeseburger.

"Baby, what are you having?" James asked, looking at the menu. "I think I'm going to try the spinach salad." He gazed at her. "Are you having your usual?"

"No. I'm not really that hungry," she lied. "I guess I'll have the house salad." She was starving and wanted some beef really badly.

The waitress appeared and he gave their orders. Then his eyes totally focused on her. "What is Jami doing at your house?"

"What are you talking about?"

"When I called a few days ago, she answered your phone. I know how anal you are about strangers in your home. You would never allow me to have any of my friends over."

Kendall smiled and placed her menu on the table. "That little insecurity was due to you, Mr. Matthews. Remember me coming home early from a conference and finding you in my bed with that nurse?"

James actually looked a little embarrassed. "Yeah. That was a bit of bad luck. I didn't mean for you to catch us in bed."

"Obviously." Kendall was so ready for this lunch to be over. "Look, James, let's not relive that day. It's over and done with. I caught you in bed, we divorced, end of story."

"It doesn't have to be."

"What?"

"It doesn't have to be the end."

"James, what on earth are you talking about?" She held up her hand. "And don't spin me a tale."

"Same ole Kendall. Straight to the point. What I'm talking about is us. It's not too late for us to pick up the pieces. Before you start with your rejection, hear me out, baby."

He continued, not giving her a chance to answer. "Kendall, the reason I was sleeping with so many women was because I wanted your attention."

Kendall gasped. "What?"

"You weren't paying any attention to me, so I had to do something."

She took a deep breath, determined not to lose her temper. It was a hard fight, but she won. "So instead of talking to me, you chose to sleep with every nurse in a twenty-mile radius. You told me I was too stiff in bed."

"A real woman would have wanted to please her man," James said. "I wanted you to be more adventurous."

Kendall instantly thought of Cole and the things they had been doing in and out of bed. She'd become more spontaneous with Cole encouraging her. She had never been the problem. Now that she'd taken the blinders off, she saw the real James. The problems in their marriage had had little to do with her and everything to do with James.

"So what do you say, Kendall? Want to give that writer the boot?"

"Give me one good reason why I should?" She knew he couldn't. "Honestly, why would you want to get back with me?"

"You know we're good together. The doctor and the pharmacy sales rep. We belong together."

"Do you love me?"

"Of course I do."

"Oh, that's why you left me hurt that night on the skater's path."

"No, I saw that guy coming toward us and I wasn't sure who he was or if he had a weapon. I knew he wouldn't hurt you, so I left."

It was a typical answer and one she'd heard a million times before. Each time she'd confronted him about his sleeping around, he'd always turn it around in his favor. He was an excellent salesman. He could make anything sound like a good idea.

"Kendall, you know what you mean to me."

She knew exactly what she meant to him. With both Briarwood and InfaCare in his territory he could be top salesman with little effort on his part. "How's your mother?"

"Mom? She's fine."

"How's her breast cancer?"

James had the good sense not to lie this time. "She doesn't have it."

"Really," Kendall said, waiting for him to embellish his earlier lie.

"Yes, it was a mistake on the tests." He glanced around the room.

The waitress appeared with their orders. After making sure everything was fine, she disappeared.

James stared at his salad. "Wow, there's a lot of stuff in this thing. What's in it?"

Kendall didn't have to look at his plate; she knew exactly what was on it, since it was one of her favorite meals. "Spinach, red peppers, green peppers, green onions, mushrooms, and boiled eggs in an Italian vinaigrette."

"I thought you didn't eat eggs," James said, carefully inspecting his food.

"I'm a vegetarian. Actually, the politically correct term is lacto-ovo-vegetarian. Traditionally, I can eat the milk and eggs of animals. I can also eat anything I damn well please, for that matter."

His eyes popped up at her tone. "Well, good for you. How's your salad?"

"Fine." She picked at her house salad, wishing it was a cheeseburger.

"Now, getting back to us. What do you think?"

"I think it's a horrible idea. James, we were married for eight miserable years."

"It wasn't all bad," he said.

"It certainly wasn't good." Kendall sipped her water, hoping James would take the hint and stop talking about the past. She hated opening up old wounds. Dredging up the past would do nothing but rekindle the hate she'd felt all those years ago.

"I know I wasn't the best husband, Kendall. All I'm asking for is a chance."

She didn't have to think about it for one second. James was all about James. Their marriage had ended because he was selfish.

Charlie sat in his corner office, not knowing exactly what his next move was. He'd just received a courtesy phone call from Gabriella Hunt's attorney. She wanted her son back and was prepared to sue for custody.

He knew Gabriella was probably just blowing smoke, hoping that the threat of a very public custody hearing would have Cole ready to sign on the dotted line. But there was a hiccup in her little plan: Taylor. Since he was sixteen and had come to Texas of his own free will, Gabriella couldn't really cry kidnapping.

Charlie was concerned about both Cole and Kendall. Charlie hoped his sister was strong enough to deal with two very conniving women. If not, he'd be there to prevent her from getting hurt again. As much as he valued his friendship with Cole, as well as his business relationship, he'd chuck it all to protect his baby sister.

He picked up the phone and dialed Cole's home number. He knew Taylor wasn't there, which was good since Charlie needed to discuss the teenager. Charlie listened as the phone rang and rang.

And rang.

Finally Cole picked up. "What?"

"Bad morning?" Charlie asked, wondering if Gabriella's attorney had already contacted him.

Cole sighed. "The worst. Holly just kicked me in the gut, and I'm still reeling from it."

"She's not supposed to come anywhere near you. Is she still there?" Charlie slipped from concerned friend to attorney in a matter of seconds. "Does she think she's above the law because she works at CNT?"

"Charlie, please. One lunatic at a time. To answer your questions, no, she's not here. She did her punching by phone."

Charlie knew what Holly was capable of. He'd seen the destruction she'd caused in Cole's life first-hand. "I'm almost afraid to ask. What did she say?"

"She informed me that she'd had an abortion while we were dating. She didn't want the baby because a maternity leave would have jeopardized her career."

Charlie was speechless. He knew while Cole said he didn't want any more children, he would have welcomed a baby simply because it was his. "Cole, I'm sorry, man. She's been bad news from the day you met her."

"You don't have to tell me. I don't need this drama right now. I came home to lead a quiet life, and lately it's been anything but."

"I hope none of that had anything to do with my sister," Charlie said in his big-brother role. "Kendall has had her share of the blues and doesn't need any more."

"No, Charlie, none of it has to do with Kendall. At least not directly. I'm sure you know she has Jami and her son Dylan staying with her for awhile."

"Yeah, Mom mentioned it. Something about the husband taking drugs and threatening the kid. I think it's great Kendall is reaching out to the people on her staff. She's asked me to represent Max in his divorce proceedings as well as Jami. Kendall had been so focused on her work, I'd begun to wonder if that's all she thought about."

"Me, too. I'm glad we were both wrong," Cole said. "Charlie, what's up? You don't normally call early in the morning."

"I hate to add to your drama pile, but Gabriella's attorney called me this morning."

"Now what?"

"Cole, Gabriella wants to sue you for coercing Taylor to come to Texas," Charlie said.

When Cole didn't let out a string of expletives, Charlie became concerned. "Cole, did you hear me?"

"I heard you. It's going to be one of those days, isn't it? Next, Kendall is going to call me and tell me she's taking James back."

Charlie didn't believe that for one second. "What would make you believe that? She's so over that loser."

"So why is she having lunch with him at that upscale vegetarian restaurant? Max called earlier and told me about it."

Charlie was puzzled. If that was his woman having lunch with her ex, he would have been at the place before they could place an order. "So what are you doing at home?"

"You're kidding me, right? Charlie, you know Kendall better than anyone. She'd have my nuts in a food processor if she thought I didn't trust her enough to have lunch with James."

Charlie laughed. That was his baby sister. She took no mess from anyone, especially men. "Right. That's Kendall. We don't call her the ball buster for nothing."

"Amen," Cole said.

"Spoken like a man in love," Charlie joked. "Now what do you want me to do about Gabriella?"

He took a deep breath, thinking about his problem. "Nothing."

"Nothing?" Charlie asked, wondering what his friend was thinking. "Not even a countersuit?"

"Charlie, if Taylor decides he wants to go back to New York, then it's his choice. I don't want to subject him to a nasty court hearing and publicity. He's been through enough, and I will not cause him any more pain. I'll talk to him and see what he wants."

"I understand. You've changed since you came back home, Cole. I'm not quite used to the caring Coltrane Highpoint. What happened?"

"You said it earlier. I fell in love with your sister."

CHAPTER 28

"This isn't over, Kendall." James parked the car in front of the hospital. "You'll see I'm the best thing for you. That guy doesn't love you like I do."

Kendall opened the door and got out of the car. There wasn't much to say to him when he was in that kind of mood. Refuting him right now would only escalate the problem. "James, I have to get to work. Thanks for lunch." She closed the door and headed for the entrance.

"Oh, you'll see me. It might not be today, but you're going to see me," he called out of his open window. He drove off before she could reply.

Kendall shook her head and entered the building. She had a little time before her interview with Holly, and she could really use it. She had no idea what to do about James. He was in total denial about her refusal. But as she glanced in the lobby and saw Harry Campbell, thoughts of James flew out of her brain.

"Oh great," she mumbled, walking toward the multi-millionaire, Max's father-in-law.

Harry stood the minute Kendall came into his line of vision. He extended his lean hand toward Kendall. "Hello, Dr. Matthews, it's nice to see you." He smiled. "I was in the area and hoped to have a word with Max, but

I was told he went out for lunch and to run some errands."

Kendall nodded, hoping she could get Harry out of the hospital before Max returned. "Would you like him to call you when he gets back?"

Harry took out a business card and handed it to her. "Just have him call me at this number when he returns. It's imperative that I talk to him today." He stepped closer to Kendall and whispered, "I'm sure you're aware of the problems between him and Katie. I'm hoping they can work it all out."

Again Kendall nodded. She knew there was nothing to work out, especially since Max now had proof of Caitlin's infidelity. Which probably explained Harry's sudden appearance at the hospital. "I'm sure everything will work out as it needs to, Harry."

He smiled at Kendall. "Thank you." He glanced at his Rolex. "I have to get back to Dallas. Tell Max I'm sorry I missed him." He headed for the exit doors.

Kendall watched Harry as he left the hospital. After letting Jami know she was back, Kendall headed for the gym. She figured Max was there, and she was correct. Max was on the treadmill, running at top speed. Sweat poured down his face. His hair was completely soaked, and his T-shirt was molded to his slender body. She knew exactly what he was doing, and she had to stop him.

She decreased his speed until he was standing still.

"Kendall, what are you doing?" he asked between breaths.

"Max, you can't outrun your demons. You're going to have to face them. Harry was here looking for you."

Max stepped off the treadmill and reached for the towel hanging on the bars and wiped his face. "I saw him when he drove up in the Benz. Caitlin must have told him about the pictures. He probably wants to buy them."

"What are you going to do?"

He looked at her with sad blue eyes. "First, I'm taking the hottest shower ever, then I'm going to talk to Charlie to see exactly where I stand."

Kendall raised a hand to his shoulder. "Max, I know how it feels to be lied to and betrayed. I understand what you're going through. You can't keep this bottled up inside you."

He looked at her sideways. "That's pretty good talk coming from a woman who kept everyone at arm's length, including me. Until Cole came onto the scene you wouldn't let anyone get close enough to even kiss you. I don't want to end up like that, Kendall. I felt so sorry for you letting life pass you by. I don't regret pushing you toward him. You two guys are good for each other. I don't know why you can't admit it. I love Jami and will do anything and everything to be with her."

Kendall stared at him. Max always cut to the chase and, when needed, gave her a kick to the gut. "How can you know you love Jami already?"

"Because I just do. It's hard to explain, but we have this connection that defies all kinds of logic. I feel like a kid at Christmas when I'm around her. My heart starts beating twice as fast when she smiles at me. Yeah, I know my life is a mess right now, and hers isn't much better, but if we can survive the next few months, we can make it." He struggled out of his T-shirt. "What about you, Kendall? How long are you and Cole going to play this silly game? I know you love him and I know he loves you, but neither of you has admitted it to the other."

"I want to tell him, but now is not a good time."

Max shook his head and walked toward the men's locker room. "There's no such thing as a good time. I say tell him now. With all the craziness going on in our lives, it's heartwarming to know someone is in your corner." He walked into the men's room, leaving Kendall alone with her thoughts.

Why couldn't she tell Cole how she felt? What did she have to lose? He already had her heart, so really, she had nothing to lose and everything to gain. She hoped the decision to tell him wouldn't bite her in the butt later.

"Please tell me you didn't go there with Cole," Jason said, shaking his head in disappointment. "Holly, you just opened up a can of worms. You're not going to be able to talk your way out of the situation this time."

They were having a late lunch at a small bistro near their hotel. Holly was dining on a salad and Jason was chowing down on a ribeye steak. "I know I shouldn't have told him, but I had to do something."

"So you figured a little lie would make him run back into your arms."

She leaned back in the uncomfortable chair. "A little misinformation never hurt anyone. I did have an abortion. That part wasn't a lie."

"Yeah, but he wasn't the father and you know that. You just made a horrible situation worse. When Cole gets wind of what you've done, you can kiss that anchor gig good-bye, and this time Herb isn't going to save your ass."

She waved away Jason's remark. "Cole's not going to know that I lied, 'cause I'm not going to tell him. He thinks he has life all wrapped into this neat little ball since he's back here. Let's see if the good doctor will be so loving if she thinks Cole is responsible for a child's death. Think about it: Her life's work is getting people pregnant. It would be like a slap to her ego. She couldn't be with someone who killed a child." She grinned at her sheer brilliance in concocting the ultimate plan. The look on Jason's face told her he didn't share her enthusiasm.

"Holly, you've lost it. First of all, he didn't kill the baby. You did. Second, he wasn't even the damn father! Why don't you just give up this stupid idea, do the interview tomorrow, and get out of Arlington before you do something insane and lose your job and what little credibility you have left?"

"Too late for that," Holly said ruefully. "The game has already started and I'm going to finish it. Cole agreed to meet me later to discuss the whole abortion thing."

"And that's going to prove what?"

Holly hated having to explain every little detail, but knew Jason wasn't going to let up until he was privy to her plan. "Once Cole and I are together, he'll realize how much he misses being with me. We were good together."

"Holly, you cost that man a seven-figure book deal and he was ostracized by the publishing industry for a year. Now you sit there calm as you please, professing how good you two were? He hates you and has a restraining order against you. I'm sorry, Holly, you know you're my girl, but here's where I draw the line."

"Jason, you still have to help with the story."

"Yes, I do, because I do value my job. Holly, I know you want Cole back, but honey, Cole has moved on. You should too."

Meeting Holly to discuss anything was always a bad idea. Today had been different. Cole had hoped their meeting would be quick and to the point, but it was with Holly. And she did everything in her own time.

She had threatened to tell Kendall about the abortion if he didn't take her back. She'd finally taken complete leave of all her senses, he'd thought. After all she'd done to him, why would she think there was any circumstance that would make him go back to her? It was completely insane.

After challenging her to make good her threat, he'd stormed out of the hotel restaurant and headed to his mother's house. He had another mess to fix.

Taylor met him at the front door. "Hey, Dad. Gram is cooking a roast, mashed potatoes, and broccoli." He followed Cole further inside the house after he closed the

door. "She made my favorite, chocolate cake, for dessert."
He smiled proudly at his father. "I helped her make it."
Taylor fell onto the couch and turned on the TV.

Cole loved seeing Taylor's wide grin. It was worth
everything he had to endure. "That's good, son. I need to
talk to you." He sat down on the couch.

Taylor looked at Cole and saw the serious look on his
face. He turned off the TV and faced him. "What's up?
Are you going to propose to Kendall?"

"No, not yet, anyway. I need to talk to you about
your mother," Cole said, rubbing his hands together.
"She wants to sue me for custody, claiming that I coerced
you to come to Texas. Now, you're sixteen and can make
your own decision. If you want to go back to New York,
I won't stand in your way."

"Dad, what are you asking me?"

"I know we're just getting to know each other, Taylor,
and I don't want you dragged into a nasty court battle.
She's doing this to get back at me for you coming here.
I'm asking you if you want to stay here. If you want to
return, I won't contest the lawsuit. If you do want to stay,
I'm going to have a legal battle on my hands. You need to
be aware of what's happening. When the press gets wind
of this, they will descend on you like locusts."

"So this is all about Mom," Taylor said in a cold
voice. "She wants me back because it's cool if you're a
single woman raising your child. She doesn't really want
me. I hardly saw her the last few months I was there. She
was always going to rehearse for the Broadway play she
was in, or something."

"Taylor, I know your mother loves you in her way," Cole said, hoping to take some of his son's hurt away.

Taylor swiped the tears. "Well, I happen to think her way sucks. I'm not going back. Even if you don't want me here, I'm not going back to New York. I'll stay here with Gram."

"Taylor, I want you with here. I love you, no matter where you are. Your happiness is the most important thing to me."

"Even more than Kendall's?"

"Yes, even more than Kendall's. You will always come first." Cole sighed. He hated Gabriella for all the hurt she'd caused Taylor. Cole should sue her for that alone. "No matter where you are, what you do, I will always love you."

"I love you, Dad." Taylor hugged his father suddenly. "I'm so glad I came here. I don't want to go back."

"You won't have to," Cole reassured his son. He returned the tight embrace, not wanting the moment to end. "I had to know where you stood on the matter." Cole straightened and looked deep in son's eyes. "I needed to know you were ready to face the wrath of your mother."

Taylor wiped his face again. "I'm ready."

Cole hoped this was a good idea. He walked to Kendall's house and knocked on the door. Hopefully, she was alone. He really needed to talk, and he knew she'd be brutally honest.

The door opened and his heart swelled. Kendall wasn't alone, she was carrying a sleeping Dylan in her arms. She smiled at him and motioned him inside.

"I was just going to put him to bed," she whispered. "Jami and Keerya went out for the evening." She started for the stairs.

Cole followed her silently, then stopped in his tracks as the words sank in. "You're babysitting?" he asked a little too loudly. Dylan stirred in her arms, but Kendall lulled him back to sleep.

"Lower your voice," she hissed. "It's not that unusual, Cole. I've babysat my nieces and nephews over the years." She stepped on the first stair. "I'll be right back."

"Catch me letting you do this alone." Cole wasn't about to miss the sight of Kendall in such a domestic setting. It might be his only chance after he told her of Holly's threat.

Kendall blew him a kiss and continued to Dylan's room. Cole followed and watched in silence. Kendall changed the tyke into Spongebob Squarepants pajamas and eased him into bed, all without waking him. She turned on the intercom system and turned off the lights, but left on a tiny nightlight. She waved Cole outside and then she closed the door.

"I was reading him a story and he fell asleep." She grabbed Cole's hand and started downstairs. "I'm glad you came by. I missed you."

Was this the same woman who couldn't stand the sight of him just a few short months ago? She was nurturing and holding his hand. He could get used to this woman.

"Hey, we don't have to go downstairs, do we?"

Kendall looked at him with the look. The look that said that she wanted what he wanted, but it wasn't going to happen. "Yes, we do. I have to talk to you about something."

Cole sighed. Nope, he wasn't getting any anytime soon. "I have to talk to you as well."

"Oh, sounds interesting."

"I hope you still feel that way when I'm finished," Cole said, regretting the conversation already.

They reached the couch in silence. Kendall offered him a glass of wine, but he refused it. He needed a clear head, and wine would only make him want Kendall more.

Kendall turned on the intercom mounted on the wall. "You know, when I bought this place, I never thought I'd have a use for the intercom other than playing Mozart throughout the house. Now I use it whenever Dylan takes a nap." She smiled in amazement. "Hard to believe they've only been living here a month."

Had it only been four weeks since Jami moved in with Kendall? It was something both women had needed. Kendall had reached out to someone who really needed her help, and Jami had found she had someone to lean on. "Yeah, it seems like it was only yesterday. Wasn't that the last time we had sex?"

She laughed. "Oh, you're such a man." She moved closer to him, snuggling up next to him. "What did you want to talk about?"

"What did you want to talk about?"

Kendall looked at him. "Yours sounds a lot worse than mine, so you go first."

Cole didn't want to bring Holly into the room, but he had to tell Kendall what was going on. "Okay, you might as well know the whole truth. I never thought any of this would happen, and I surely don't intend for it to play out at Briarwood or InfaCare."

She sat up straight. "Okay, now you've got my attention. What's going on with you?"

He took a deep breath and told her the sordid details. He hated having to rehash any of it, but he had to. He finished the story, and waited for a reaction, expecting her to tell him to leave her house. She surprised him.

"So what's the next step? You can't let her think she'll get away with something like this. I have half a mind to cancel the interview tomorrow and let her stew in her own juices."

Cole cleared his throat, too afraid to believe what Kendall just said. "You're not pissed?"

"Of course I'm upset, but not at you. Cole, you have a past just like I have a past. We can't do anything about it but learn from our mistakes."

He rubbed her arm gently. "I hope you still feel that way after my next news."

She twisted in his arms. "You have more good news?" she asked sarcastically.

He leaned down and kissed her, letting his hands roam over her body, easing her onto his lap. "Smart ass," he murmured against her lips.

She ended the kiss, but didn't move from his lap, thank goodness. "You were saying?"

"My ex's lawyer called Charlie today." He wanted to lead into it slowly.

"I know, Charlie told me," Kendall said softly.

Cole wasn't sure who to be mad at, Kendall or Charlie. "My attorney broke a confidence and told you my business?"

"Oh, will you calm down. You know he is my big brother, besides being your best friend. He knew you were going to tell me anyway, and he wanted me to know what I was getting into. What does Taylor say? Poor thing, he's been through the wringer."

He just couldn't get used to the caring Kendall. "Yes, he has. He says he wants to stay with me, so I'm sure Gabriella is going to continue with the lawsuit. Even if she does drop it, it will still get in the media. Are you ready for that? I'm sure you're going to come up, and my donation to your hospital."

Kendall rolled her eyes toward the ceiling. "If you think I'm going to let a little thing like some Broadway actress try to bully me or my man, you must be nuts. We've got the best attorney in North America on our side."

Cole almost choked on the emotions lodged in his throat. "I'm your man?"

"Yes. You think I sit in just any man's lap? You think I'd risk exposure for just anyone? Cole, I'm willing to risk it all for you. I love you."

Cole had doubted she'd ever actually admit it. "Baby, I love you, too. I've loved you since the minute I laid eyes on you." He kissed her long and hard. He tried to inhale her mouth and tasted her tears. "Kendall, what's wrong?"

She shook her head and zoomed back in for another kiss. Cole moved out of the line of her swollen lips. "No, baby. Not until you tell me what's wrong. You don't know how long I've been waiting to say those words to you. Now that I've said them, I can't take them back. I won't take them back."

Her tears were running full force now. She placed a hand on either side of his face and kissed him. "There's nothing wrong, Cole. In fact, everything is finally all right." She kissed him again and rose from his lap. She held out a hand. "Come on."

"You don't mean . . ." He stood carefully, hoping his erection wasn't too noticeable.

"Only if you promise to be quiet." She led him upstairs and into her bedroom. She turned on the intercom and sat on the bed and began undressing. "If you wake Dylan, you have to put him back to sleep."

Cole slipped out of his clothes in record time. "You've got a deal." As he got into bed and drew Kendall into his arms, he remembered she had something to tell him, but as he kissed her, the thought flowed out of his mind. He had a much more pressing need to make love to the woman he loved.

CHAPTER 29

Friday morning, Jami prepared her son for the day. She'd hoped he would cooperate that morning since they were running behind schedule. She grabbed her purse and begged her son to get a move on. "Come on, baby. We're going to be late."

Dylan was dressed in shorts, a T-shirt, and sandals. "Where's Aunt Doll? We eat together."

Jami looked down the hall to the master bedroom's closed door. Kendall was still asleep. It was near seven o'clock in the morning, and she was still not awake. "She's sleeping. We'll see her later." Jami headed down the stairs. "Maybe we can stop at McDonald's to get some breakfast. How's that sound?" She waited for her son's response, but she didn't get one.

She turned around, hoping and praying her son hadn't gone into Kendall's room. He had a bad habit of just walking into her room without knocking. Jami ran back upstairs and that was exactly where she found him, inside Kendall's bedroom and standing near the bed. But Kendall wasn't alone. Cole lay next to her. They were huddled together on one side of the bed.

"Mommy, Aunt Doll is sleeping." He looked at Jami with big eyes. "How come she's not up?"

Jami hoped she could get her son out of the room before Kendall or Cole awoke. "Shh, baby. Aunt Doll is probably tired. Let's let her sleep." *Please God, don't let her find us in her bedroom.*

"Jami?" Kendall's very sleepy and startled voice stopped her in her tracks. "Jami?"

"I'm sorry, Kendall. I had no idea," Jami babbled. "It's just that Dylan was looking for you." She expected to be fired and homeless in the next thirty minutes.

"It's all right, Jami," Kendall said in an amused voice. "You should see your face right now." She glanced at the bedside clock. "Tell Max I'll be in around ten." She turned over and snuggled closer to Cole, effectively dismissing her.

Jami grabbed her son and they left the room. She still couldn't get used to the new Kendall. Jami had noticed the changes in her boss's emotional makeup. There was a time when Kendall wouldn't have allowed anyone to catch her in an embarrassing situation, such as being in bed with Cole. But she had just laughed it off. Jami realized her boss was really in love. She wanted that same kind of love.

Cole's eyes opened at the sound of the bedroom door closing. Kendall was still lying beside him, trying to feel him up. So who had been in the room? He moved closer to her, giving her better access to his body. "Was that Jami?"

Kendall looked up at him. "Yes." She kissed him. "Dylan was looking for me."

Cole tried to gauge her reaction. He knew how much she valued her privacy. "I'm sorry, Kendall. I should have gone home last night, but you wore me out. I was too tired to move."

She was still caressing him. Gentle strokes, hard strokes, but she was working magic and his erection grew at each touch. "Hmm, it doesn't feel like you're tired now. You feel hard."

"I'm hard anytime I'm within two feet of you," Cole admitted. "Now, how about easing my discomfort, baby." He kissed her, easing her body on top of his.

"All you had to do was ask, Cole," she said.

The look on her face brought back the incredible memories of the night before. They'd admitted they loved each other and he had confessed everything and Kendall hadn't sent him packing. Then he remembered. Kendall had mentioned she also had news, but he'd forgotten. Damn. He was acting just like her ass of an ex-husband, James. He watched in despair as Kendall straddled his body. She was right where he needed her, but what was a brother supposed to do? He had to show her he wasn't just about good sex. He took a deep breath, placed his hands on her slim hips and pushed her away from his erection. "Baby, last night you said you had something you wanted to talk about."

Kendall stared at him. "You want to talk about James now?" She nodded to his very erect body part.

"Yes, I want to talk about it now. Last night you listened to me talk about my problems, now it's my turn."

He eased her off his body. "We're going to talk, and if there's time before you have to be at the hospital, we'll resume our other conversation."

She blew out a tired breath. "A man wanting to talk instead of having sex? What are the odds?" She smiled. "I guess that says something about you, huh? All right, James and I had lunch yesterday."

"Really?" He feigned ignorance.

"Oh, stop. I know Max snitched. Anyway, we went to one of my favorite vegetarian restaurants in Arlington. I guess he was trying to show me how much he'd changed."

"They have a vegetarian restaurant here? Wow!"

Kendall playfully hit him. "You know, you could support my lifestyle a little bit. Anyway, James always had a bad habit of lying to me. Eventually I always found out the truth and he was busted. He'd told me the reason he'd returned was because his mother had been diagnosed with breast cancer, but that was a lie."

Cole could read the writing on the wall. "And you called him on it."

"Yeah. And to make matters worse, all through lunch, I wanted a cheeseburger. Me. I've been a lacto-ovo-vegetarian for the last ten years of my life, and I was craving red meat."

Her admission was like music to his ears. "So we eat steaks tonight in celebration?"

"Well, at least you're not patronizing me," she said, shaking her head.

"Baby, I have to know. Do you feel anything for James?"

"Sorrow, maybe, but little else. James can be very determined, and he seems to think he and I should reconcile. He knows all about you, so you'd better watch your back. He's not above doing something to you to get to me."

Cole didn't doubt it for one minute. "I'll be careful. Between our exes, we could be on one of those talk shows."

She looked at him, then moved on top of him again. "You don't have to tell me. Now that all that's been resolved, I say no more talking, at least with our mouths."

Cole was all for that. He kissed her as he eased inside her body, taking them all the way to paradise and then some.

By the time Cole returned to his house, he barely had time to shower, dress, and get to the hospital to tape the PSA and do the interview. It was an afternoon he was not looking forward to at all.

His phone rang just as he was getting out of the shower. He hurried to it, hoping it was his son. He was taking him to the hospital to watch the taping of the interview. But it wasn't his son. It was his ex-wife. He knew Charlie had given her attorney his home phone number. With a sigh, he picked up the phone. "Hello, Gabriella."

"Cole."

"What can I do for you?" Or *to* you.

"It's about Taylor. He wants to come home. Do you really want me to initiate this nasty lawsuit against you?"

"Gabriella, do what you have to. I've told Taylor what you're planning to do. I gave him the option of returning to New York if he wants."

"So?"

"He's not coming back to New York, so let the games begin. I can have him testify about all the lies you've told him over the years about me. I don't know how good your suit is going to look then."

"I can say you coerced him into coming to Texas," Gabriella said in the voice that had won her many movie awards. "I can say you aren't a good role model."

"Ditto, babe. See you in court." He hung up the phone and continued getting dressed.

One crazy ex down, one to go, he mused. He glanced at the clock. Kendall should be at work by now, he thought. Their morning session had lasted longer than he had anticipated. But it was worth every minute of it.

His cell phone rang. "What is it now?" He snatched up the phone, unfolded it, and grumbled into the phone, "What?"

"Mr. Highpoint?" a male voice asked.

"Who wants to know?" Cole hadn't recognized the voice.

"My name is Jason. I work with Holly."

Great, now she's conned some poor schmuck into doing her bidding. "What is it now, Jason? Tell Holly the answer is still no."

Jason cleared his throat. "This is about Holly, but not what you think. I'm risking my job just calling you."

"I'm listening."

"Since her meeting with you didn't go as she expected, Holly has come up with some kind of crazy scheme to make you take her back. I really think she's not in her right mind, and you should be very careful. You remember what she did to you the last time."

How could he ever forget? "Oh, yes, I remember. You have any idea of what she plans to do?"

"Since her first plan didn't work, she's looking at the doctor. She might just misquote her. I wouldn't put anything past her."

Cole didn't doubt what Holly was capable of for one second. "Look, Jason, I really appreciate the heads-up. I'll be on the lookout." He ended the call and threw the phone on the bed. Today might have started out great but, with the last two phone calls, his life had just taken a nosedive. He had to save Kendall.

Kendall walked into the hospital, instantly noticing the chaos. Cameras were being set up near her office. The hallway was littered with cameramen, reporters, and a lot of people she didn't want involved with this project. Kendall locked eyes with Holly. She was dressed in a dark suit.

"Kendall, I'm so glad you finally made it." Holly looked at her slim gold watch. "We just have time to run through the segment before we start taping. Is Cole with you?"

"No, he's bringing his son with him. I'm sure he'll be here shortly. I don't need to rehearse anything unless you've changed the questions you gave me yesterday."

"I might throw in a few new questions. I'll need to check with Cole first."

"I'll be in my office," Kendall said, walking down the cluttered hallway. She entered the room and took a deep breath. Holly almost seemed normal. Maybe Cole was overreacting because of their past together. Kendall hoped so.

Jami opened the door and stepped inside. "I want to talk to you, Kendall." She closed the door and walked to her desk.

Kendall watched her friend take a seat in the leather chair. "Sure, Jami, what is it?"

Jami took a deep breath. "I can't apologize enough for Dylan this morning. I have enjoyed staying in your home, and I love working for you."

Kendall gasped, then laughed. "Jami, I'm not going to fire you for Dylan being a little boy. We usually eat breakfast together, and he couldn't find me. It's expected. I had intended for Cole to go home last night, but we fell asleep. So I should be apologizing to you. You know you're welcome to stay at my place as long as you want."

She stood. "Thank you, Kendall. I think you should know that Holly has been here all morning asking very impertinent questions about you."

That had Kendall's attention. "Like what?"

"She knows that I'm living with you. She wanted to know how many times Cole stayed over. She wanted to know if you got along with Taylor, and she wanted me to go through your bills. I didn't give her any information because I felt it had nothing to do with the interview. I don't trust her, Kendall."

"I don't, either." Kendall walked to her friend and hugged her. "Thank you for telling me, Jami. Holly wants Cole back."

"But he doesn't want her, does he?"

Kendall shook her head. "No, he says it's definitely over, and he only went along with this interview thing 'cause it was so important to me."

"Yes, that's what Max said. I just want you to be careful around her. Something about her is making my skin crawl." Jami left the room.

Kendall sat in her office waiting for all the players to get in place. When she heard the commotion in the hallway, she ran out of her office. As if the day couldn't get worse, Karl, Jami's husband, was making an appearance.

He stood in front of the nurses' station, calling Jami every name in the book and then some. Kendall wanted to defuse the situation before Max got involved.

"Karl, now is not the time to do this." She approached the large man. As she came within smelling distance of him, her nose turned up at his rancid odor. Kendall glanced at the cluster of people and waved them away. The fewer people involved in this mess, the better.

"You damn bitch," he roared at Kendall, but pointed at Jami. "You got her thinking she don't need me, and she's not going to live without me."

Kendall realized Karl was high as a kite. She didn't have much experience handling drug-induced fits, but knew making him angrier wasn't the answer to the problem.

She looked at Jami's frightened face. Tears were streaming. "I'm sorry, Kendall. I called and told him that I'm going to file for divorce," Jami croaked.

In any other circumstance, it would have been the right thing to do, but today, of all days, it wasn't. "Karl, why don't we go talk about this in my office? Maybe we can figure out a solution to satisfy everyone."

He rubbed his head as if he were thinking about her proposition. "I need you to just shut up." He paced the area in front of the desk and began talking to himself.

Kendall really didn't like that. She noticed Holly slowly making her way to the front of the crowd. Surely, this stupid woman could see this was a volatile situation.

But Holly had her own agenda. She started throwing questions at Karl, sending him into a more agitated state. "Mr. Lewis, what do you plan to do today? Are you going to take the doctor hostage?"

Kendall took a deep breath. *Thanks, Holly. If he wasn't thinking about it, he is now!*

Karl looked in Holly's direction. "You'll be the first to know." He stared at his wife. "How could you do this to us? You know I love you. You know you can't make it without me. I'll make sure of that!"

Kendall had to do something. The situation was a powder keg and Karl held the match. The more he spoke, the more afraid Jami became.

Before she could think of a plan, Karl came up with one of his own. He stepped toward Kendall. "I'm tired of you messing up my life. I knew she had nowhere to go, but you took her in. If I could have gotten past your guard, I would have killed you and then her."

Kendall opened her mouth to speak, but suddenly felt a crushing blow and everything went black.

Cole entered the hospital just in time to see Kendall hit the floor, hard. Some large African-American man stood over her limp body with a gun in his hand, aiming it at her.

Cole took off in a full run and tackled him hard. When they hit the floor, the gun went off. With the sound of voices ringing in his ears, he wondered if he'd been shot. He couldn't die. Not now. Not when he and Taylor had reconciled. Not when he'd found Kendall and discovered what love really was.

"Cole, are you all right?" Max asked.

He heard his friend. That had to be a good sign. He rolled over and opened his eyes. "I'm not dead."

"No, Karl accidentally shot himself." He nodded toward Karl's limp body. "The best docs are working on Kendall. Karl hit her with the butt of his gun."

Cole struggled to sit up, using a nearby wall for support. "Go work on Kendall. She's going to be pissed if you're not by her side."

Max smiled. "You got that right. Sit tight, I'll be back." He went over to Kendall just as they loaded her on a stretcher.

If Cole had had the strength, he would have been by Kendall's side, but the hallway kept spinning. When his brain was finally working again, he remembered his son had accompanied him. Where was Taylor?

"Dad, are you okay?" Taylor sat beside Cole on the floor. "They took Kendall upstairs. Max was examining her, then he looked real funny. You know, like on *ER* or something."

The information finally filtered through. Kendall's office was on the ground floor of the hospital. The second floor held the critical care unit and surgical department. If Kendall was there, something was wrong. Cole had to find out what was going on. He attempted to stand, but his legs wouldn't work.

"Dad, Max said you had to sit still."

"Something is wrong with Kendall," Cole said. "I have to find out."

"No, Dad. You can't do anything right now. You can't even move," Taylor said.

"You're right. I want to help, but . . ."

"I know that feeling," Taylor said, wrapping his arm around his father.

Holly witnessed Cole and his son's tender moment after all the chaos settled down. She felt tears racing down her cheeks. She tried to wipe them away, but it didn't seem to work. The faster she swiped them away, the faster they came. She realized she was crying, not just a sniffle here and there, but really crying!

Jason came up beside her and handed her a small box of tissues. "Hey, you never cry."

She turned to him and, for the first time in their three-year friendship, saw him for the jewel he was. He'd been by her side when no one else would acknowledge her existence. He'd talked her out of some of her more insane ideas and listened when she ranted like a mad-woman when Cole wanted nothing to do with her.

She hugged and kissed him. "Thank you for being my friend."

He smiled down at her, wiping her eyes. "You know I can't let you go to jail. Who'd go to the baseball games with me?"

Holly looked over at Cole and his son, then back at Jason. "I'm so glad I didn't go through with my plan. I have to tell Cole how sorry I am."

Jason shook his head. "Honey, I think you should leave well enough alone."

Holly looked up at him. He was right, of course. She should just leave well enough alone. "All right, Jason, let's go home."

CHAPTER 30

A few hours later, Max walked into Kendall's hospital room. Due to her condition, she'd been admitted.

"Max, whose idea was this?" Kendall asked. She tried to look stern but, in the generic gown with all kinds of machines hooked up to her body, she looked scared. "I feel fine. My headache is going away."

This was going to be hard. He pulled one of the chairs near the bed. "Normally, you wouldn't have to stay in the hospital. But there's a little hiccup in that."

She rubbed her head. "What did Karl hit me with? I'm filing charges as soon as you find my clothes."

"Kendall, we need to talk."

She stared at him. "You sound serious. What's wrong? Is Jami all right? What happened to Karl?"

"Will you just slow down? I'll tell you what I can, but first I need to ask you something."

She struggled to sit up. "What?"

"Have you been feeling off lately?"

"I've been eating a lot of meat lately. My cholesterol is up, isn't it? I'm going to kill Cole."

Max was getting nowhere fast. He was going to have to take control of the situation, or this was going to turn into a comedy act. It was going to have to be tough love or nothing. "Kendall, you're pregnant."

She looked sideways at him, then laughed. "That's funny, Max. Not."

"I'm not kidding, Kendall. You're knocked up. About three weeks, as far as I can tell. But that's not the big news."

"Max, I'm not pregnant. There's no way I can be pregnant."

"You and Cole were having sex. Either you guys didn't use any protection or you're lucky enough to be the one person that defies latex."

"I just can't be," she whispered. "They said it wasn't possible."

"Start from the beginning," Max said. He'd known her long enough to know when she was hedging.

She reached for a tissue and wiped her eyes. "Remember when I caught James in bed with the nurse? Sure you do. Well, I had just discovered I was pregnant. After that I went away for a month and I had an abortion. There were a few complications with it, and the doctor told me that conceiving would be very unlikely."

Everything after that fell into place. "You came back and divorced James and started InfaCare for the baby you lost." He shook his head. "Damn you, Kendall, you've been carrying this around for the last five years. You couldn't even tell me?"

"No one knows. I couldn't bear to tell anyone. I just focused on work. I just don't understand how I can be pregnant."

"Well, try to get your head around the fact that you are pregnant. Here's something else to ponder: You're having twins." He grinned at her. "I think you and Cole deserve some kind of award, considering you didn't use any fertility drugs."

"Twins! Are you nuts?" Kendall sank back against the pillows. "Cole is going to have a cow."

"Probably so. Do you want to know the rest of the story?"

"I don't know."

"It's good," Max said. "When Cole saw Karl knock you out, he tackled Karl. They struggled, then the gun went off and Karl was shot. He wasn't killed, but he might wish he were. After being charged with bringing a loaded gun into the hospital, beaning you over the head, and threatening Jami, he's going to be in jail a long time."

"Good. How's Jami?"

"Waiting to see you. Cole is still downstairs. I'll go get him. He wasn't seriously hurt, just had the wind knocked out of him."

She nodded. "Thanks, Max. Don't tell him about my condition."

He kissed her on her forehead. "I won't, but I will call Zenora. She'll be so happy."

She rubbed her stomach. "Are we talking about my mother?"

Kendall wiped her eyes after Jami's visit. Was this what she had to look forward to for the next eight months? Now she waited for Cole's appearance. She wondered how he would take the news. Would he blame her?

Cole walked in with a dozen roses. He set them on the counter, then leaned over the bed and kissed her. "I was so worried. Taylor is downstairs talking to Jami."

He looked as tired as she felt. "I don't remember much of what happened, but Max brought me up to speed. I can't believe you tackled Karl. Thank you."

"He hurt you," Cole said simply. "I had to do something. If I had my way he'd be dead right now."

More tears. "That's the sweetest thing anyone ever said to me. I love you, Cole. Before you say anything, I have something to tell you." She took a deep breath. "I'm pregnant."

"What? That's not funny."

"I know, that's why Max had to tell me twice." She waited for a response.

He stood and paced the room. "How far along?"

"About three weeks."

He chuckled. "Guess it happened that time I took you to lunch."

She remembered that day well. They never made it to the restaurant. Instead they had stopped at the motel and feasted on each other. "Yes, probably so. I know this wasn't on your agenda."

He stared at her. "Who says?"

"Cole, you and Taylor have just started mending fences and you have this lawsuit thing going on."

"None of that matters. You matter. My baby matters."

"Babies," she corrected.

"Say what?"

"According to Max, I'm having twins."

Cole sat down in the chair with a thud. "Two babies? I can't believe this. How on earth did that happen?"

Kendall laughed. "Remember, you were the one always begging for just one more time." She remembered Taylor. "How do you think Taylor will take the news?"

"I'm sure he'll be happy."

"How about his father?"

"I'm stunned, of course, but as the shock is wearing off, I'm happy." He sat on the bed and held her hand. "What's Zenora going to say?"

Kendall shrugged. "Should be interesting. Max said he'd call her for me." She couldn't wait to see the look on her mother's face when she found out. She wiped her eyes. "I can't believe I'm crying again. This has to stop!"

"Baby, it's okay. The most important thing is that you're all right," he said. "Whatever you need, I'm here for you."

Kendall regained some of her composure as he wiped her face. "Thank you, Cole." She took the tissue from him. "I'm sorry. I didn't mean to lose it like that. If this is too much for you, you can tell me."

"You always think you can get rid of me. But baby, you'll see, I want it all. You, the babies, us being together, I love you and want you in my life. We need each other. I know that you're going to be on bed rest, and I think you should move in with me and Taylor."

Kendall shook her head. Her mother would kill her. "No, I can't live with you. Besides, my place is bigger than yours. I was thinking of hiring a nurse to stay with me."

"Like hell," Cole said.

"And I agree."

Kendall knew that voice. It belonged to her mother. Zenora walked into the room, followed by Charlie and rest of her family. "Oh, no," Kendall groaned, rubbing her still flat tummy. This was not going to be pretty.

Her mother walked to the bed and lovingly caressed Kendall's forehead. "Yes, honey, we know. And I have to say I agree with Cole and I also agree with you. You're going to need help, but you shouldn't live with him." Zenora's brown eyes glanced in Cole's direction. "Well, Cole, what are you going to do? Are you going to allow my grandbabies to be born out of wedlock?"

"Mom," Kendall pleaded. "Please, not now."

"Yes, Zenora. This is between Kendall and me. No one else is going to decide when we get married."

Kendall noticed he didn't say *if*. Getting married was a foregone conclusion, apparently. That would have bothered the old Kendall, but the pregnant Kendall didn't mind one bit. She glanced at her mother, waiting for the retort that would send Cole running for the nearest airport and out of her life. But no sharp retort came. Her mother nodded. "I like a man with some backbone," was all she said.

Cole laughed as he rose. "I like a woman who can make me think fast on my feet. I see where Kendall gets it from."

Zenora smiled. "I need to speak to my daughter alone."

Cole nodded. "I see where she gets that bluntness from, as well. I'll go call my mom and give her the news." He left the room, followed by all of Kendall's family except her mother.

After the door closed, Zenora faced her. "Baby, are you sure you're all right?" She rubbed Kendall's arm. "You feel warm."

Kendall glanced at her mother. "I still feel pretty out of it, but I'm happy about the turn of events. I just have to be careful for next eight months. I really want this so I'm going to do what's necessary, even if that means lying in bed every day."

"What about your work?"

To Kendall nothing compared to the lives growing inside her. "I'll take a leave of absence until I decide what I'm going to do."

Zenora nodded, pouring Kendall a glass of water. "You know, honey, Cole can well afford for you not to work, if you were married." She handed her the glass.

Kendall smiled. No matter what, her mother would still be her mother. "Mom, let's handle one crisis at a time." She sipped the water and nearly dropped the glass when Cole bolted into the room. "What are you doing back so fast?"

He flopped down on the edge of the bed, taking the water glass out of her hand. "You never gave me an answer."

"You never asked me a question."

He thought for a minute. "True. So I'm asking now. Will you take me, with Taylor as part of the deal?"

Kendall wanted to say yes. It was on the tip of her tongue. "Do you take me, the babies, and Jordan?"

He studied her for a moment, then glanced at Zenora. "Yes, with no doubts."

"Ditto."

EPILOGUE

Six months later

Kendall glanced at her quickly expanding body in the large mirror in the bedroom. She looked as if she were hiding a beach ball under her maternity sweater.

She reflected on the events of the past few months. Holly went back to New York without her interview. The news show ran the clips of Karl hitting Kendall on the head instead, and donations for InfaCare poured in. Not only did she receive enough for the cancer wing, she was able to hire a full-time staff. James returned to Boston after failing to secure Briarwood and InfaCare for his sales route.

Kendall heard Jordan as he climbed up the stairs, which meant Cole was right behind him with her breakfast. True to his word, he waited on her hand and foot, making all of her meals. Since she'd become pregnant her vegetarian lifestyle had taken a backseat to cheeseburgers, steaks, barbecued ribs, and pork chops.

"Honey, what are you doing up? You know the rules," he said, motioning her back to the bed. "You can only be up for two hours, and you're having lunch with Staci later today."

She laughed as she sat on their king-sized bed. "I know, sweetheart, but I just wanted to see how I looked in regular clothes. I hardly ever get to wear anything but pajamas or oversized lounging clothes. Besides, I thought you were the one who always wanted to break the rules."

He leaned down and kissed her gently on the lips. "Not in this case. You and the babies are too important to me." He placed the tray across her thighs. "Now eat. Your mom is coming over in an hour."

Kendall looked down at the eggs, bacon, toast, and juice. She couldn't have coffee. Cole thought it wasn't good for the babies. "You know, you were so much more fun before we got married five months ago."

He smiled. "You are just as much fun now. And I love you more each day, even if you do kick me in your sleep. Now eat."

Kendall reflected on their brief marriage. It hadn't been the roller-coaster ride she had envisioned with Cole; instead it had been a nice transition into wife, stepmother, and mother-to-be. Cole had been wonderful and patient. Taylor even spoiled her when he wasn't in school.

After much discussion and deciding to start fresh, both Kendall and Cole had sold their respective houses and had a new one. They now resided in a six-bedroom, four-bath, three-car-garage home in South Arlington. Cole had a room to write in, which was where he'd be as soon as Kendall's mother arrived.

He didn't like leaving her completely on her own when he was working in another section of the house. The very idea of Cole being so considerate brought tears to her eyes.

"What is it?" Cole wiped her eyes with a napkin. "You promised no more tears. Max is starting to question my masculinity."

She sniffed. "He's not. Max is riding on cloud nine now that his divorce is final and Jami accepted his marriage proposal."

"Okay, maybe not. But you know what that does to me. Cut me some slack."

Her tears made him cry. Which made him the most masculine man she knew. "I'll try."

He smiled at her. "I love you."

"I love you more," Kendall said, picking up her fork to eat her breakfast.

"I don't think that's possible."

"Maybe not, but I'm sure going to try."

THE END

ABOUT THE AUTHOR

Celya Bowers was born and raised in Marlin, Texas. After attending Sam Houston State University in Huntsville, Texas, she relocated to Arlington, Texas where she was bitten by the writing bug. After joining several writer-based groups, she found what she'd been missing.

Being a die-hard romantic, she developed a love for reading very early. Being the youngest of six and living in a small town, reading soon became her favorite pastime.

Currently she works part-time as a substitute teacher in the Arlington School District and attends college full-time, while keeping up with her writing. In her spare moments, she loves catching up with old friends, surfing the Internet, and listening to audiobooks. She is also on the executive board of her local Romance Writers of America Chapter.

Her dream destination is still Ireland and she hopes to get there one day very soon.

Please visit her website at *www.celyabowers.net.*

2009 Reprint Mass Market Titles

January

I'm Gonna Make You Love Me
Gwyneth Bolton
ISBN-13: 978-1-58571-294-6
$6.99

Shades of Desire
Monica White
ISBN-13: 978-1-58571-292-2
$6.99

February

A Love of Her Own
Cheris Hodges
ISBN-13: 978-1-58571-293-9
$6.99

Color of Trouble
Dyanne Davis
ISBN-13: 978-1-58571-294-6
$6.99

March

Twist of Fate
Beverly Clark
ISBN-13: 978-1-58571-295-3
$6.99

Chances
Pamela Leigh Starr
ISBN-13: 978-1-58571-296-0
$6.99

April

Sinful Intentions
Crystal Rhodes
ISBN-13: 978-1-585712-297-7
$6.99

Rock Star
Roslyn Hardy Holcomb
ISBN-13: 978-1-58571-298-4
$6.99

May

Paths of Fire
T.T. Henderson
ISBN-13: 978-1-58571-343-1
$6.99

Caught Up in the Rapture
Lisa Riley
ISBN-13: 978-1-58571-344-8
$6.99

June

Reckless Surrender
Rochelle Alers
ISBN-13: 978-1-58571-345-5
$6.99

No Ordinary Love
Angela Weaver
ISBN-13: 978-1-58571-346-2
$6.99

2009 Reprint Mass Market Titles (continued)

July

Intentional Mistakes
Michele Sudler
ISBN-13: 978-1-58571-347-9
$6.99

It's In His Kiss
Reon Carter
ISBN-13: 978-1-58571-348-6
$6.99

August

Unfinished Love Affair
Barbara Keaton
ISBN-13: 978-1-58571-349-3
$6.99

A Perfect Place to Pray
I.L Goodwin
ISBN-13: 978-1-58571-299-1
$6.99

September

Love in High Gear
Charlotte Roy
ISBN-13: 978-1-58571-355-4
$6.99

Ebony Eyes
Kei Swanson
ISBN-13: 978-1-58571-356-1
$6.99

October

Midnight Clear, Part I
Leslie Esdale/Carmen Green
ISBN-13: 978-1-58571-357-8
$6.99

Midnight Clear, Part II
Gwynne Forster/Monica
  Jackson
ISBN-13: 978-1-58571-358-5
$6.99

November

Midnight Peril
Vicki Andrews
ISBN-13: 978-1-58571-359-2
$6.99

One Day At A Time
Bella McFarland
ISBN-13: 978-1-58571-360-8
$6.99

December

Just An Affair
Eugenia O'Neal
ISBN-13: 978-1-58571-361-5
$6.99

Shades of Brown
Denise Becker
ISBN-13: 978-1-58571-362-2
$6.99

2009 New Mass Market Titles

January

Singing A Song...
Crystal Rhodes
ISBN-13: 978-1-58571-283-0
$6.99

Look Both Ways
Joan Early
ISBN-13: 978-1-58571-284-7
$6.99

February

Six O'Clock
Katrina Spencer
ISBN-13: 978-1-58571-285-4
$6.99

Red Sky
Renee Alexis
ISBN-13: 978-1-58571-286-1
$6.99

March

Anything But Love
Celya Bowers
ISBN-13: 978-1-58571-287-8
$6.99

Tempting Faith
Crystal Hubbard
ISBN-13: 978-1-58571-288-5
$6.99

April

If I Were Your Woman
La Connie Taylor-Jones
ISBN-13: 978-1-58571-289-2
$6.99

Best Of Luck Elsewhere
Trisha Haddad
ISBN-13: 978-1-58571-290-8
$6.99

May

All I'll Ever Need
Mildred Riley
ISBN-13: 978-1-58571-335-6
$6.99

A Place Like Home
Alicia Wiggins
ISBN-13: 978-1-58571-336-3
$6.99

June

Best Foot Forward
Michele Sudler
ISBN-13: 978-1-58571-337-0
$6.99

It's In the Rhythm
Sammie Ward
ISBN-13: 978-1-58571-338-7
$6.99

2009 New Mass Market Titles (continued)

July

Checks and Balances
Elaine Sims
ISBN-13: 978-1-58571-339-4
$6.99

Save Me
Africa Fine
ISBN-13: 978-1-58571-340-0
$6.99

August

When Lightening Strikes
Michele Cameron
ISBN-13: 978-1-58571-369-1
$6.99

Blindsided
Tammy Williams
ISBN-13: 978-1-58571-342-4
$6.99

September

2 Good
Celya Bowers
ISBN-13: 978-1-58571-350-9
$6.99

Waiting for Mr. Darcy
Chamein Canton
ISBN-13: 978-1-58571-351-6
$6.99

October

Fireflies
Joan Early
ISBN-13: 978-1-58571-352-3
$6.99

Frost On My Window
Angela Weaver
ISBN-13: 978-1-58571-353-0
$6.99

November

Waiting in the Shadows
Michele Sudler
ISBN-13: 978-1-58571-364-6
$6.99

Fixin' Tyrone
Keith Walker
ISBN-13: 978-1-58571-365-3
$6.99

December

Dream Keeper
Gail McFarland
ISBN-13: 978-1-58571-366-0
$6.99

Another Memory
Pamela Ridley
ISBN-13: 978-1-58571-367-7
$6.99

Other Genesis Press, Inc. Titles

A Dangerous Deception	J.M. Jeffries	$8.95
A Dangerous Love	J.M. Jeffries	$8.95
A Dangerous Obsession	J.M. Jeffries	$8.95
A Drummer's Beat to Mend	Kei Swanson	$9.95
A Happy Life	Charlotte Harris	$9.95
A Heart's Awakening	Veronica Parker	$9.95
A Lark on the Wing	Phyliss Hamilton	$9.95
A Love of Her Own	Cheris F. Hodges	$9.95
A Love to Cherish	Beverly Clark	$8.95
A Risk of Rain	Dar Tomlinson	$8.95
A Taste of Temptation	Reneé Alexis	$9.95
A Twist of Fate	Beverly Clark	$8.95
A Voice Behind Thunder	Carrie Elizabeth Greene	$6.99
A Will to Love	Angie Daniels	$9.95
Acquisitions	Kimberley White	$8.95
Across	Carol Payne	$12.95
After the Vows	Leslie Esdaile	$10.95
(Summer Anthology)	T.T. Henderson	
	Jacqueline Thomas	
Again My Love	Kayla Perrin	$10.95
Against the Wind	Gwynne Forster	$8.95
All I Ask	Barbara Keaton	$8.95
Always You	Crystal Hubbard	$6.99
Ambrosia	T.T. Henderson	$8.95
An Unfinished Love Affair	Barbara Keaton	$8.95
And Then Came You	Dorothy Elizabeth Love	$8.95
Angel's Paradise	Janice Angelique	$9.95
At Last	Lisa G. Riley	$8.95
Best of Friends	Natalie Dunbar	$8.95
Beyond the Rapture	Beverly Clark	$9.95
Blame It On Paradise	Crystal Hubbard	$6.99
Blaze	Barbara Keaton	$9.95
Bliss, Inc.	Chamein Canton	$6.99
Blood Lust	J. M. Jeffries	$9.95
Blood Seduction	J.M. Jeffries	$9.95

Other Genesis Press, Inc. Titles (continued)

Other Genesis Press, Inc. Titles (continued)

Other Genesis Press, Inc. Titles (continued)

Other Genesis Press, Inc. Titles (continued)

Meant to Be	Jeanne Sumerix	$8.95
Midnight Clear (Anthology)	Leslie Esdaile	$10.95
	Gwynne Forster	
	Carmen Green	
	Monica Jackson	
Midnight Magic	Gwynne Forster	$8.95
Midnight Peril	Vicki Andrews	$10.95
Misconceptions	Pamela Leigh Starr	$9.95
Moments of Clarity	Michele Cameron	$6.99
Montgomery's Children	Richard Perry	$14.95
Mr Fix-It	Crystal Hubbard	$6.99
My Buffalo Soldier	Barbara B. K. Reeves	$8.95
Naked Soul	Gwynne Forster	$8.95
Never Say Never	Michele Cameron	$6.99
Next to Last Chance	Louisa Dixon	$24.95
No Apologies	Seressia Glass	$8.95
No Commitment Required	Seressia Glass	$8.95
No Regrets	Mildred E. Riley	$8.95
Not His Type	Chamein Canton	$6.99
Nowhere to Run	Gay G. Gunn	$10.95
O Bed! O Breakfast!	Rob Kuehnle	$14.95
Object of His Desire	A. C. Arthur	$8.95
Office Policy	A. C. Arthur	$9.95
Once in a Blue Moon	Dorianne Cole	$9.95
One Day at a Time	Bella McFarland	$8.95
One in A Million	Barbara Keaton	$6.99
One of These Days	Michele Sudler	$9.95
Outside Chance	Louisa Dixon	$24.95
Passion	T.T. Henderson	$10.95
Passion's Blood	Cherif Fortin	$22.95
Passion's Furies	AlTonya Washington	$6.99
Passion's Journey	Wanda Y. Thomas	$8.95
Past Promises	Jahmel West	$8.95
Path of Fire	T.T. Henderson	$8.95
Path of Thorns	Annetta P. Lee	$9.95

Other Genesis Press, Inc. Titles (continued)

Peace Be Still	Colette Haywood	$12.95
Picture Perfect	Reon Carter	$8.95
Playing for Keeps	Stephanie Salinas	$8.95
Pride & Joi	Gay G. Gunn	$8.95
Promises Made	Bernice Layton	$6.99
Promises to Keep	Alicia Wiggins	$8.95
Quiet Storm	Donna Hill	$10.95
Reckless Surrender	Rochelle Alers	$6.95
Red Polka Dot in a World of Plaid	Varian Johnson	$12.95
Reluctant Captive	Joyce Jackson	$8.95
Rendezvous with Fate	Jeanne Sumerix	$8.95
Revelations	Cheris F. Hodges	$8.95
Rivers of the Soul	Leslie Esdaile	$8.95
Rocky Mountain Romance	Kathleen Suzanne	$8.95
Rooms of the Heart	Donna Hill	$8.95
Rough on Rats and Tough on Cats	Chris Parker	$12.95
Secret Library Vol. 1	Nina Sheridan	$18.95
Secret Library Vol. 2	Cassandra Colt	$8.95
Secret Thunder	Annetta P. Lee	$9.95
Shades of Brown	Denise Becker	$8.95
Shades of Desire	Monica White	$8.95
Shadows in the Moonlight	Jeanne Sumerix	$8.95
Sin	Crystal Rhodes	$8.95
Small Whispers	Annetta P. Lee	$6.99
So Amazing	Sinclair LeBeau	$8.95
Somebody's Someone	Sinclair LeBeau	$8.95
Someone to Love	Alicia Wiggins	$8.95
Song in the Park	Martin Brant	$15.95
Soul Eyes	Wayne L. Wilson	$12.95
Soul to Soul	Donna Hill	$8.95
Southern Comfort	J.M. Jeffries	$8.95
Southern Fried Standards	S.R. Maddox	$6.99
Still the Storm	Sharon Robinson	$8.95

ANYTHING BUT LOVE

Other Genesis Press, Inc. Titles (continued)

Still Waters Run Deep	Leslie Esdaile	$8.95
Stolen Kisses	Dominiqua Douglas	$9.95
Stolen Memories	Michele Sudler	$6.99
Stories to Excite You	Anna Forrest/Divine	$14.95
Storm	Pamela Leigh Starr	$6.99
Subtle Secrets	Wanda Y. Thomas	$8.95
Suddenly You	Crystal Hubbard	$9.95
Sweet Repercussions	Kimberley White	$9.95
Sweet Sensations	Gwyneth Bolton	$9.95
Sweet Tomorrows	Kimberly White	$8.95
Taken by You	Dorothy Elizabeth Love	$9.95
Tattooed Tears	T. T. Henderson	$8.95
The Color Line	Lizzette Grayson Carter	$9.95
The Color of Trouble	Dyanne Davis	$8.95
The Disappearance of Allison Jones	Kayla Perrin	$5.95
The Fires Within	Beverly Clark	$9.95
The Foursome	Celya Bowers	$6.99
The Honey Dipper's Legacy	Pannell-Allen	$14.95
The Joker's Love Tune	Sidney Rickman	$15.95
The Little Pretender	Barbara Cartland	$10.95
The Love We Had	Natalie Dunbar	$8.95
The Man Who Could Fly	Bob & Milana Beamon	$18.95
The Missing Link	Charlyne Dickerson	$8.95
The Mission	Pamela Leigh Starr	$6.99
The More Things Change	Chamein Canton	$6.99
The Perfect Frame	Beverly Clark	$9.95
The Price of Love	Sinclair LeBeau	$8.95
The Smoking Life	Ilene Barth	$29.95
The Words of the Pitcher	Kei Swanson	$8.95
Things Forbidden	Maryam Diaab	$6.99
This Life Isn't Perfect Holla	Sandra Foy	$6.99
Three Doors Down	Michele Sudler	$6.99
Three Wishes	Seressia Glass	$8.95
Ties That Bind	Kathleen Suzanne	$8.95

Other Genesis Press, Inc. Titles (continued)

Tiger Woods	Libby Hughes	$5.95
Time is of the Essence	Angie Daniels	$9.95
Timeless Devotion	Bella McFarland	$9.95
Tomorrow's Promise	Leslie Esdaile	$8.95
Truly Inseparable	Wanda Y. Thomas	$8.95
Two Sides to Every Story	Dyanne Davis	$9.95
Unbreak My Heart	Dar Tomlinson	$8.95
Uncommon Prayer	Kenneth Swanson	$9.95
Unconditional Love	Alicia Wiggins	$8.95
Unconditional	A.C. Arthur	$9.95
Undying Love	Renee Alexis	$6.99
Until Death Do Us Part	Susan Paul	$8.95
Vows of Passion	Bella McFarland	$9.95
Wedding Gown	Dyanne Davis	$8.95
What's Under Benjamin's Bed	Sandra Schaffer	$8.95
When A Man Loves A Woman	La Connie Taylor-Jones	$6.99
When Dreams Float	Dorothy Elizabeth Love	$8.95
When I'm With You	LaConnie Taylor-Jones	$6.99
Where I Want To Be	Maryam Diaab	$6.99
Whispers in the Night	Dorothy Elizabeth Love	$8.95
Whispers in the Sand	LaFlorya Gauthier	$10.95
Who's That Lady?	Andrea Jackson	$9.95
Wild Ravens	Altonya Washington	$9.95
Yesterday Is Gone	Beverly Clark	$10.95
Yesterday's Dreams, Tomorrow's Promises	Reon Laudat	$8.95
Your Precious Love	Sinclair LeBeau	$8.95

Order Form

Mail to: Genesis Press, Inc.
P.O. Box 101
Columbus, MS 39703

Name _____
Address _____
City/State _____ Zip _____
Telephone _____

Ship to (if different from above)
Name _____
Address _____
City/State _____ Zip _____
Telephone _____

Credit Card Information
Credit Card # _____ ☐ Visa ☐ Mastercard
Expiration Date (mm/yy) _____ ☐ AmEx ☐ Discover

Qty.	Author	Title	Price	Total

Use this order

form, or call

1-888-INDIGO-1

Total for books _____
Shipping and handling:
  $5 first two books,
  $1 each additional book _____
Total S & H _____
Total amount enclosed _____
Mississippi residents add 7% sales tax